UNDER THE CLOUD

A Novel

Violet Nesdoly

SparrowSong Press

UNDER THE CLOUD

Copyright © 2020 by Violet Nesdoly

Scripture quotations marked NKJV are taken from the Holy Bible, New King James Version®. Copyright © 1982 by Thomas Nelson, Inc. Used by permission. All rights reserved.

Scripture quotations marked MSG are taken from The Message. Copyright © 1993, 1994, 1995, 1996, 2000, 2001, 2002. Used by permission of NavPress Publishing Group. All rights reserved.

ISBN: (the following numbers have been assigned through SparrowSong's ISBN Canada account)

Paperback: 978-0-9735842-1-9
PDF: 978-0-9735842-2-6
Kindle (mobi): 978-0-9735842-3-3
Kobo: 978-0-9735842-4-0
EPub: 978-0-9735842-5-7

Published by SparrowSong Press
7 – 20771 Duncan Way
Langley, BC Canada V3A 9L4

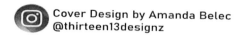 **Cover Design by Amanda Belec**
@thirteen13designz

Formatting: Rik Hall - Wild Seas Formatting

Cataloguing Information:
Nesdoly, Violet E., 1946-
Under the Cloud / Violet Nesdoly
Fiction, Historical fiction, Bible fiction

For my readers, who have encouraged me by asking for more. And for my heavenly Counselor, who gave me no peace until I completed this project.

Table of Contents

Author's Note

When I published *Destiny's Hands* in 2012, I was sure I was done with fiction-writing. To my surprise, though, readers asked for more—another story. Since I had already lived so long with the Israelites and especially one family, a continuation of their saga made the most sense.

As I considered the characters in that book, there was one whose life I was interested in exploring further—Bezalel's fictional younger sister Zamri. *Under the Cloud* is her story and the story of a generation of wilderness wanderers. One of the big challenges of telling this tale through her eyes was to portray a spirited woman living out her dreams and destiny in a male-dominated culture.

I have included a few poems—narration that tells or interprets aspects of the story Zamri does not personally witness or comprehend.

A set of discussion questions follows the story. These are designed to help you understand some of my intentions in writing, and to help you find and apply timeless principles for your own life.

I have tried to follow the events of the biblical exodus as they are narrated in the Bible. Endnote numbers throughout link you to an Endnote section, following the questions, that give the Bible references of the incidents mentioned and enacted.

Thank you for reading!

Introduction

After much inward struggle, Bezalel, gifted artisan and goldsmith, leaves his position in Pi-Ramesses as one of Pharaoh's gold shop workmen. He joins his family (Grandfather Hur, father Uri, mother Noemi, and younger sister Zamri) in their exodus from Egypt.

Leaving the goldsmith shop puts him on a path of questioning the purpose of his talent. That all changes when Moses announces that Yahweh has chosen him (Bezalel) to be in charge of constructing a holy tent and its furnishings for worship. His story is told in the book *Destiny's Hands* (©2012, Violet Nesdoly, Word Alive Press).

In *Under the Cloud*, we continue the exodus journey as experienced by Zamri, Bezalel's younger sister.

Cast of Characters

Characters are listed by households in alphabetical order. Main characters are indicated in bold. Characters who appear in the Bible are referenced. Characters with no Bible reference cited are fictional.

Aaron – (Exodus 4:14) Moses' brother, High Priest.

> Eleazar (Exodus 28:1; Numbers 20:28) – Aaron's son who became High Priest after Aaron died.

>> Phinehas (Numbers 25:7) – Eleazar's son, Aaron's grandson, who was also a priest.

Abiram – (Numbers 16:1) Leader of a rebellion against Moses. Pallu's father.

> **Pallu** – Son of Abiram, he pursues Zamri and asks for her hand in marriage.

Aunt Sarah – Zamri's aunt, mother to Reisa and Jaffa.

> Reisa – Zamri's cousin, daughter of Aunt Sarah.

>> Simeon – Reisa's son.

>> Talia – Reisa's daughter.

> Jaffa – Zamri's cousin, daughter of Aunt Sarah, Reisa's younger sister.

Bezalel – (Exodus 31:1-5) Grandson of Hur, son of Uri and Noemi, sister of Zamri. He was put in charge of crafting the tabernacle and its accessories.

> Sebia – Bezalel's wife.
> Ari – Bezalel and Sebia's daughter.

Caleb – (Numbers 13:6) Son of Jephunneh, Father of Iru, Elah and Naam, represented Judah as one of the Canaan spies.

> **Devora** – Wife of Caleb, married after her first husband Sethur (Asher's spy to Canaan – Numbers 13:13) died.

Achsah (Joshua 15:16-17) Daughter of Caleb and Devora, sister of Iru, Elah, and Naam.

Cherut's Mother – Mother of Cherut who married Naam (Caleb's youngest son).

Elah – (1 Chronicles 4:15) Middle son of Caleb, a shepherd, husband of Zamri.

> **Zamri** – Granddaughter of Hur, Daughter of Uri and Noemi, sister of Bezalel. This book's main (point-of-view) character, through whom the story is told.

> Kenaz – (1 Chronicles 4:15) Elah and Zamri's son.

> Nara – Midianite girl Kenaz brings home from battle.

Grandfather Hur – (Exodus 31:2; 17:10,12) Father of Uri, Grandfather of Bezalel and Zamri, friend of Moses.

> **Uri** – (Exodus 31:2) Son of Hur, father of Bezalel and Zamri, husband of Noemi.

> **Noemi** – Wife of Uri, mother of Bezalel and Zamri.

Iru – (1 Chronicles 4:15) Caleb's oldest son.

> **Merab** – wife of Iru.

> **Aliyah** – Iru and Merab's oldest daughter.

> Haviva – Iru and Merab's second daughter.

Joshua – (Exodus 17:9; Numbers 13:8) Moses' assistant and Canaan spy who joined Caleb in encouraging early conquest of Canaan.

Korah – (Numbers 16:1) A Levite rebel.

Miriam – (Exodus 2:1-8; 15:20-21) Moses' and Aaron's sister, an Israelite leader, prophetess, and Zamri's inspiration.

Moses – (Exodus 7:1-7) Leader of the Israelites.

Naam – (1 Chronicles 4:15) Caleb's youngest son.

Cherut – Naam's wife.

Raanan – Naam and Cherut's oldest son.

Basmat - Raanan's wife.

Rebecca – Raanan & Basmat's daughter.

Enat – Naam and Cherut's daughter (second child).

Lavi – Naam and Cherut's second son (third child).

She'era – Lavi's wife.

Oholiab – (Exodus 31:6) Tabernacle craftsman, Bezalel's friend.

Saria – Oholiab's wife.

Obed – Oholiab & Saria's son.

Paltiel – Cetura's husband.

Cetura – Zamri's childhood friend and wife of Paltiel.

Yaron – Cetura and Paltiel's son.

Shoshan – Bezalel's friend, Sephy's husband.

Sephy (Sephora) – Zamri's childhood friend, wife of Shoshan.

Chaim – Shoshan and Sephy's first son.

Matan – Shoshan and Sephy's second son

Part One: Spring

Chapter One

Head down, shoulders slumped, Bezalel trudged into our campsite. It was after sundown and he was finally home following another long day of work.

"How is the job coming along?" Grandfather Hur asked.

"Don't ask!" Bezalel's uncharacteristically sharp answer silenced the conversation. We all watched from our seats around the courtyard campfire as he stumbled to the tent and lifted the flap.

Mother jumped up. "He'll be hungry," she said following him into the tent.

"I apologize for his disrespect," Father said to Grandfather.

"No need," Grandfather said. "I wondered if a day would come when this job would overwhelm him. What he needs is a good night's sleep."

Bezalel, my big brother the goldsmith, had been working long hours—sunrise to sunset long—supervising the crafting of the utensils and tools for Yahweh's special tent, the tabernacle. In fact, Moses had put him and Oholiab the weaver in charge of making the tent itself.

This time at Mount Sinai had been stressful for Bezalel. He was only twenty, young to be the overseer of so many workmen, hundreds he told us one time he wasn't too tired to just eat and stumble to his sleeping mat. They had been working at the project for months.

A few days ago, he said they were nearly done and mentioned something about Moses inspecting their work. In the last few days he had been especially jumpy but he had never snapped at Grandfather before.

I was surprised then, when the next day he arrived at the tent just after our midday rest — a smile on his face.

"You're home early" Mother exclaimed, as she added water to the pot for his drink.

Bezalel joined us in the shade of our awning. As we waited for the tea to steep, Grandfather Hur asked again, "So, how is the work coming along today?"

I cringed, remembering Bezalel's sharp retort of yesterday. But there was no annoyance on his face today. Instead, a smile lit his whole countenance. "Finished," he said. "We finished late yesterday. Today Moses did his inspection."

"Did he like it?" asked Mother. "Was he happy with it?"

"Yes. He looked it over carefully — even measured some pieces comparing them to the instructions he had given us. And it was all good. He was pleased."

"What did he say?" Mother pressed. She loved to hear her children praised — all the details.

"I don't recall exactly what he said," Bezalel replied. "But after the inspection was done, he blessed us."

The slight crack in his voice had me studying his face. There was a glisten in his eye. I couldn't remember the last time he had cried. Moses' words must have meant a lot to him.

"What now?" I asked.

"I have one more assignment from our leader, Nahshon," he said. "He has asked me to make our tribe's special tabernacle gifts — a silver platter, a silver bowl, and a gold pan. I will also need to oversee workmen of the other tribes making theirs. And then," his face brightened, "I can get to work on my wedding present for Sebia."

My heart fell. I had been hoping he would want to spend some time with me, exploring beyond the camp, maybe playing one of the games we played in Egypt, or even just talking. But Sebia had changed all that. Since she had come into his life he was all moon-eyed and distracted every minute he wasn't working. Would I ever get my big brother back? [1]

* * *

We had been trekking through the dessert for almost a year, led by Moses and a cloud that went before us by day and lit our way at night. I could scarcely remember being in Egypt and yet it felt like our leaving had just happened. The waxing and waning of the moon helped me see how time was passing. This evening we would have a new moon, Grandfather Hur told us, marking the beginning of a new year — a special event.

This day, a few days after the work on Yahweh's holy tent was completed, was a special day for Bezalel too. Today the craftsmen were to help Moses set up the tabernacle. Bezalel looked as tense as he had before Moses did his inspection.

We planned to watch. Grandfather had reserved a place for our family because of Bezalel's position. Mother said my friends Sephora (we call her Sephy) and Cetura could join us. As soon as they arrived, we set out for the plain outside the camp where the tent was to be erected.

The air was still chilly from the night. I shivered as

it seeped through my cloak. We found our spot from which we had a good view. The workmen were already scurrying around, carrying golden planks to the site and snapping them into specially made holders. As they worked, a golden enclosure grew before our eyes.

Next, workmen came carrying bundles of fabric and skins. They covered the enclosure, tenting it first with a dark curtain. On top of that they laid red-dyed animal skins.

Sephy watched closely. She loved fabrics of every kind. "That dark covering is woven goat hair," she said. "The skins don't look like ram or calf, though. I wonder what animal they're from."

As soon as the gold enclosure was covered, four workmen carried in a gold box. Its top had a beautiful golden lid with figures mounted on it. From where we sat, they looked like winged men. The box had rings at its four corners, with golden poles through the rings. Four men, with the poles resting on their shoulders, carried it. This must be the Ark of the Covenant that Bezalel had told us about.

Two other workmen carrying a weaving drew my attention. Sephy's too — she caught her breath. "Look. It's embroidered in the same shape as the wings on the box! And do you see the colours? I wish I could see it up close." But we couldn't even examine it from a distance, for the men had disappeared with it into the tent.

They were followed by more workmen carrying a table and bread, a lamp stand, a beautiful gold altar, and a container from which flames leaped. Everything was made of gold that sparkled and flashed in the strengthening desert sun. It was magnificent!

From time to time I caught sight of Bezalel as he

brought more objects from the tent where they were stored and helped here and there, fitting carrying poles into rings, lifting articles onto other worker's shoulders, even carrying some of the things himself. It was hard to read his face from this distance but he seemed relaxed now, even laughing with his friends. I recognized Shoshan.

I noticed Sephy's eyes on them too. A smile played around her mouth.

Cetura, sitting on Sephy's other side, followed our glance. "Tell her, Sephy," she said, giving her a nudge.

"Tell me what?" I asked.

"There's nothing to tell," said Sephy, though her dancing eyes contradicted that.

"Can I say?" asked Cetura, and then before Sephy answered, she continued, "Shoshan's father has asked Sephy's if they can marry. "

"Is this true?" I asked. But Sephy didn't have to say anything. Her downcast eyes and pink cheeks were answer enough.

I didn't know why I was shocked. After all, Sephy wasn't quite a year older than I was. She'd be sixteen very soon, and at my fifteenth birthday, just a few weeks ago, everyone was teasing about finding a husband for me. But my friend getting married? And to Shoshan of all people! I'd just never thought of my brother's friend as being someone's husband.

An exclamation from Grandfather Hur drew my attention back to what was taking place. Four men were carrying a gleaming basin, cauldron-sized. Moses motioned them to place it outside the doorway of the gold enclosure. As a parade of workmen filled it with water, more workers came carrying another large altar, square with curved shapes, like horns, on the corners. Others brought tools—shovels, pans, and a grate. They placed them on the outside of the enclosure as well.

Now the workmen brought out poles and lengths of fabric. They planted the poles at intervals around the tent and its outer area, then fastened the fabric to them, creating a fence around the tabernacle and its courtyard.

As time passed, more and more people gathered and began surrounding the tent. In order to see, we left our spot and crowded near to the fence, along with everyone else.

When everything appeared to be in place, the crowd grew silent, as if in anticipation. All of our eyes were on Moses, who had been supervising what had gone on. He paused and someone handed him a golden pitcher.

"What is he doing now?" I asked Father.

Grandfather Hur, who knew a lot about these things, said, "I believe he has asked for oil."

We watched as Moses began to pour golden liquid from the pitcher onto the objects that had just been set up.

"Why does he do that?" asked Cetura.

"It's called anointing. It's a way to mark these objects as set apart for Yahweh," Grandfather said.

As we talked, Moses disappeared inside the tabernacle and stayed there for a long time. When he reappeared, he went to the brass cauldron. Pouring oil into his hand, he smeared it all around the edge of the cauldron, down the sides and over the base. Then he went to the altar and anointed it and the things around it—pails, grates, shovels, and forks.

Next, he went to the tent itself and poured oil on all four sides. The steady desert breeze carried its smell to us—the spicy fragrance of cinnamon.

When he was finished, Moses summoned his brother Aaron and Aaron's sons. Before us all, Aaron took off his outer clothes and Moses gave him fresh new ones—a white tunic over which he pulled a sleeveless blue robe that jingled as he shifted it into place. Next, Moses covered Aaron's robe with a garment that looked like an apron. "That's an ephod," Father said.

Again, Sephy gave a little gasp at the sight of its crimson and blue embroidery. Now that we were closer, we could see the details. I don't know much about fabrics but even I could see that this was a very special garment.

Moses next lifted a strange and sparkling object from the collection in front of him and placed it over Aaron's shoulders. It had glossy black stones on each shoulder and in front, covering Aaron's chest, many jewels with writing on them. He fastened these garments snug to Aaron's body with an fancy sash.

Finally, Moses positioned a white turban on Aaron's head, held in place by a gold band over his forehead and strips that met in a crown on the top. Then he poured anointing oil onto Aaron's forehead. It dripped down his face onto his beautiful clothes.

Moses dressed Aaron's sons in similar tunics, robes, and sashes. Then he anointed them. Finally, all four of them, with oil still glistening on their faces, took fire, loaves of bread, and burning incense, and entered the tabernacle, disappearing from view.

When they came out again, Moses and Aaron lit a fire under the courtyard altar, then called for a lamb and a basket of grain. Right before us they killed the lamb and placed it on the altar.

My mind wandered back to the time many months ago, just after we got to Mount Sinai, when Moses had made a similar sacrifice. Then the blood that was sprinkled on all of us touched Bezalel and, in an instant, healed his broken hand. Would something like that take place today? I glanced around but didn't notice anything unusual.

Moses, finished with the animal, washed his hands in the cauldron. As he did this, I noticed the sky. The light of the sun had dimmed momentarily as the cloud that was sitting on top of the mountain moved. Slowly the cloud drifted toward the tabernacle and descended until the top was hidden within it. As I watched it come to rest, my eyes were blinded with the radiance that came from within the cloud itself.

Under the descending cloud the workmen staggered and fell. Glowing brightness poured through the doorway of the enclosure. Even Moses, who stood in front of the door, sank to his knees.

Meanwhile, the lamb and the grain on the altar had burst into flame—all on their own.

A shiver went through me, my heart pounded, and my hands grew clammy. Was this bad or good? Was Yahweh pleased with His tabernacle, or not? I looked away from the brightness to find Bezalel but couldn't locate him in the crowd of workmen. They were all kneeling or lying face down on the ground.

"Yahweh be praised!" Grandfather Hur sat rocking back and forth, his arms high, his face lit up in ecstasy. "It is Yahweh's glory come down. Our Bezalel has served him well!"

For some reason, I couldn't stop my hands and feet from trembling. And I was speechless. So were my friends. What had we seen today? Yahweh's presence so near was reassuring but disturbing too.

When we left for home little later, I remembered, as if it were a dream, the news about Sephy's possible betrothal. That too felt unreal. It seemed like just yesterday we were playing with our dolls.[2]

Chapter Two

With the tabernacle set up, it felt like change was in the air for all of us. But the next morning as I made my way to the spot where my friends and I gathered manna, I was preoccupied with the changes that would come about with Sephy and Shoshan's betrothal.

My friends were already there and busy. I greeted them and set to work. We filled our baskets working silently, side by side.

"You are quiet today," Sephy said at last.

"A lot on my mind," I answered, giving her a tiny smile.

"Are you angry with me?" she asked. She was good at picking up on my feelings.

"Why didn't you tell me your father was arranging your betrothal?" I blurted, embarrassed that, despite my determination to stay calm, my voice quivered.

Sephy looked at me sharply, then looked down, as if considering her words. "I was afraid you'd be upset that it was me and not you."

"You thought Shoshan might want to marry *me*?"

"He spends so much time at your tent," Cetura said. "Before his father talked to Sephy's we thought it would be you."

"He spends time there because he's Bezalel's friend," I said. "He never comes to see me!" Then another thought hit me. "Maybe he visits so often to see *you*, Sephy. You're often there. To be truthful, marrying him, marrying anyone really, is the farthest thing from my mind."

Sephy looked relieved, but also puzzled. "You mean you don't want to marry?"

"It's not that I don't want to marry. I do, of course. And have children—sons—lots of sons. But ... not yet."

This was the first time I had actually admitted there was a resistance within me to following the expected order of things. What was it that I did want? I had no special talent or gifts like Bezalel did. Neither was I good at the things women were expected to do—cooking, weaving, mending. In my imagination, I saw the woman I admired—Miriam—waving her timbrel and singing at the top of her voice as she led us in the victory dance the morning after we crossed the Red Sea. Even though she was old, she was strong and brave and seemed above caring whether others approved of her or what she did. Actions like hers and the married life, of being someone's meek wife, hardly went together. [3]

"When you find the right man, I'm sure you'll change your mind." Sephy's voice broke into my thoughts. A smile played around her mouth.

"What about you," I asked Cetura. "Are you keeping something from me too?"

"I wish," said Cetura, who was the oldest of the three of us but, to be truthful, not as pretty as Sephy.

"Anyway," said Sephy, starting to gather manna again, "Shoshan's father hasn't come to make the official request. It may never happen."

"Or it may," I said, "and you'll begin life in Canaan not only in a new home but with a husband."

* * *

During that day, I saw another sign of change coming. Midmorning a parade passed our encampment.

Mother, I, and all of us looked up from washing clothes to watch the unusual sight of six wooden carts, each pulled by a team of yoked oxen, plodding by toward the tabernacle.

"What's that for?" I asked Mother.

"I'm not sure," she said. "For Moses and Aaron to ride in, or perhaps to move the parts of the tabernacle when we leave this place."

Later, Father and Grandfather assured us that moving the tabernacle was indeed what the carts were for. Each, along with the oxen, was a gift to the priests and Levites to help carry the boards, posts, coverings, and skins of the tabernacle. But it turned out the carts were only the beginning of gift-giving for our new worship place.

Bezalel came home exhausted late that night. As usual, it was hard to get anything out of him when he was this tired. But Grandfather Hur did. In answer to his questions Bezalel told us he had finally finished helping each tribe cast their tabernacle gifts. These were in addition to the carts and oxen. "Our leader Nahshon gives Judah's gift tomorrow," he told us. "Why don't you come and watch?"

* * *

The next morning found Mother, Father, Grandfather Hur, Bezalel, and me along with a good number of other Judah tribespeople, near the entrance to the tabernacle courtyard. We huddled in our cloaks against the chill morning wind waiting for Nahshon to appear.

I took three-year-old Simeon, cousin Reisa's little boy, for a walk while she attended to Talia, her baby. We were just a short distance from the congregation when our tribe's lion ensign came into view.

Behind the ensign bearer walked Nahshon in an ornate wine robe that flapped in the breeze. In his hands, he carried a silver platter. Behind him another man carried a silver bowl and following him another had a gold pan. They were followed by a parade of men who led a small herd of animals — bulls, rams, kids, a couple of oxen, and goats.

As Nahshon approached the tabernacle fence, Moses, Aaron, and Aaron's sons — wearing their new white and blue priest clothes — came toward them. The bells that bordered the bottom of their tunics tinkled in the crisp air.

"Oh, esteemed Moses and you Levites, we present gifts from Judah," Nahshon began. "This platter and bowl of fine flour and oil we present for the grain offerings." He handed the platter he had been carrying to Moses, took the golden bowl from the man carrying it, and handed it to Aaron. Next, he took the pan and handed it to one of Aaron's son. "This pan is full of offering incense," he said.

He motioned for the men leading the animals. "These are the animals required for the sacrifices." Going to each beast and touching its head as if bidding it farewell, he named what it was for. "This young bull, this ram, and this yearling male lamb are for our burnt offering."

A group of young men from Levi tribe came from outside the tabernacle and took charge of the animals as they were presented.

Nahshon beckoned the next person. "This goat kid is for our sin offering," he said, and handed the animal's lead rope to another Levite.

"These oxen and yearling rams, goats, and lambs are for our peace offering." In a similar way he carried on, presenting the remainder of Judah's gifts.

When all the animals had been taken away, Nahshon stood with his head bowed before Moses and Aaron. Moses placed his hand on Nahshon's head. "May the shalom and blessing of Yahweh rest on you and the whole tribe of Judah," he said. Nahshon raised his head and smiled, looking relieved. Then he and those with him turned to go. We followed behind.

"Did you make those gold and silver things?" I asked Bezalel.

"Yes. And many more. Each day another tribe will come and bring similar gifts to Moses."

Mother's face was furrowed in a frown. "Why do Moses, Aaron, and his sons need so many things? So much fine flour! Why, it would make wonderful bread — a welcome change to the tiresome manna. And all those animals? What will Moses do with them?"

"They were what Moses commanded," Bezalel said.

"Yes, but what is he going to do with them?"

"Sacrifice them," said Father.

"Burn them?"

"I believe the priests and Levites are to eat some of the meat," Father said.

"Well, that's hardly fair," said Mother. "Why do they get all the meat while there's none for us?"

Mother's questions cast a cloud over my day. I knew what she had said would rile Grandfather Hur. Now, not surprisingly, he responded.

"You may not understand this, Noemi. But Yahweh who freed us from Egypt by sending plagues and doing miracles, and who goes with us now in a cloud, has

14

commanded these things. If He wants them, why would we not willingly give them?"

"Hmm," Mother muttered, but she said no more. [4]

* * *

It was still cold when mother woke me to do my job of gathering manna a few days later. "It's too early," I complained.

But she gave me no peace. "Today we must again meet at the tabernacle remember? Everyone must go. We don't want to be late and stuck at the back of the congregation."

I was not the only one out early enough to see the sun reddening the boulders of the mountainside and brightening the slopes of Mount Sinai. I snugged my goat hair robe around me as I joined the others, filling my family's basket with the sweet round wafers that had been our food for almost a year.

Mother had the water boiling on the fire outside our tent when I got back. She was chatting with other women from our clan's circle of tents which made up our encampment.

The space in the middle was a hive of morning activity. Like my mother, other women also tended cooking fires near tent entrances, while men and boys watered sheep and goats staked nearby. Children laughed and chased each other around the open area in childish games.

I felt a tug on my cloak. It was Simeon. "Catch me, Auntie" he called. I lunged toward him as if to follow. He darted away and I laughed.

"I can't play right now," I said, "or I'll spill all this food."

Mother took the manna from me, dumped a good half of it into the water. Even though its taste was mild, I looked forward to the boiled gruel that would soon take away the morning's hunger pangs.

After we'd eaten, Mother, Father, Grandfather, Bezalel, and I made our way to the tabernacle site. Moses had said to gather at the entrance. We were among the first to get there and had a good view of the tabernacle, the altar, and the brass basin that were put up a week earlier.

I saw that Aaron and his four sons were already there, standing at the door of the tent dressed in their priestly robes. "They are here early," I said.

Grandfather, who was beside me, replied, "They have been here all week."

"All week?" Then I remembered how Judah gave its gift and how the other tribes would have been delivering theirs.

Now Moses appeared and entered the tabernacle court. He looked dark and weathered beside the priests with their white head coverings and white and blue clothing. He talked briefly to Aaron and his sons then beckoned to others.

In response, men from the tribe of Levi entered the courtyard leading animals. I saw a goat kid, calf, lamb, bull, and ram. Maybe these were some of the beasts Nahshon had given to Moses earlier. Another man carried a basket.

Moses turned to face the crowd that was still assembling and motioned for silence. When we had quieted, he called out in a booming voice, "This is the thing which the Lord commanded you to do. Watch closely what happens here today and the glory of the

Lord will appear to you."

"What does he mean?" I asked.

"You remember how the cloud came down on the tabernacle when it was set up?" said Bezalel. "Perhaps we will see something like that again."

I was not sure I wanted to again experience something so awe-inspiring, yes, but also frightening.

Meanwhile, Moses spoke to Aaron and the priests began working in the tabernacle courtyard.

Aaron's sons led a calf to him and with his gleaming knife he slit its throat. The animal's legs buckled as the priests held it over the basin to drain its blood. Aaron dipped his finger in the blood and smeared some on each horn-shaped corner of the altar, then poured the rest out at the base, staining the desert floor dark wine.

His sons cut the animal apart. Some pieces they placed on the altar, below which a fire was burning. Flames leaped to lick at the portions. Soon the air was full of the scent of burning flesh and smoke. Other pieces of the animal they threw in a heap and still others they washed then placed on the altar.

One by one they killed the animals. The smell of roasting meat made my mouth water. We hadn't eaten meat for a long time.

Though the sacrifices took a good while to complete, for some reason I could not take my eyes off what was happening. Maybe that was because the light from cloud seemed to be getting brighter. It was as if Yahweh Himself was watching.

At last all the animals had been sacrificed and the altar fire burned low. Aaron stood facing us and I saw his once-clean priest clothes were stained with blood and char, though his hands, which he raised toward us in blessing, were clean.

In a voice softer than Moses' but still strong and clear he spoke:

"The Lord bless you and keep you.

The Lord make His face shine upon you and be gracious to you;

The Lord lift up his countenance upon you and give you peace."

Then he and Moses went into the tabernacle.

"What happens now?" I asked.

"We wait," said Grandfather Hur.

We waited for a long time. That was one thing I was learning. You couldn't rush Moses when he was with Yahweh.

At last Moses and Aaron came out of the tent and stood before us. They both raised their hands toward us and said, together,

"The Lord bless you and keep you

The Lord make His face shine upon you..."

As they were speaking, light from the cloud grew brighter and brighter. Then a roar came from within it and flames leaped out, engulfing the charred pieces of sacrifice still smouldering on the altar. The sacrifice caught on fire again in a brilliant flame.

The crowd gave a collective gasp and someone began to cheer. I stood to join in but my legs had become as weak as reeds. I couldn't stay upright, and I fell to the ground.

How long I remained there, I don't know. Gradually I became aware of the movement of those around me— Father, Mother, Grandfather. I sat up and dared to look again at the tabernacle. The whole enclosure was still bathed in radiance. Moses and Aaron were prostrate.

Two of Aaron's sons were up though. They staggered toward the tent door with incense censers in their hands. Smoke drifted from the censers. They walked so unsteadily I had the thought that one of them might trip, fall, and burn himself.

As they got to the door of the tabernacle and were about to go in, I heard the roar again, then saw flames leap, this time from the inside of the tent. Fire engulfed the men and they dropped to the ground.

There was a collective gasp from the crowd.

Moses and Aaron roused and walked to where Aaron's sons were lying. Moses reached out his hand to one to give him a hand up, but the man on the ground lay motionless.

Moses and Aaron crouched down beside them and shouted. Moses took one of their hands in his and held it as if to feel for signs of life. Aaron placed his hand near the face of the other. There was still no movement from either of the men.

Moses rolled them over, then he and Aaron rose heavily to their feet. Somewhere in the crowd a woman screamed, a scream of despair that trailed into a death wail.

"What happened?" I asked. "Why did the fire come at them and burn them?"

Grandfather Hur looked shaken. "I don't know," he said.

In the meantime, Moses called other men from the tribe of Levi to move the bodies. They wrapped them in their priestly clothes, using their tunics as litters to carry them. People opened a path to let them by. They passed near us and I smelled smoke, incense, and the scent of something sour. Grandfather smelled it too. "Maybe they were confused with wine," he said.

The atmosphere in the crowd had changed. Smiles had been replaced by the silence of stunned disbelief and quiet mutters of confusion. Though Moses and Aaron continued their activities inside the tabernacle and courtyard, people began to leave. Our family too gathered our water jugs and mats to trudge home.

Mother seemed particularly disturbed. "Why would Yahweh lash out like that?" she asked Father on the walk. "What a cruel thing to do. This God of Moses' makes no sense." [5]

Chapter Three

Another week passed. As the one-year anniversary of our leaving Egypt approached, our family prepared to celebrate the Passover feast. Father chose another perfect lamb. This time it wasn't a pet like Curls. By now I knew better than to get attached to a lamb like I did to him.

We searched the tent for leaven and destroyed it all. While Mother baked unleavened bread with the little flour we had left, she sent me out to look for bitter herbs. Cetura and Sephy were on the same errand. The three of us clambered around on the rocks and scoured the crevices for greenery. We found no parsley, peppermint, or lettuce here but there was spicy oregano, lemony homath, and horsemint.

Back at home, Father slaughtered the lamb. He rigged a tripod over the cooking fire near our tent and after skinning the animal, hung it to roast. Meanwhile I helped mother with the meal.

I was not good with food like she was. Neither was I as particular and fussy. But she insisted that I help her. "You want to be a good wife someday, don't you?" she asked.

Why did everyone think of us girls as being only wives? Did Miriam's mother hound her about marriage too? She seemed to have gotten along very well without a husband!

The smell of roasting meat soon filled the air. It came not only from our fire but from the cooking fires all around us. My stomach rumbled and my mouth watered.

Inside the tent, we placed the cushions around the mat that would soon hold our food. Already set out was the salad of oregano, homath, and mint, and the matzo or unleavened bread.

At last the lamb was ready. As the sun was beginning to set we gathered around the food. Grandfather Hur held his hands out over us in a blessing before we started. He thanked Yahweh for leading us this far on our way out of Egypt and to the Promised Land. He gave thanks for every part of the meal — the lamb and its blood that kept the Death Angel away a year ago in Egypt, the matzo free of the defilement of leaven, the bitter herbs symbolizing generations of slavery we left behind...

Finally, he was finished and we could eat the food we had been smelling for the last hours. As I took in a mouthful of meat and matzo, I was transported back to our house in Egypt. All around us then there were bundles. We were ready to leave, just as Moses had instructed us. We were all exhausted from packing and making the meal. After eating, mother and I had fallen asleep on the floor only to be awakened by the screams and wails of the Egyptians whose sons had died at the hand of the Death Angel.

The others around our table were apparently remembering the same things. "No Death Angel to fear this year," said Grandfather Hur.

"No Egyptians bringing us their gold and clothes and begging us to leave," said Bezalel.

"No door frames to paint with blood," said Father.

"I can't wait till I have a door frame again!" That was Mother for you. She brought us back to earth. "Now eat up. We don't want to have to burn this precious meat." [6]

* * *

It was a few days after Passover when we were called to assemble once more. Now that the tabernacle was up and things were happening, it was exciting!

The standards of each tribe ringed the area where we gathered. We milled around with hundreds of others near our Lion banner. Messengers mingled amongst us as they instructed us to gather into clans and file past our leader Nahshon.

He sat near our Judah ensign, with a man on each side, scrolls before them, styluses in hand. The line moved slowly but finally our family stood before him and his helpers.

"Recite your family line and age, Nahshon instructed Grandfather Hur. As Grandfather spoke, one of the men wrote in his scroll. Father gave the same information. When it was Bezalel's turn, Nahshon asked, "How old are you son?"

"Twenty years old—almost twenty-one."

"Good. Tell us, then, your lineage and name."

"Bezalel, son of Uri, son of Hur of the tribe of Judah."

He didn't ask mother or me for our names and ages, though, or write anything as we passed by. Neither did he record the names of Reisa, Simeon, and Talia.

"Why are they doing this" I asked Father. "What does it mean?"

"It's a census. Moses needs to know how many men are available—probably for war."

"War? When will we need to go to war?"

"There are nations and tribes living in the Promised Land where we're headed. Though Yahweh has promised it to us, He has told Moses we will not be able to inhabit it without a fight," said Grandfather Hur.

A breath of fear chilled the delight I felt. If there was a war, would Grandfather, Father, and Bezalel have to fight? People were killed in battle, I knew. I couldn't imagine any life, here or in the Promised Land, without all of my family. [7]

* * *

It took a month for the census to be completed. Then one day word came from our leaders. We were moving. I went out and studied the cloud, which still rested over the tabernacle. Even though it stayed stationery, we were to move?

"Why?" Mother asked, as she began bundling our clothes.

"Moses says it is to be so," said Grandfather Hur. "According to Nahshon we are now to camp in order of tribes. We'll be organized according to the armies of fighting men that were just counted."

"I don't like this talk of fighting," Mother muttered.

"Well, we are getting closer to the Promised land," Father reminded her.

Mention of the Promised Land churned up the excitement I had felt earlier. Could it be that our time in this hot and cold, dusty, barren, harsh place would really be over soon? I could only imagine how wonderful it would be to live in a house again, though I didn't like the thought of war any more than Mother did. I gathered my things and began rolling and tying up bundles of clothes and covers.

We hadn't moved for months. Pulling down our tent and getting our animals roped together for the move took us longer than when we did it every day. At last we were ready to set out.

Grandfather, as our family head, had been told

where we were to go. We joined the crowds of others, streaming toward the plain around the tabernacle. Walking even this short distance laden with our belongings brought back memories—not good ones! At last we reached the spot marked with Judah's banner. Grandfather met friends and began to talk with them. Father and Mother chose a patch of level ground. I helped clear away rocks and then Father and Bezalel erected the tent under Mother's exacting eye. They were about to pound the stakes that secured its ropes to the ground when Grandfather Hur returned.

"No," he said. "We must turn the tent so that the opening faces the tabernacle."

"But that means our entryway will be open to the hot late-day sun," Mother objected.

Father, though, didn't argue. "We'll move it," he said.

I was glad he made that decision. After seeing what happened to Aaron's sons, I didn't want us to take the chance of making Yahweh angry.

I helped Mother organize the tent the way she liked it and then got permission to find my friends. Wandering through the confusion of our tribe getting settled, I finally found Cetura, a good walk from where we were camped.

"What about Sephy?" I asked. Do you know where she is now?"

"No. We'll have to find her in the camp of Dan. And who knows where that is. Maybe your mother can help. She was from the tribe of Dan, wasn't she?"

Indeed, Mother was from Dan. However, I knew that it would be no use to ask her, for she would have no better idea than we had so early in the move.

"Maybe we can find her on our own," I suggested. I knew well, from Mother, what Dan's banner looked like. How hard could it be to find Sephy with the tribal ensigns waving above us throughout the multitude?

We walked in the direction of the tabernacle and soon found ourselves, having passed the tents of Judah, wandering amongst the encampment of Levi. To the right I saw a donkey ensign — Issachar.

When we got to the border of the tabernacle courtyard, I saw there were tents as far as the eye could see on all sides with tribal banners so distant, they were impossible to make out. The immensity of our company hit me. We could walk all day and not find Sephy.

Meanwhile people were bustling by. Surely someone would know where the tribe of Dan was camped.

"Do you know where to go?" Cetura asked.

"Not exactly. Maybe we should ask someone."

Cetura, who was always very proper, looked questioningly at me. I knew that girls didn't usually ask for directions from strangers. Still, I was sure Miriam would do such a thing.

I glanced about for some woman from whom to ask directions and my attention was caught by a handsome stranger. His eyes were on me and when I looked at his face, our eyes met for a second. Quickly I looked down, but already he was approaching.

"You ladies look lost," he said. "Can I help you?"

I ignored him and started walking again, as did Cetura. But he fell into step beside her. "Ladies, I'm happy to help," he said.

"We're looking for the camp of Dan," Cetura said at last. We exchanged uncomfortable looks. Somehow my face had gone burning hot and I didn't look up.

"I happen to be going that way," he said. "You're in luck because it's not far. Just around the corner and past the tents of Naphtali."

We walked along in awkward silence until, for some reason I looked at him again to see his eyes boring into me. His hair was black and curly, his olive skin smooth and tanned. There was a hint of a smile around his mouth and his eyes were lively. I quickly looked down again.

"Where are you ladies from?" he asked, looking at Cetura for an answer.

His smile and friendly manner had obviously reassured her for she smiled back, though tentatively. "We're from Judah," she said. "We are looking for our friend."

Something inside me rose up in warning and I walked along without saying anything, hoping Cetura would say no more. My family would be aghast at us walking openly with a man we didn't know.

"Do you like your new camp spot?" he asked. He seemed harmless enough. He looked about Bezalel's age, maybe a little older. Surely, he was a brother to someone like Bezalel was to me. I knew Bezalel would never wish me harm, and so why was I suspicious of him?

"Yes, it's fine," Cetura said, "though Judah's camp is very big. It will take a while to get familiar with everything."

"And what about you?" he asked, looking directly at me.

I glanced into his face again, and again those eyes — burrowing into me, their flick over my form, then up again to my face — were entirely unnerving. My whole body went hot and I looked down. "It's okay," I say. "Our family is together, and that's the important thing."

"And whose family might that be?'

The forwardness of his question annoyed me and I felt resistance rising. Why was he trying to pull all this information out of us when we didn't know anything about him? "You ask a lot of questions," I said, trying to keep my voice light.

"Oh, I'll tell you about myself," he said, as if reading my mind. "I'm Pallu, of the tribe of Reuben, son of Abiram. And I'm perfectly safe."

"I'm sure you are," said Cetura, looking over at me as if to say, *don't be rude*. And then, perhaps annoyed that Pallu kept looking at me, told him all. "My name is Cetura and this is Zamri. As I mentioned, we're from the tribe of Judah. I'm from the family of Hamul, she's from the family of Hur."

"The relative of Bezalel the goldsmith?" he asked, looking at me with even more interest.

I looked up and met his eyes again. "Yes," I said.

We had reached the Eagle and Snake ensign of Dan and, looking around, I wondered how, even though we were here, we would ever find Sephy in this crowd — or explain Pallu's presence to her. Then I heard her voice. "Zamri! Cetura! You found me!"

I looked around to see her running toward us. And Pallu had disappeared into the crowd. [8]

Chapter Four

"We have a job to do," Mother said one morning a few days later. "We need to weave more tent panels to make a room for Bezalel and his bride."

My heart fell. I had planned on going to Cetura's. I had an idea of how to make timbrels and her mother didn't mind us making a mess. But now Mother was all bustle. As she pulled out the basket of goat hair we had collected, along with a couple of spindles and a loom, I knew I had no choice but to stay home.

"I don't know how to spin or weave," I said, hoping this would be reason enough for her to release me from this task. When we were still in Egypt and Mother was too weary to teach me, I'm sure my excuse would have worked. But things had changed.

"Well, it's time you learned." she said. "I've arranged for the aunts and cousins to join us. We'll work together. You will enjoy it."

After she got the loom set up and the spindle threaded, she sat on the cushion beside me to demonstrate how spinning was done.

I'd watched her many times. It didn't look that difficult—the way she spun the spindle against her thigh and fed the raw hairs to be drawn in and twisted into thread. But when I tried to copy her, I found I needed at least two more hands. Soon the spindle's shaft was a tangled mess of unevenly spooled yarn.

As we worked to untangle what I'd done, a couple of aunts and cousins arrived. They had their own spindles and looms. Mother left me so she could welcome them and tell them what she wanted done.

Soon everyone was at work. But my tangled spindle was hopeless. I set it aside and watched my young cousin Jaffa, Reisa's little sister. She was not yet eleven but under her blur-quick hands, the stream of yarn flowed with steady grace.

"How do you do that?" I asked.

"Easy," she said, and proceeded to demonstrate, but so quickly I couldn't follow her busy motions.

Mother had set Aunt Sarah to weaving the black yarn into a tent panel. I cast my tangled spindle aside and went over to watch her at the loom. This looked more like something I could do. After a while I asked, "Can I try?"

"Do you know how?" she asked.

"I've been watching you."

"Here, let me explain while I show you."

She took the wooden shuttle with yarn attached to it like a giant needle, and slowly wove it in and out, through the threads that were stretched the length of the loom. She showed me how to snug them tight before threading the shuttle through the threads the opposite way. Then she handed the shuttle to me and I clumsily maneuvered it in and out, and then started back.

"Make sure you check that it's tight," she said, showing me how much space I had left between the rows. After watching me for a couple rows more she left me to work on my own. As I wove the shuttle back and forth, I thought how surprised and pleased Sephy would be to see me doing this thing she loved and was so good at.

Gradually I got into a rhythm. As my hands became accustomed to the in and out motion, my need to concentrate lessened and I found myself listening to the conversation around me. Mother and the aunts talked about what had happened over the last few weeks and how magnificent the tabernacle looked. They thought Bezalel and his crew had done an amazing job crafting all the golden objects — observations that I knew would make Mother happy. They also talked of other things. One of the cousins was expecting a baby and hoped we wouldn't be traveling again soon. The aunts wanted to know more about Sebia. There had been rumours, one of them said, that in Egypt she had a shady past. I perked up my ears.

Mother didn't reply to that but instead changed the subject. How were they enjoying the manna, she asked, and had they discovered any new ways of serving it? I detected sarcasm in her voice.

Mother came over to me to check my work. "Zamri, this is much too loose!"

There was a sharp tone in her voice. I interpreted it as her being upset but about more than just my work. She was probably bothered by the gossip about Sebia.

I worked to tighten the weave, then stood up to stretch my arms and wriggle stiff shoulders. "I need a break," I said. Mother nodded.

On the way back from the latrine, I thought about Sephy again. She would so enjoy our spinning and weaving gathering. Surely mother wouldn't miss me for the short while it would take for me to fetch her.

I was well past the tents of Judah and on the path that connected the encampments to the east and north of the tabernacle when I saw him again. Pallu. He was standing beside the pathway, watching the passersby.

My heart pounded and my face grew hot. I pulled

my head covering further forward and turned my face away as I passed where he was standing. Had he seen me? I hoped not. Why did his presence send both fear and excitement through me?

* * *

I easily found Sephy's tent this time. She was in the courtyard of their encampment and when she saw me she ran to greet me.

"Zamri, it's so good to see you. I have such news!" She grabbed my hand, drew me inside the tent, through the common section and to the women's room behind it. She motioned me to a cushion and when we were both seated, leaned near and whispered, "Father and Shoshan's father are meeting today." Her black eyes sparkled. "I've overheard Mother and Father discussing wedding contract and dowry." Her voice hiccupped in a giggle. "It's really happening!"

"You're about to be officially betrothed?"

"It looks that way!"

I gave Sephy a big hug. I was so happy for her—and Shoshan.

"Wedding doings with us too," I said. "I came to see if you'd like to join the work gathering in our tent. We're weaving panels to make a room for Bezalel and Sebia."

Sephy gave a squeal of delight. "How exciting!"

"I could use your help. Maybe you could teach me some of what you know."

"I'd love to!" Sephy said.

We went in search of her mother and with her permission were soon on the way back to our tent. As we walked, I kept glancing around. Would I see Pallu again? But he was nowhere in sight. My disappointment surprised me.

On approaching our tent, I heard Jaffa's voice calling out, "Zamri's back!"

"Where did you go?" Mother came to meet us, disapproval furrowing her forehead.

"To get Sephy. She's going to help me."

"Why didn't you tell someone?"

"I only thought of it when coming back from the pits," I said. "It would have meant a lot of extra walking."

Back at the tent the aunts and cousins looked up, some with curiosity others with frowns on their faces. Aunt Sarah said, "Don't get too independent, Zamri. You'll want a good husband soon—and men like compliant women."

I said nothing, but in my mind, I answered back. *Who says I even want to marry, especially a man who wants a meek wife?*

Chapter Five

Two days later I was still half asleep when I heard Grandfather Hur. There was urgency in his voice as he talked to Mother and Father. "The cloud has moved. I think we'll be traveling again soon."

I grabbed my robe and joined everyone to look at the sky outside the tent. Sure enough. The cloud had lifted from its place over the tabernacle and was now high above us to the north and east. It reminded me of all the other times the cloud showed us it was time to move on. I felt excitement and dread.

"Oh no," Mother said. "I had hoped to get the tent panels done before we had to pack up."

Bezalel put his arm around her shoulders. "Don't worry Mother. All will come together at the right time."

"Well, we'd better start packing and readying the animals." Father headed toward our sheep and goats. Mother went back into the tent and returned with the manna basket. "Here you go," she said, handing it to me.

I trudged to my customary spot for collecting the day's food. Cetura was there and someone was with her. Pallu. My heart began to pound and I felt my face grow hot. But before I had a chance to change direction, Cetura saw me and waved. Her face glowed as she watched me approach. Could it be Pallu's presence that brought that sparkle to her eyes?

Pallu looked up now from filling his own basket. "Oh, it's the goldsmith's sister," he said. I glanced at his face. His eyes laughed, teased, and challenged.

I felt like I needed to explain my presence. "Mother

sent me out," I said. And then I babbled on. "I need to hurry. The cloud has moved. It looks like we will break camp today."

Pallu and Cetura looked up. "Aren't you the observant one to notice with those pretty eyes," Pallu said.

His personal comment hung in the air. I glanced at Cetura. Her face was bent in concentration over her task. Maybe she hadn't heard. I buried my face in the folds of my cloak and busied myself with picking up the white rounds.

As if unaware of how his comment had affected me, Pallu went on. "I don't know why we have to move with that ridiculous cloud anyway. I think it's just something Moses has invented because he doesn't know what he's doing — or where he's going."

"You don't believe that Yahweh's presence lives in the cloud?" Cetura said. "How do you explain what happened over the mountain and at the tabernacle?"

"What do you think?" he asked. I looked up to see that Pallu was now beside me, addressing me.

I didn't know what to say. Of course I believed that Yahweh's presence was in the cloud and that He led us with it. Pallu's confidence that it wasn't so unnerved me. I said nothing as I kept piling manna into my basket.

"Not talking?" he asked. He came near, crouched down, leaned his face close to mine, and reached out to tug at a bit of hair that had escaped my headdress. His fingers brushed my cheek. "What's going on under those black curls?"

I recoiled. No man from outside my family had ever touched me in this way.

"Come now, I won't hurt you," he said gently,

releasing my hair. "I'm perfectly harmless, right?" He looked at Cetura.

I glanced at her face. The light that had been there earlier had gone out. She looked at us numbly. "I guess."

"Please, I have to hurry," I said as I stood, drew back a few steps, then squatted down again to my gathering. My thoughts were so jumbled I didn't even notice when Pallu and Cetura left or that I was collecting way more manna than our family would eat in a day.

Back at the camp our things were in the usual disarray of packing up.

"That took you long enough," Mother said. "Here, dump enough for breakfast in this pot. Then go pack."

I did as she said. In the privacy of the tent I touched cool palms to my still-hot face. It felt like everyone around could see where Pallu had touched me. What a relief to be away from probing eyes.

What did his words and touch mean? Was this the beginning of courtship? Was this how men and women came together? Did he want me? Was this how Shoshan let Sephy know he wanted her?

I began bundling my clothes, hair combs, the gold chain that Bezalel had made for me. But my mind was still on Pallu. I didn't feel happy about him, like Sephy felt about Shoshan. In fact, I didn't want to tell anyone and hoped Cetura wouldn't say anything. What could she say?

"Are you almost done, Zamri?" Mother called. "Hurry. We need to collapse the tent."

I tied the last of my bundles and emerged from the tent with them. While I was eating my portion of boiled manna, a messenger from Nahshon came by our camp. He gave instructions to Father and Grandfather about

Judah being the first tribe to leave camp and that we must listen for signals from some trumpets. They would tell us when to begin to move. Judah's soldiers were to lead the way. Father and Bezalel would need to march with the army. The rest of us were to follow behind, but stay together as a tribe.

I was glad of that. There was no chance that I would run into Pallu as we were traveling. [9]

* * *

"Can I have a drink from your water skin," I asked Mother. "Please? I emptied mine a while back."

Mother's expression of grim resignation didn't change as she trudged beside me. "I suppose," she said at last and handed me the skin. "But don't empty it. I need it to last till we stop."

On this second day out from Sinai, the early novelty of moving on had been replaced by the memories of all those hot, thirsty steps we had taken to get there. I could tell by the look on Mother's face and the tone of her voice that her patience had already worn thin. So had mine.

Thankfully, a little farther on we stopped. Grandfather Hur helped us put up a makeshift shelter. Under its shade, we were protected from the burning midday heat as we ate our manna. The water in our skins, refilled from the supply strapped to one of our goats, was warm, but at least it was wet.

I kept thinking of Pallu, replaying what happened the day we left. Did he think of me, I wondered? What did he think of me? I tried to shove thoughts of him from my mind with distractions. I gave Simeon a drink from my water skin and took crying Talia from Reisa's swaddling bands to give her arms and shoulders a rest.

As we set out in the late afternoon, Mother was

cheerier. "At least we're on the move again," she said. "After all that time at Sinai, never making progress, now there's hope of getting to the Promised Land."

I imagined what the Promised Land would be like. No more moving at the whim of Moses or a cloud. No more walking through sand, clambering over boulders, and pulling burrs from clothes by the evening fire.

"Will Bezalel and Sebia still live with us?" I asked.

"Oh yes," Mother said. "But we'll have a proper house there, I expect, and not be living in a crowded tent."

My imagination wandered back to Pallu. Suppose his attentions were serious. Suppose he wanted to marry me. I shoved the thought aside and yet it kept coming back. If I married, I would have to move away from my family to my husband's home. Of course, the time of entering a new land would be a good time to start a new home. But would marriage, even to someone as handsome as Pallu, be worth giving up my dream of being like Miriam? Not that I'd have any say in the matter, for if my family arranged for me to marry, I knew I would have to marry. I needed to know more about Pallu. Maybe a talk with Cetura would help. I could find out what she knew about him and his clan.

After we'd walked for a while I asked Mother for permission to join Cetura. "I suppose," she said. "But don't be getting lost or distracted."

I hurried along beside the families of Judah until I spotted my friend. But when I caught up to her, she seemed less than thrilled to see me.

I greeted her family and then we walked by ourselves. "Are you angry with me?" I asked.

"Why should I be angry?" she said. But there was

annoyance in her voice.

"Because of what happened with that man—Pallu?" I felt my face burn even as I said his name.

"Pallu and I were talking when you came along and spoiled it all by flirting with him."

"Flirting? I never said or did anything you could say was flirting!"

She was quiet for a long time, then said, "I suppose you're right."

"What do you think of him? What did he say to you before I got there?"

"He seemed very nice. He didn't say much. He was friendly and helpful. Said I was a good worker."

"Where does he come from again?"

"Reuben. Remember he told us? I asked my parents about him. There are rumours that his father Abiram is one of Moses' critics."

A chill came over me. I knew how my family, especially Grandfather Hur, felt about those who complained against Moses. So much for him, unless I wanted trouble with Grandfather, Father, and Bezalel. Mother's quiet grumblings were enough for one family.

* * *

"I'm cold!" Simeon whimpered as we set out again early the next morning. Reisa was busy with baby Talia, so I took Simeon's hand. "It will warm up soon enough."

Reisa, Simeon, and I walked together in silence. Around us we heard the conversations of others.

"I really preferred staying at Mount Sinai to this," Aunt Sarah said.

"But at least we're moving," Mother replied. "The more I think of it, the more I wish we'd moved on sooner."

"Are you questioning Moses again?" Grandfather Hur said. "That comes to no good you know."

I saw Mother and Aunt Sarah exchange knowing looks, but their talk stopped for a while.

As we walked on and on, the desert chill dissipated in sunlight and soon we were sweating in the heat. Simeon, who had long ago left my side to race off with children his age, returned to Reisa, tugged at her robe, and whined, "I'm hot and thirsty. Can we stop?"

"Here, have a drink," I offered, opening my water skin.

By the time we finally halted for our midday break, the atmosphere was heavy with complaints and grumbling. While we rested, a messenger came by. He was not the usual messenger that came from Nahshon.

"For anyone who would like to discuss travel conditions, there will be a meeting on the eastern edge of the camp when we stop for the night," he said. "Pass the message on."

"Sounds like trouble," Grandfather Hur muttered after the man left.

"Moses has to expect something like this," Mother countered. "Surely he knows he can't keep putting us through these hardships without resistance from the people."

I thought of Pallu and the things I'd heard him say about Moses. I wouldn't be at all surprised if Pallu was at that meeting.

* * *

The late afternoon trek was no more pleasant than the morning one. We were all exhausted when we finally stopped to set up camp for the night. Still, I wanted to go to the meeting the messenger had talked about. I dared not speak of it, though, for I knew Grandfather Hur and Mother would forbid it. Also, though I didn't admit it even to myself, but I wanted to see Pallu again.

I had a plan. I told Mother I was going to the latrine. I said it quietly and no one from the encampment offered to join me. On the way back to our tent, I detoured past the east border of the camp.

Sure enough, in the light from the cloud overhead I saw, in the distance, a cluster of shadowy shapes gathered around some flares. Even from far away I heard loud, angry voices.

"Does Moses have any idea where he's leading us?"

"Why did we stop now? It would make far more sense to travel further during the cool of night."

"I'm for taking my family and turning back to Egypt."

When I reached the crowd, I scanned the people around me. By the light of the flares I saw, some distance away, Pallu beside a man that looked a lot like him, only older. That must be his father. I pulled my head covering farther over my face. I didn't want Pallu to see me.

I got jostled and felt closed in as more and more people joined the gathering. Individual words were lost in the mutter and mumble. Then a man spoke above the rest.

"People, Moses has made us miserable again by driving us through this desert. I've called you together to decide on a plan of action. What do you propose we...“

From nowhere a bolt of blinding light struck him. It was like lightning, but came from the starry sky!

There was shocked silence as flames rose and engulfed him. Then, as the flames leapt and spread to others, screams shattered the stillness as those nearby comprehended what was happening. I got pushed back, crushed, and stepped on as people staggered backward, recoiling from the fire. Some who were covered with flames broke from the crowd to roll on the ground. Quickly the crowd scattered. I turned and ran but not before glancing back once more to see that the fire raged on.

* * *

I was happy when Cetura joined me in the manna fields the next morning. It felt good to tell someone what I had seen the night before (leaving out Pallu, of course). "Grandfather Hur was out looking for me," I concluded. "He and mother were very upset with me."

No trumpet signal told us to pack up this morning. Did this mean we would get a break? I almost dozed off to sleep again when Mother pulled out the loom and put me to work. Grandfather Hur went to talk with the men. He returned with Father and Bezalel. They all looked serious.

"Many died last night," Grandfather said. The fire never went out until someone got Moses and he prayed. He has called this place 'Taberah' — burning."

"What did they do to deserve such a punishment?" Mother asked.

"The usual it seems — grumbling and complaining about the conditions, no water, Moses, the trip in general."

Mother shook her head. "Too harsh," I heard her mutter.

I kept thinking of Pallu. Did he survive the fire? Was he still alive? [10]

Chapter Six

We were now several days away from Taberah and Yahweh's burning punishment. At first, everyone had carried on in chastened silence. It was almost as if we were afraid that whatever we said would invite Yahweh's unpredictable anger. But now the grumbling had started again.

"Why did we ever come along on this journey with no end?"

"I know. I'm sick of walking. Sick of no water. Sick of sand, wind, and this tasteless manna."

"Remember the fish we used to have in Egypt and all the beautiful foods from our gardens—cucumbers, melons, garlics, and leeks?"

"Stop! I can't stand it."

This was the talk I overheard from women gathering manna next to me. Some of them were dressed in Egyptian clothes. Others appeared to be Hebrews.

The women's talk of the foods of Egypt got my mouth watering. I could scarcely remember the last time I had dug my teeth into a cool melon or enjoyed the sting of fresh garlic on my tongue.

This morning, it looked like we were stopping because the cloud hovered over the tabernacle and the trumpet signal for us to move on had not sounded. Nearing the camp from collecting our day's food, I was sure I heard weeping. Threading my way through the tents I saw women and men standing by tent openings, wailing. At our tent, Mother had joined with them.

Grandfather Hur, along with Father and Bezalel who joined us when we camped for a time, looked at each other helplessly. "Don't think you'll sway Moses with those tears," Grandfather Hur said.

Mother didn't stop, though, until a runner came to our tent with a message for Grandfather. Moses had called a meeting and requested his presence.

Mother looked on apprehensively. I imagined her thoughts: Did this meeting mean Moses would do something about the complaints? Or was more trouble on the way?

Grandfather Hur returned after a few hours. "Moses has asked me to serve as one of seventy elders again," he said. "The entire congregation is to come to the tabernacle tomorrow for the commissioning.

* * *

Grandfather Hur left early the next morning. Later all of us joined the families from Judah and other tribes that gathered around the tabernacle.

It was hard to see through the press of people, but Father found a large level boulder, big enough for all of us to stand on. From this vantage point I could see Moses. Near him was a crowd of men—Grandfather Hur among them. Beside me Jaffa helped lift Simeon to give him a view of what was happening.

Though people were still assembling, Moses raised his arms for silence. Then he called out, "Yahweh has told me of your complaints and how you are pining for the food of Egypt and for meat. You have wept in Yahweh's hearing saying, 'Who will give us meat to eat? For it was well with us in Egypt.' Therefore, the Lord will give you meat, and you shall eat.

"Consecrate yourselves, for tomorrow you shall eat meat—not for one day or two days. Not for five days or ten days. Not even for twenty days, but for a whole month."

The crowd erupted in a cheer, which became a buzz of excited conversation.

"Meat? Did he say meat? And for a month?"

"But how can this be?"

"Does he expect us to butcher our sheep and goats?"

Moses' clear voice broke into the chatter. "You will indeed eat meat until you are sick of it. Until it comes out of your nostrils and you loathe it because you have despised the Lord who is among you and have wept before Him saying, 'Why did we ever come out of Egypt?'"

Beside me Mother looked as uncomfortable as I felt. Had Moses been listening in on our conversations? Did Yahweh know our very thoughts?

Moses continued.

"Now for another matter. God has told me to choose helpers. I have chosen seventy men to aid me in leading you. Come to them first with your disputes, quarrels, and complaints."

Moses now spoke quietly to the men around him and they spread out to surround the tabernacle. As I watched, I saw that the cloud that sat above the tabernacle was moving, getting bigger, and spreading wider until it not only covered the entire tabernacle but the men around it. A voice rumbled from within the cloud. I heard what sounded like words but didn't understand them.

It was frightening. I buried my face in my hands. These times when the cloud acted so mysteriously left me feeling completely exposed and full of regret for all the times I had doubted Yahweh and grumbled along with everyone else. I would never do it again, I promised myself.

Simeon's cry, beside me, was full of fear. I opened my eyes to take his hand and noticed that the cloud around the men had lifted somewhat. Some of them were lying face down on the ground. Others stood with hands and faces raised, speaking and shouting. Seeing they still lived and were worshiping reassured me.

For the first time this day, my eyes went from the tabernacle court to the crowd around me. As I scanned the faces I saw, not fifty paces away, Pallu, staring at me. For a second our eyes connected.

My heart lurched. He was not killed at Taberah!

Now for some reason I looked forward to gathering manna tomorrow. But before nightfall, Moses' promise of meat visited us in a way that consumed all our attention for the remainder of this day and many days to come.

* * *

Quail

Someone cried "Quail!"
We heard it above the hissing sand-wind
saw a cloud on the distant horizon
dark and locust-like.

We heard above the hissing sand-wind
the flap and whir of wings
—dark and locust-like—
a cloud that splintered into a thousand birds.

The flap and whir of wings...
quail were everywhere
clouds splintering into a million birds.
We trapped them with bare hands.

Quail were everywhere!
Even just-weaned babes caught them
trapped them with bare hands.
We would eat meat tonight!

Even just-weaned babes caught them.
What would we do with baskets full of birds?
We would eat meat tonight
and tomorrow and tomorrow and tomorrow...

What could we do with baskets full of birds?
We roasted them, smoked them, dried them in the
sun
for tomorrow and tomorrow and tomorrow
till our stomachs ached, cramped, gurgled, railed.

Roasted, smoked, dried in the sun
we'd had our fill and still there were more.
Our stomachs ached, cramped, gurgled, and railed
over rotten stench of death in the camp—and the
wail.

We'd had our fill and still there were more
of those clouds on the distant horizon
the rotten stench of death in the camp and the
wail...
Now no one cried "Quail!"

* * *

Mother was especially sick after eating too much
meat. There were days I thought we would lose her, for
her stomach, long emptied, didn't tolerate even tea or
water, though I managed to squeeze some liquid into her
mouth from a soaked cloth.

After many days, she began to rally—not like six
others from our encampment who died. As for me, I

never thought I'd prefer manna to anything, let alone meat. But I did. I even craved manna's bland, comforting sweetness.

We camped for an entire month. Some would have liked to stay longer because of the graves they had to leave behind. Grandfather Hur told us Moses called this place "Kibroth Hattaavah" meaning "Graves of Lusters." I was so grateful Mother wasn't in one of them! [11]

Chapter Seven

Jaffa and I caught sight of it during morning manna gathering some weeks after moving on from Kibroth—a lone tent outside the camp. "What is that tent doing off by itself?" I asked Cetura.

"No idea."

I asked about it when I got home. Grandfather Hur nodded as if this was no surprise to him. "It's Miriam," he said.

"Why? What happened?"

"She and Aaron were questioning Moses' leadership. They've been stirring up criticism over his wife. Yesterday God called the three of them to the tabernacle. Some of us witnessed what happened—an argument, then the cloud fell on them and Yahweh's voice spoke from the cloud. When it lifted, Miriam was covered in leprosy."

Leprosy? Miriam had leprosy?

"What will happen to her?" I asked. I knew lepers weren't allowed to be around others. Yet I couldn't imagine leaving behind someone sick and alone, especially when that someone was an important person like Miriam.

"That's to be seen," Grandfather said. "Aaron apologized for both of them and begged for Moses' prayers. Perhaps God will heal her. We will be staying here to await the seven prescribed days before Aaron inspects her to see if her leprosy remains." [12]

Mother, who had been listening along with me, shook her head and muttered, "Yahweh is very strict.".

* * *

Next morning when Jaffa and I went out to do our morning chore, I couldn't stop looking at Mariam's tent. Was she lonely, I wondered, or sad, or scared? Leprosy was so dreaded, surely no one would go to see her, though someone from her family must leave her food and water. Could this be a chance for me to see her up close, perhaps even talk with her?

"It's Miriam in that tent," I told Cetura, who was already busily collecting manna. I related what Grandfather Hur told me. "Let's go over and cheer her up," I said.

Cetura and Jaffa looked at me aghast. "Are you mad?" Cetura asked. "Of course not! You would become unclean like her."

"We wouldn't go close. Just near enough to let her know we haven't forgotten her."

Cetura wasn't swayed. I got to work. But the sight of that lone tent haunted me. When Cetura left for the camp and Jaffa went with her, I stood, stretched, and gazed again at the solitary tent. Should I? With no one from our encampment around, it seemed like the perfect opportunity.

I picked up my basket and strode toward Miriam's tent till I was close enough to see her sitting alone outside the opening, under an awning that shielded her from the sun. She saw me coming and called out, "Unclean! Unclean!" Her voice was rough and gravelly.

"I know," I said, stopping some distance away beside a solitary empty basket that sat on a rock. I didn't know what to say next and suddenly felt embarrassed. *Why did I ever do this?* I was ready to turn and run but before I did, she called out, "Who are you?"

"Zamri," I said, "daughter of Uri, son of Hur, of the tribe of Judah."

"Oh, I know your grandfather," she said. "Her voice had smoothed and her wrinkled face softened into a smile. She didn't look sick.

"I brought you some food," I said. As she watched from a distance, I transferred some of the manna from my basket into the empty one beside me.

What now? Encouraged by her seeming interest, I decided I would say to her what I had intended.

"I like how you played the timbrel at the Red Sea and how you danced."

"Why, thank you, child. I have always felt Yahweh's fire in me to play and dance."

"Someday I'd like to lead the women just like you did." My dream tumbled out.

Miriam looked thoughtful. "Being a leader is a difficult thing for a woman," she said. "Yahweh's way of doing things doesn't always make sense to us... as I'm still discovering."

There was an awkward silence between us. "Well, I'd better go," I said and picked up my basket. But before I took a step Miriam said, "Stop!" She stood up, took a few steps toward me, then halted abruptly, as if remembering her condition. "I can't come any closer," she said. "But from this distance, let me bless you." She raised her face toward heaven, and reaching her hands toward me said, "God bless you and keep you, my daughter. God smile on you and gift you. God look you full in the face and make you prosper." [13]

* * *

On my lone walk, back to our encampment I thought about Miriam's words. I must find a way to make a better timbrel so I could answer the call within *me* to sing and dance. I began humming the melody of the song that Miriam led us in after the Red Sea crossing. I was still on that cloud of imagination when I neared a group of youths. Instinctively I lowered my gaze.

I hadn't gone six steps past them when I heard a voice from behind, obviously raised to attract my attention. "It's the goldsmith's sister."

In the next instant Pallu was beside me. "What are you doing here — and by yourself?"

I held out my basket of manna in answer. Our eyes met and I felt my heart pound in my chest. "What is that to you?"

"Perhaps more than you think," he said. He walked beside me for a few steps then strode in front of me, blocking my path. I stopped. In the next instant, he leaned his face close to mine and whispered, "Kiss me."

I stumbled backwards in horror and shock. I hoped his friends nearby hadn't heard him. When he did things like this, he frightened me.

In a flash, he changed. He stepped back from me and his face broke into a smile. "I was only teasing," he said. "But you need a husband to keep you in line and look out for you."

* * *

After that I couldn't get Pallu out of my mind. I thought about his curly black hair and full beard, his swarthy, muscular arms, but most of all his eyes, piercing and black as coals. I imagined him beside me, his height and the masculine force of his actions. Over and over I recalled his words. What did they mean?

But what about my dream of living alone and strong like Miriam? I felt confused. What was wrong with me?

* * *

Every morning when I went to gather manna now, I made sure I went with cousins Jaffa or Reisa, or worked near Cetura. I didn't want to meet Pallu alone again—but at the same time, I did!

Every day too, I checked to see whether Miriam's tent was still pitched beside the camp. Five days after my encounter with her, it was gone. That day too, I caught sight of Pallu.

He was gathering manna a distance away. Some girls I didn't recognize stood over him. They were talking back and forth and laughing.

I drank in the sight of him, stealing glances from under the head shawl I pulled over my eyes. I didn't want Reisa to notice.

He looked like he was having a good time. The girls did too. The sound of teasing, playful laughter drifted from them. They seemed to know each other well.

My chest tightened with a feeling I hated but couldn't seem to resist. It was the way I felt when Bezalel began paying more attention to Sebia than to me. I was jealous.

Why did I feel this way? Pallu and I had no real connection. I had no claim on him—or he on me. But then, what did his request for a kiss and his mention of marriage mean?

I looked down and focused on my task. But the temptation to look at them again was too strong and I stole another peek.

Just then two sharp trumpet blasts pierced the air, shattering the leisureliness of conversation and laughter. It was the signal to move.

Reisa and I rushed to fill our baskets and then

hurried back to camp.

Chapter Eight

We walked for many days following the cloud. I hadn't met or spoken with Pallu again. But sometimes when I was gathering manna or on my way to and from the pits, I sensed someone watching me. Always when I looked around, though, there was no one.

We often stopped at midday to rest during the heat and then pressed on again when the sun lost its strength. On many days we travelled past dark, pulled along by the cloud that, at night, glowed with its own flame-like light. We could make good time then as we walked faster to stay warm in the desert's chilly hours. The most important thing, though, was that we were moving in the direction of the Promised Land.

"We might actually get there in time for next Passover," Mother said one day, her eyes twinkling.

As we walked, I heard others talk about the future. "We'll live in houses again."

"I hope the land is good for gardens."

"Can you imagine having all the grain we need for bread and olive oil, not to speak of water?"

My thoughts turned to my own future. What a perfect time to start life as a wife. But then I recalled the last time — already days and days ago — when I saw Pallu with the girls buzzing around him like bees around a flower.

As we walked, I lost track of time in the sameness of the days. At our stops, I assisted in setting up the tent, fetched water, helped mother make a fire and prepare the manna. After we ate, I wrapped myself tightly in my robe against the frigid air and, huddled in the tent with others of my family, drifted into sleep with the sensation that I was still walking. It seemed I just got to sleep when mother's call awakened me to again gather manna before we packed and trudged on. Only the Sabbath rest day broke the rhythm of travel and its demands.

And then, on a day like all the others, we arrived at a large oasis. Word spread that this was Kadesh Barnea. Grandfather Hur, who kept track of dates, announced that on this day a year ago we had left Mount Sinai.

We set up camp in the usual arrangement. Though we put up our tent hurriedly as we always did when traveling, Mother was fussier than usual, making sure the stakes were evenly spaced and securely hammered in, the walls pulled tight. I sensed she was hoping we would stay for a while.

The next morning when I went to gather manna, I glanced at the sky, as was my habit, to look for the cloud. Reisa and little Simeon were with me. The cloud was not in the eastern sky as it had been all the weeks of travel.

"Where is the cloud?" I asked. We scanned the heavens but it was little Simeon who caught sight of it.

"On top of the tent," he said, pointing to the tabernacle.

"Sharp eyes!" I said to him. He giggled at my praise.

"Do you think that means we'll be camped here for a while?" Reisa asked.

"I hope so."

Now Simeon tugged at Reisa's hand and she let herself be pulled along at his speed while I took my time, savouring the thought of a day, maybe days, of no walking.

"Hello, little sister of the goldsmith." A familiar voice

broke into my reverie and I startled. It was the voice I had replayed a hundred times in my imagination.

Somehow, Pallu had sneaked up beside me. I glance into his face, then lowered my gaze to hide the flush that I knew was reddening my cheeks.

"Look at me" he said not sharply, but insistently.

Unable to resist, I looked into his piercing eyes. As our eyes met his softened as did his whole face.

"Have you thought about what I said?" he asked.

"What did you say?"

"You don't remember? That you need a husband."

I didn't know what to answer. I couldn't tell him I had thought of little else. At the same time his confidence and boldness irked me.

"Why would I think of that?" I asked. "Lots of girls my age are not married."

"But they're not as beautiful as you are."

My eyes sought out his again and we stood transfixed for a moment. Then he moved a step closer and, before I could draw back, fingered a wisp of my hair, lifting it gently from before my eyes. "Perhaps I will have to do something about that," he said. Then he turned and walked away.

"Who was that?" Reisa asked when I joined her and Simeon.

"Oh, no one," I answered trying to keep my voice casual.

"Judging from the colour of your cheeks and the sparkle in your eye, that man is not 'no one.'"

* * *

Soon after arrival at Kadesh, Mother pulled out the weaving materials. She was determined to finish enlarging the tent and completing Bezalel's huppah—

the bridal chamber. She insisted I must be part of the work crew. As we set to work, I discovered that what I had learned about weaving at Sinai came back to me and I could honestly say that I preferred even weaving to walking!

We were hard at work on this when Grandfather Hur arrived back at the tent. I saw there was a spring in his step and a smile on his face. Mother noticed it too. "You have news?" she asked.

"Moses has called for a gathering of the tribal leaders. Word is that he's planning to send spies to view the land — the Promised Land!"

"Then we will really soon be done with this wilderness life?" Mother looked happier than I'd seen her in a long time.

"Don't think it's just a matter of moving in, though," said Grandfather. "There is bound to be opposition from the people who live there now. That's why we've been traveling in army formation all this time."

But it was as if mother and the others hadn't heard his last warning. They cheered at the news of spies being sent and then quickly began a lively discussion of the houses everyone would soon live in and the gardens they'd plant.

My mind went back to Pallu and what part he might have in my future. He called me beautiful. Maybe he felt about me like Jacob did about Rachel! What did he mean when he said he would do something? Would he send his father to mine to arrange a betrothal?

It was all too strange and exciting and, yes, too wonderful, to grasp. But scary too. His boldness and self-assurance put me on guard. Maybe he was just playing with me. I didn't like being taken for stupid. Or maybe he was serious. If he was, then perhaps another mother would soon be preparing a huppah for her son.

* * *

Spy Song

Go now my brothers to spy out the land
Scout the inhabitants, tell what you see.
Bring a report and some fruit in your hand.

Go through the mountains — Canaan's motherland.
View for yourselves; don't trust in hearsay.
Go now, my brothers, to spy out the land.

Calculate army size, see it firsthand,
spy out the weapons — for real, not might-be.
Bring a report and some fruit in your hand.

Explore the forests and wild hinterland.
Cipher city dwellings, note all that you see.
Go now, my brothers, to spy out the land.

Is soil productive or weakened by sand?
Take note of the vineyard, the garden, the tree.
Bring a report and some fruit in your hand.

From Zin Wilderness to sweet Hamath land
pay heed to it all and tell us what you see.
Go now, my brothers. Spy out the land.
Bring a report and some fruit in your hand. [14]

* * *

The time of Bezalel's wedding was getting closer. Even though no one had told me details of the plans, there was an air of excitement in our encampment.

The tent enlargement was complete with the new huppah for Bezalel and Sebia. This was where they would spend their wedding week and then live with us until we had our own houses in the Promised Land.

Mother had been hard at work on a dress that Bezalel wanted to give Sebia. She remade one of the garments taken from our neighbours the night we left Egypt. Every day it became more beautiful with embroidered fruits and birds stitched with gold, red, and blue threads she had salvaged from other pieces.

For the wedding feast, she had dug through our belongings, asked around, and somehow come up with a few dried dates and figs. She planned to cut these small and bake them into the manna dishes she would serve to our guests.

Bezalel was absent-minded and dreamy-eyed. When I saw him like this, it was hard to believe he was once in charge of all the tabernacle workmen.

Then one night, after the evening meal, as the swift twilight came on, he beckoned me to join him outside the tent. There he pulled something from the folds of his cloak. It was made of gleaming wood, bent in a perfect circle with spaces that held brass disks. They caught the pink glow of the dying fire. A timbrel!

"For my special little sister, who has a singer and dancer inside her," he said, handing it to me. "I haven't heard your song for a while. Maybe this will inspire you to start singing again."

The disks jingled merrily as I took it. I was surprised by how heavy it felt—yet how comfortably it fit my hand.

"Thank you!" I whispered, past the lump in my throat.

"I want you to know that you'll always be special to me," Bezalel said, giving me a hug. I looked up at him through tear-blurred eyes. I had my brother back... but only for a few moments.

"Bezalel!" It was Shoshan. A minute later he was beside us and giving Bezalel a playful fist-bump on the shoulder. "The big night at last!"

I left them and went inside the tent with my new treasure. "Look at what Bezalel gave me," I said to Mother.

She gave it a quick glance but seemed distracted.

"Is this Bezalel's wedding night?" I asked. Her knowing grin and wink gave me the answer, as we heard more male voices—Oholiab and others with whom Bezalel had worked on the tabernacle.

Bezalel's face beamed. He was excited and as tense as a bowstring. He chatted and laughed with his friends as more and more people arrived—musicians with pipes, lyres, drums, and timbrels. I kept the rhythm of their song with my new instrument. Then, when all was ready, the whole company left on the trek to Sebia's tent in the camp of Asher.

Meanwhile Mother nervously revived the fire. When the coals glowed to her satisfaction she set pans of fig-manna above them to bake and then, for at least the tenth time, checked that all was ready in their huppah.

I felt tense too. Would the party turn out well? And what about later? We had lived with plenty of women around—new women too when cousins married and brought their wives. But we'd never hosted a big celebration like this or had a stranger, another woman, living with us in our tent.

At last we heard the music and singing, faint at first, then ever louder till the noisy procession arrived. The guests gave a cheer as the couple and their troupe entered the encampment. Bezalel acknowledged the greeting with a smile but today he did not stop to chat, visit, or reply to the good-natured teasing of his friends.

Sebia's face, faintly visible under a veil, looked radiant. Her auburn hair flowed loose under a golden crown that Bezalel must have fashioned for her. She wore the dress mother had made. It fit her perfectly and the golden embroideries glittered like stars in the night. She looked like a queen.

And Bezalel looked like a king. He also had a crown on his head. It gleamed against his wavy black hair.

Bezalel and Sebia walked toward us holding hands. As he led Sebia into the tent and the room that had been prepared for them, he gazed down at her as if to reassure himself that it was really her, that this was really happening.

Mother beckoned me to help her serve our guests, as we awaited the shout from Bezalel that they were completely wed.

I mingled with the guests, offering baskets of specially prepared manna. At one point, I again had the strange sense that someone was watching me. I glanced around. Could Pallu have joined the party? He was nowhere in sight. But my attention was captured by a youth. Our eyes met momentarily and he quickly looked away, as if embarrassed.

* * *

Sebia was now part of our family. The first week Bezalel and she spent almost every moment together. Once, when Mother sent me to their huppah around midday with food and they were up and dressed I said to Sebia, "Isn't it a little early for you to be up?"

Later Bezalel caught me alone. "Why were you

sarcastic to Sebia?" he asked. "Don't you like her?"

I didn't know what to say. The lump in my throat didn't allow me to get any words out anyway. If I knew how to put it into words I'd tell Bezalel how I wished he and I were best friends again like before Sebia. And how now that she was with him all the time, he hardly ever teased me or gave me a hug.

"It's different with her here," I muttered at last.

"Please be kind to her," he said. "You'll come to love her. I promise."

After their wedding week, Sebia offered to help in the kitchen. Mother hesitantly accepted, then watched her like a hawk—every little thing, like how she arranged the firewood, prepared the manna, tidied up after herself—which she hardly ever did.

That's one thing that really annoyed Mother—Sebia's untidiness. She'd forget to put a basket back in place or arrange the firewood neatly and mother would go behind her and straighten it all up as she shook her head in disgust and uttered sighs of annoyance.

The state of their huppah was another stone in Mother's sandal. After a few outright requests that Sebia straighten the bed and fold the robes and tunics that littered the floor, it seemed she'd given up. Each time Mother had reason to enter their room, she came out with her face clouded, her mouth a grim line.

It made me long for the day I'd be on my own—with Pallu?

Maybe it was silly to think that way. His father still hadn't paid mine a visit. Would he ever? And even if we were betrothed, it would be a year before we would marry anyway.

Yet I dreamed—no longer dreams of being like

Miriam. Bezalel's timbrel reminded me of the changes inside of me. Since I had played it at his wedding celebration I hadn't touched it. Instead, I'd tucked it out of sight. Looking at it made me feel confused, even sad, like I was giving up something precious and good. Still, I couldn't help myself. Now my thoughts kept returning to Pallu and the possibility of making a home with him in the Promised Land.

Judging from the conversations around me, a lot of people were thinking about the same thing.

"When do you think the spies will come back? They've already been gone two weeks." And then it was three weeks... four weeks.

"When we get to the Promised Land we'll have our own property again," people reminded themselves.

"Once we get settled, I'd like to start a dress-making business," cousin Reisa said. "It will be so wonderful to have time to weave beautiful cloth. I can hardly wait to throw out these rough, dusty clothes."

Oholiab, Saria, and little Obed come to visit Bezalel and Sebia. While I played with Obed just outside the tent door, I overheard them talk about opening shops to work with metal and fabric. We were all eager for the next season.

* * *

Now that the tent enlargement was long finished and there was an extra set of hands to help with cooking and clothes washing, tent repair and the animals, collecting firewood, hauling water, and gathering manna, I had some free time. After a few days of begging, Mother finally let me visit Cetura.

When I arrived at their tent, Cetura's mother greeted me with uncharacteristic enthusiasm. "Cetera has news for you," she said, all smiles, as she beckoned me into the women's quarters.

Cetura rose from the mat where she was working on a basket and gave me a hug. "Guess what?" she said. And then, without giving me time to reply, "I'm betrothed!"

Both Cetura and her mother laughed at the surprise on my face. "Who is the happy man?" I asked.

"Paltiel," Cetura replied, blushing.

The name was not familiar to me. "Do I know him?"

"Probably not," said Cetura's mother. "He is the son of Azlan, a childhood friend and distant cousin from my tribe."

"And he's very handsome," Cetura said, beaming.

"You will be moving," I said, realizing suddenly that I'd be losing another friend.

"Not far," said Cetura. "The tribe of Issachar camps just to the north of us. And not for at least a year. I know it's early, but will you be one of my wedding maids?"

"Yes of course."

"And what about you?" Cetura's mother asked me. "I would expect a pretty girl like you to have inquiries."

I smiled, shook my head, and said nothing. Later, though, when Cetura and I were alone, I confided to her what Pallu had said to me. I thought she would be pleased. But instead, the smile left her face and she was quiet.

"What?" I asked, eager to hear her response.

"I hope he doesn't ask you," said Cetura.

"Why?" I was surprised and hurt. I thought she'd be happy and excited for me.

"Because after he started showing such an interest in you I asked around about him. He has a reputation of being a lady's man. And his father is one of Moses' sharpest critics. Father said there's a rebellious streak in his family."

"Well, he thinks for himself," I said. I felt my face grow warm with annoyance and I knew I shouldn't say what I said next but it just tumbled out. "I think you're saying these things because he wasn't interested in you."

"Don't be upset," Cetura said. "I'm not telling you this to make you angry but because I care about you."

"Really?" I heard the sarcasm, thick in my voice. I didn't feel like talking with Cetura anymore. I rose. "Well, I'd better be going." Then I just left, without exchanging our usual farewell hug or saying goodbye to her mother.

On the way home I thought about what Cetura had said. I recalled the day I watched Pallu surrounded by girls as he was gathering manna. I also remembered how I saw him at Taberah beside an older man who could have been his father. But surely the seriousness of their criticism of Moses was being blown up by the gossip-mongers. I wouldn't give up my dream of a future with Pallu for such a flimsy reason. Why had Cetura spoiled the day by saying what she had?

* * *

The spies had now been gone for over five weeks. One morning as I arrived back at the tent with a load of fuel, I saw Father welcoming a man into our tent. He looked familiar. Mother put a pot of water on our cooking fire to make a drink. She shooed me into the women's quarters where I picked up the loom to resume work on a weaving—listening with half an ear to what the adults were saying.

"You are well?" I heard the stranger say.

"Yes, well," said Father. "And you?"

"Could be better. This waiting around isn't making you impatient?"

"The spies should be back soon," said Grandfather. "Then we'll surely be on the move and soon into the Promised land."

"Let us hope. It has taken Moses long enough to keep his promise. But I come on a different matter today."

"Please, speak your business," said Father.

"I am Abiram, of the Tribe of Reuben. I'm here because my son Pallu insisted I come. You have a daughter?"

"Yes," said Father. "One. Zamri."

"As Pallu's father, I am here to arrange the union of our houses through the marriage of our children."

I felt myself go all hot and prickly. The man was Pallu's father. No wonder he looked familiar. And it was happening — the thing I had thought and dreamed about for the last weeks! My heart pounded as I strained to hear Grandfather's or Father's reply. But there was only silence. It stretched on and on.

Pallu's father spoke again. "Why are you hesitating? We are a good, influential family in our tribe. Your daughter could do much worse."

Grandfather Hur replied at last, "We do appreciate the offer. And we know your position and influence. That is the problem. We have heard of your criticisms of Moses. We want no part of that."

"Indeed," echoed Father. "We support our leader."

"You can't be serious! Such a thing would cause you to turn down my offer? I am prepared to pay an excellent bride price if that would change your mind."

"I assure you, it will not," Grandfather said.

My heart was still thumping, my palms sweaty.

Surely Grandfather's and Father's initial refusal was all part of the way these things were bargained. From Father's tone, I got the feeling he might be on the verge of saying yes. But as patriarch of the family, Grandfather had the last word.

"Well, arranging the betrothal of my son and your daughter is what I came to do," said Pallu's father. "I will not prolong my visit or impose on you further." He sounded annoyed.

"Oh, you are not imposing," said Mother. "Will you have more to drink?"

"Thank you, no."

I held my breath, waiting for Father or Grandfather to stop him from going and to carry on with negotiations. But there were no such words from them, only regrets that they were unable to make the visit a success, polite words of thanks, and a blessing on his household.

Pallu's father left with parting words. "Should you decide to change your minds and join our houses, you know where to find me. Anyone from the tribe of Reuben can direct you to my tent."

I was stunned. The very thing I had been hoping for and dreaming about had happened. But my family had spoiled everything. I was so upset, I couldn't think straight.

Meanwhile in the main room of the tent a discussion was going on.

"Are you sure you made the right decision?" Mother asked. "Abiram and his clan are powerful in Reuben. Marriage into that family would be good for Zamri and for us."

"Position and influence are nothing if they push for

the wrong things," Grandfather Hur said.

Father picked up the argument. "Abiram's reputation of resisting and criticizing Moses is well known. Do we want our daughter—and so ourselves—connected to a rebellious house like his? Of course not!"

"Perhaps the things you've heard are more rumours than fact," Mother replied. "We could at least have asked Zamri."

Mother's words unleashed the flow of tears I'd held in check till then. I buried my face in my hands and sobbed, quietly at first. But the immensity of what had just happened overwhelmed me and I was soon shuddering and hiccupping despite myself.

I felt Mother's hand on my shoulder. "You heard it all?"

I couldn't talk but managed a nod.

"I'm sorry," she said. "Maybe Father and Grandfather will reconsider. We still have that hope."

But later that day, another event changed everything.

Chapter Nine

"The spies have returned!" It was Grandfather Hur who brought the news to our encampment that afternoon. "They have come back with fruit from the land. Moses has called us to gather and hear their report."

The place Moses spoke to the congregation was a large flat area in front of the tabernacle on which was erected a raised platform. Our family walked together toward the meeting place but I straggled behind, still too upset by what had happened that morning to talk to anyone. The thought of the spies return I had looked forward to for so long was now as tarnished as old silver.

People were streaming from all directions toward the meeting place. Today Moses and Aaron were joined on the platform by the twelve returned spies. We stood quite near them and I studied their weathered faces and dusty clothes.

Moses waited for more people to arrive and when the area was crowded with no more space, he began. "Your tribal leaders are back. I sent them to spy out the land of Canaan, to go into the South and up to the mountains. They were to evaluate the people, their encampments, villages, and cities. Now they have returned and will tell us whether it's a good land or bad, rich or poor, forest or plain." Addressing the spies, he said, "What is your report?"

"This is where we went," one of them began.

"That is Shammua from Reuben," Grandfather Hur whispered to us.

"From the Wilderness of Zin, we went to Rehab near

the entrance of Hamath. Traveling up through the South we came to Hebron, Ahiram, Sheshai, and Telmai. Fearful giants live there, the descendants of Anak. Then we came to the Valley of Eshcol. There we cut these."

He motioned to two of his companions and together they lifted the ends of a massive branch onto their shoulders. A gasp rippled through the crowd as we saw what hung from the pole between them. Grapes! Large, round, reddish-purple globes in mammoth clusters like I'd never seen in my life.

Another of the spies took up the report. "We went where you sent us, Moses. The land truly flows with milk and honey, and this is more of its fruit."

From a basket beside him he lifted a huge red pomegranate in one hand, took several brown figs in the other, and held them up for all to see before he continued.

"But the people who live in the land are strong."

The buzz of excitement, that had risen in response to the fruit, silenced as he continued. "The cities are fortified and very large. And, like our brother from Reuben said, we saw giants, the descendants of Anak, there."

"The Amalekites live in the southland," said another of the returned men.

Murmuring went through the crowd at his words. We knew the Amalekites. If it weren't for Moses holding up his hands in prayer to Yahweh through the battle — with Grandfather Hur and Aaron helping when he tired — they would have thrashed our army. [15]

"The Hitties, Jebusites and Amorites live in the mountains," another spy continued. "Canaanites live by the sea and along the banks of the Jordan."

71

This dismaying information took but a few minutes to sink in. Ripples of concern ran through the crowd. Anxious chatter increased to a buzz of confusion until someone shouted, "Moses, are you going to send us against these tribes?"

"We'll all be killed," someone else called out.

"We barely beat the Amalekites when they attacked us before. How will we handle all these tribes coming at us at once?"

Above us on the speaker's stage Caleb, the spy from our tribe, now stepped forward. He held up his hand and called out, "Quiet. Quiet!"

When the shouting died down he spoke, addressing Moses as much as the people. "Let us go up at once and take possession, for we are well able to overcome all these things."

But the other spies shook their heads in disagreement. "No. No," they called together. "We are not able to take these people. They are stronger than we are."

Another spy interjected, "The land which we spied eats up and destroys the people who live in it. We would be annihilated by the monsters who live there. We felt like grasshoppers compared to them and that's how we looked to them."

Now from all over the crowd, people erupted in angry words, even weeping. A woman nearby rocked back and forth and beat on her chest as she moaned, "All my sons will die in battle." A man shook his fist at Moses and shouted, "You murderer! You led us into a trap."

Grandfather Hur and Father looked troubled. "Let's go," said Bezalel. "I can't bear to watch this."

We made our slow way, pushing and squeezing

through the crowd, and once out of it walked together in stunned silence to our tent. I didn't know what the others were thinking, but I was shaken. How things had changed in one day.

* * *

Anger and arguing filled the atmosphere—even entered our tent. Though Caleb had spoken in favour of entering Canaan, many, even from our tribe, disagreed with him. Mother was one of them. "It would have been better if we had died in Egypt or the wilderness," she muttered, slamming pots as she prepared our evening manna.

I slept little that night. Besides living and reliving the visit of Pallu's father, I heard voices outside. They were full of disappointment, anger, and desperation. It seemed that people were going from tent to tent trying to come up with a plan for what to do next.

"Why has Yahweh brought us to this place? He and Moses are not to be trusted."

"All the men will be killed in battle leaving our women and children vulnerable."

"Maybe we should return to Egypt."

And then Mother woke me with a shake. "It's time to get up, Zamri. Go gather our manna. But hurry. We are going before Moses again."

After a rushed breakfast, we hurried to the meeting place to find a large crowd had already assembled. Today not only were Moses, Aaron, and the twelve spies on the speaker's platform but there were other leaders, standing face to face with Moses and Aaron. It looked like they were engaged in a heated discussion. Grandfather Hur shook his head. As one of the appointed elders, he should have been included with the leaders. But no one had summoned him. "I can only imagine what those men are up to," he muttered.

Now it was one of the other leaders—not Moses—who called the crowd to order. "People of Israel," he shouted, and waited for silence. "We your leaders have met together. We agree that this whole exodus has been a big mistake. It would have been better if we had died in Egypt or the wilderness.

"Why Yahweh has brought us to the border of this Promised Land just to be killed in battle and our wives and children victimized and enslaved makes no sense to us. I'm sure you'll agree it would be better for us to return to the conditions we know in Egypt than to hazard this crazy venture into unknown and dangerous territory

"We, your tribal leaders, have decided to choose another leader—not this Moses or Aaron but someone else—to lead us in a return to Egypt."

The spies nodded their heads while some in the crowd begin to cheer. But that cheer quickly quieted as both Moses and Aaron fell to their knees and then onto their faces. The sight of them lying face down on the platform in front of us was shocking. Had Moses given in so easily?

However, two of the spies then stepped determinedly away from the others. In the sight of all, Caleb and Joshua ripped their clothes. Then Caleb shouted above the din of the crowd that grew louder every minute, "People, people, listen! The land we went through and spied out is very good. If the LORD delights in us, then He will bring us into this land. It's rich—a land that flows with milk and honey."

Joshua chimed in, "Don't rebel against the LORD.

Don't fear the people of the land. They are bread to us. Their protection is gone from them while the LORD is with us. Don't be afraid of them."

But it was no use. Rather than persuade the crowd to change its mind, the words of Caleb and Joshua seemed to fuel even more anger. One after another, people picked up stones and began hurling them toward the platform. Then, it seemed LORD Yahweh Himself intervened. Light that grew brighter and brighter settled on the tabernacle and streamed from inside it. Rumbles, like those we heard from the top of Mount Sinai, came from the light. It blinded and transfixed us. Accompanying the sound of the thunder now I heard the clatter of stones that dropped from the hands of the stone-throwers.

I don't know how long we sat there motionless in front of the tabernacle, frozen by Yahweh's fearful light and thunder. Gradually the sound softened and the light dimmed. At last Moses and Aaron moved, then lurched up on their knees, and staggered to standing.

"God has spoken," Moses said. "This is what He says: 'As I live—the things you have prophesied will come true. But these things won't happen to your children but to you. The carcasses of you who have complained against Me shall fall in this wilderness. All of you who were numbered in the census—men twenty years and older— will die here. Of those, only Caleb and Joshua will ever enter the Promised Land.

"'The land where your feet walked, Caleb and Joshua, shall be yours and your children's inheritance forever because you wholly followed the Lord my God.

"'As for your little ones, who you said would be

victims, they also will enter the land you despised. The rest of you will die in the wilderness. You will be sheepherding people with your children bearing the brunt of your faithlessness.

"'The spies were in the Promised Land for forty days. You, evil congregation, will be in the desert one year for each day they were away. Your time in the desert will be forty years. The desert will consume you and you shall die here.

"'The spies who brought back an evil report and started this complaining, will die by plague. Only Joshua and Caleb will survive.'"

No sooner were the words out of Moses' mouth than one after the other, the ten spies who opposed entering the land began to cry out. Some clutched their stomachs, some held their heads, as if in pain. And then they began falling, their limbs twisting in agony, onto the platform. There they lay — soon all ten of them — motionless.

A wail rose from the crowd and spread from front to back as all the onlookers grasped what had happened. They had died right before our eyes. Mother joined in with the wailing, but I remained silent. [16]

* * *

If the grief and shock brought about by the spies' report was bad, that night's anguish over what Moses had pronounced and then the sight of the ten spies dropping dead in front of us was ten times worse.

The reality was slowly sinking in. All our dreams for the future in the Promised Land would stay just that — dreams. If we were doomed to stay here in the wilderness for forty years, like Moses said, the youngest of us would grow old here.

There wouldn't be a goldsmith shop for Bezalel or a

market stall with beautiful fabrics for Reisa. Bezalel and Sebia wouldn't have their own home, and neither would I make a home for Pallu—which I wouldn't be able to in any case because of my family's decision.

Long after dark I was still tossing on my mat—kept awake by the coming and going, the rise and fall of voices in talk and argument outside our tent, and the chilling wails of the mourners.

But the next morning when Mother awoke me to fetch the manna, her spirit seemed lighter. "Hurry back," she said. "This will be a full day."

I went to the spot where Cetura and I collected. Cetura had arrived before me. We greeted each other and I set to work in silence beside her. After a while, she asked, "What do you think of what has happened the last two days?" Something in her voice sounded like she had been crying. When I looked at her, I saw her eyes were red and swollen.

"It's terrible," I said. "But why are you upset? You still have the hope of marrying Paltiel."

"I know. But we had such wonderful plans for a vineyard and olive groves. Now it looks like none of it will ever happen."

"How do you know?" A man's voice broke into our conversation. Pallu! I cast a quick glance up and our eyes locked. I looked down and he went on. "How do you know that what Moses says will happen like he said? The leaders have changed their minds. Plans are afoot for battle after all."

Cetura brightened. "You mean we might not be stuck out here for all those years?" She stood and lifted her partly filled basket onto her head. "I'm going to tell my family."

I wanted her to go — and I didn't. When she was gone, Pallu stepped in front of me and held out his hand to help me up. It was rough, strong, and warm. As he drew me up, he looked searchingly into my eyes. "Why did your family refuse my father's offer? Was it you?"

I felt my face go hot. His eyes were too probing and I looked down from them as I shook my head. "They never asked me," I managed to say.

"What would you have said if they had?"

I glanced up, caught his eye, and felt my face soften in a smile. It was answer enough for him. He squeezed my hand, then dropped it, wrapped his arm around me, pulled me close, kissed the top of my head and murmured, "You will be mine. We will soon enter the Promised Land, and when we do, you will be mine."

* * *

As I walked back to the encampment I was floating on air. The last few days seemed like a nightmare from which I had finally awoken.

Pallu said we would marry! How he would arrange a betrothal without Father's and Grandfather's consent I didn't know, but I had confidence he would do it. And his prediction that we would soon enter the Promised Land after all, put the future right again. That we would face it together made it perfect.

For the first time in days I noticed the sun shining on the mountains around Kadesh. The strong light threw the craggy cliffs into beautiful rusty shadow. Twittering swallows flited above my head. My happy heart joined in their song.

When I got back Mother scolded me for taking so long. Father, Bezalel, and Grandfather were needing to go to the meeting place. But I scarcely heard her scolding as I went about my tasks my mind full of Pallu—his grip on my hand, his kiss on my head, his promise, "You will be mine."

Sooner than I expected, the men were back. Father and Bezalel looked stern. Grandfather seemed angry.

"What happened?" Mother asked.

"Did Moses not relent?" asked Sebia.

"What a mess," Grandfather Hur said, shaking his head in disgust. "The leaders told Moses that we, the people, have changed our minds and are now ready to go to war. Though Moses would have none of it, they have decided to fight anyway."

"Isn't that what Moses wants?" Mother asked. "Maybe they'll be successful. Caleb and Joshua sure seemed to think so yesterday."

"Moses told them plainly they will not succeed," Father said. "He refuses to go with them."

"And he isn't allowing them to take the Ark of the Covenant into battle either," said Bezalel.

So, these were the plans that Pallu had talked about this morning. Knowing him, he would go to battle with the rest. I felt a clutch inside. Would he be okay?

Suddenly the sun that had looked so brilliant a few minutes ago didn't shine nearly as brightly.

* * *

Battle March

(Israelite army)

Here we are, ready to spar!
We're not sub-par
Won't spoil our future
With the fear of war.

We will go up
To the place
Not suffer the disgrace
Of a cowardly race.

Yes, we have sinned
But we rescind, won't be pinned
To this desert place
We and our kin.

(Moses)

Why do you transgress
The command of the Lord,
It's a serious challenge
You can't afford.

The Amalekites & Canaanites
Are looking for a fight.
They'll give you a fright.
With all their might, they'll put you to flight.

I smell defeat. You're enemy meat.
You will get beat.
I know you'll fall by the sword
Because you've turned from the Lord.

I stay behind
The ark does too.
I don't expect God
Will be helping you.

(Amalekites & Canaanites)

They're climbing our hill
Let's get ready for the kill!
Give them their fill —
An Amalekite pill.

A Canaanite attack
That'll make them back-track
For we know they lack
Warfare skill.

(Chorus)

Israelites run
as fast as you can
Or they will kill you
to a man!
Down the hill
and to Hormah's sand.
This fight you wage
by your demand
surely won't win you
the Promised Land. [17]

Chapter Ten

It was all going bad again. The plan to go to war didn't work. Our army was defeated and humiliated by the Amalekites and Canaanites. Our men had to run for their lives. Many were killed.

No one from Judah joined the army so my family was fine. But what about Pallu? Had he joined the battle? Was he still alive?

Around us the talk was gloomy as hopes for a soon entry to the Promised Land had been dashed again. And there was blame—especially of Moses. Even in our tent.

"We should never have come. Why were we so foolish as to trust that man?" Mother muttered these things when Grandfather was out of earshot.

When Father, Bezalel, and Sebia heard Mother, they were quiet. Father sided with Grandfather and Bezalel had a strong loyalty to Moses after working under him on the tabernacle. Sebia, despite her seeming meekness, had surprising inner strength that kept her from being swayed by others.

I felt torn—between Grandfather, Father, and Bezalel on one side and Mother and Pallu on the other.

Three days after our humiliated army returned from battle I was out gathering manna when I heard footsteps. I looked up. It was Pallu! I stood as he approached and without thinking reached for his hand. "You live!"

"Yes, I live," he said, taking my hand in both of his. Immediately I felt self-conscious. People from my encampment were nearby. I pulled my hand away.

"Follow me," Pallu mouthed. I picked up my basket

and followed him to a spot where we were obscured by scrubby brush.

"Don't give up hope," he said, looking into my eyes. "I have it on good authority that changes are coming soon. There's a lot of unhappiness with Moses. He wouldn't come with us to battle or let us bring the Ark of the Covenant. People are blaming him for our defeat."

"What will change?" I asked.

"Moses isn't the only one capable of leading. In this company, there are hundreds of leaders, men with more battle experience and good sense than Moses will ever have."

"You mean someone else will become our leader?"

Pallu winked at me, smiled his rakish smile, and the sun in my sky shone again. How could it not?

Now he pulled me close, nuzzled the top of my hair and kissed the top of my head. "I can't wait till you're mine," he murmured.

The thrill of his closeness was accompanied by a shiver of apprehension. What if someone from my encampment saw us and told Father, or Grandfather?

I pulled away. "I'd better get going." I hurried back to our tent with my basket only half full.

After we'd eaten Grandfather left and we continued with our morning chores. But a short while later he returned, running and out of breath. "Come quickly," he said, summoning Father and Bezalel. "Rebellion has broken out."

* * *

The men left. Mother, Sebia, and I exchanged concerned glances, then went back to our tasks.

Was this the beginning of the rebellion Pallu had told me about this morning? Was Pallu's father one of the rebels? I couldn't concentrate on the spindle in my hand and the thread I was weaving got all tangled. I threw it down. "Can I go to see what's happening? Please?" I asked mother.

"I'll come with you," she said. Sebia wanted to join us as well.

The crowd was large at the meeting place. I found a rock to stand on. Elevated in this way I could see just above the heads around me.

Moses was standing on the dais in front of the crowd. I watched as a man hoisted himself onto the platform and walked determinedly toward him. The chatter of the crowd quieted as the two met. Though he was dressed in the same white clothes as Aaron's sons, the priests, I was sure I had never seen him with them before.

The man's voice rang out. "You, Moses, and your brother Aaron take too much upon yourselves. Everyone in this crowd is set apart by Yahweh. The LORD is among us all. What gives you the right to raise yourself above us?"

At this, a crowd of men near the platform raised their fists and cheered. I was certain I saw Pallu's father with them, his fist raised high with the others. This must be the plan to choose a new leader that Pallu had described this morning.

Moses didn't answer. Instead he fell flat on his face in front of everyone, as he had the last time rebels challenged him.

A buzz went through the crowd. Then he rose and the crowd grew silent.

"Tomorrow morning Yahweh Himself will show who is His and holy, and will cause that person to come near Him. Here is the test. Korah, you and all your company, take censers and put incense in them before the LORD tomorrow. It shall be that the man whom the LORD chooses is the set-apart, holy one.

"You Sons of Levi take too much on yourselves. Hear now, is it a small thing that the God of Israel has separated you from the congregation? That He has allowed you to come near Him to do the work of the tabernacle of the LORD and to stand before the congregation to serve them? Is coming near Him in this way not enough for you? Do you insist on being priests as well? Your rebellion is against Yahweh, not Aaron and me!"

Moses stopped speaking and looked over the crowd. Then he called out, "Dathan and Abiram, sons of Eliab, where are you? I understand you also have a complaint. I will speak with you now."

A flash of prickly heat came over me when I heard the name "Abiram" That was Pallu's father. I gripped Sebia's shoulder to keep from falling off the rock as a wave of dizziness came over me.

On the stage, Korah pointed to the man I recognized as Pallu's father. But he didn't move from his place. Instead he shook his head vigorously and shouted, "We will not come up. Is it a small thing that you have brought us out of a land flowing with milk and honey to kill us in the wilderness? You act like such a prince over us.

"On top of that, you haven't brought us to a land flowing with milk and honey, nor given us the promised inheritance of fields and vineyards. We will not come up or in any way acknowledge your authority."

Moses listened closely to Abiram's outburst. When

he was done, Moses kept his piercing eyes on him for a long time but said nothing. At last he turned his attention back to Korah. "I expect you here tomorrow, Korah, you and all your company, as well as Aaron." With that Moses left the platform.

As the crowd broke up, all around us people talked about what they had just seen and heard.

"Why won't Moses listen to good sense?"

"Even leaders from his own tribe have lost faith in him."

"What can he do if these hundreds are against him?"

Personally, I was not surprised it had come to this. Abiram and Korah had said things today that I'd heard others say too.

Among our family there was no conversation. We walked back to our tent in silence.

My mind was in a turmoil. The plan to replace Moses was playing out way sooner than I thought. What if Korah and Pallu won? Would my family betroth me to Pallu then?

What if they lost? A shiver went through me as I thought of what had happened to others who crossed Moses—Aaron's sons, dead in an instant, the rebels at Taberah killed by fire, the ten spies dropping of plague right before our eyes.

But there were so many against him. I got the sense from the talk around us that our family was one of the few that were loyal to Moses.

As we sat together at the evening meal, Grandfather said to me, "Now you see, Zamri, why we refused Abiram's request to betroth you to his son."

"You don't know that Pallu is like him," I answered back, looking straight at him.

"Rebellion spreads in a family," Grandfather said. "We hope you haven't been infected." I caught his sideways glance at mother. She didn't look up but gave a small shrug of her shoulders and uttered an almost imperceptible grunt.

After the meal, I went outside to get away from everyone. If only they knew the real Pallu, they would not say such things about him and his father. I had a bad feeling about the next day.

I stood looking up at the stars, shivering in the cold desert air, feeling scared and alone. Then there was a hand on my shoulder. Bezalel. He had my warm cloak draped over his arm. "Here," he said, "put this on. You're shaking."

I snuggled into the garment. "Thank you," I said, looking up at him. It had been so long since we'd been together like this.

"What is it?" he asked. "Why are you so upset? There will be other men. I know several who would be overjoyed if you were wearing their betrothal ring"

I looked up at him, my eyes filling with tears. "You don't understand," I said. "We care for each other."

"You know him well then?" Bezel asked, looking displeased. "How is that?"

"I have run into him here and there," I said. "Like you met Sebia. He is one of a kind."

"He has not touched you, has he?"

"No," I lied. "We just talk."

"Well little sister," he said, his tone softening, "Yahweh will work it out. You'll see. Someday you'll be someone's wife. Maybe Pallu's. Maybe someone else's. I just hope you are as happy as Sebia and I." Then he took my hand and led me back into the warm tent.

* * *

I woke the next morning feeling happy—for a minute. But then I recalled all that had happened, all that was unknown, and my sense of well-being quickly became apprehension. After morning chores and our meal, we joined the river of people moving toward the tabernacle.

There was no one on the platform today. Just inside the tabernacle boundary, Korah and the men who were with him yesterday were picking up brass censers, filling them with glowing coals, then placing incense onto the coals. Soon the air was thick with smoke and the smell of burning spices.

The men with prepared censers stood, their backs to us facing the tabernacle entrance. A little way from their company were Moses and Aaron. Aaron too had a censer in his hand.

When all the censers were loaded, Korah vaulted onto the platform and called to the crowd, "Gather round. Come close and watch. Today the LORD will show who should really be leading us." Then he jumped down, someone handed him his censer and he took his place with the others.

Even as Korah moved into place the cloud that rested above the tabernacle began to descend, becoming brighter and brighter as it lowered. Soon it was so bright I couldn't look at it. Thunderous rumbles came from within it.

I detected movement within the crowd in front of the tabernacle. With eyes dazzled by the brightness I barely made out what looked like Moses and Aaron, on their faces again.

The brightness intensified. The rumbling from

within the cloud built to a crescendo pitch. All around people were putting their hands over their ears, closing their eyes, or looking away. As the sound gradually faded, I asked Grandfather beside me, "What does it mean?"

"It's not finished," he said. "Look, Moses stands."

Moses and Aaron were again on their feet. Moses walked, unsteadily at first, as if he lacked strength, through Korah's men and ascended the platform steps. Looking over us, he raised his hand for silence and called out, "Yahweh says, 'Get away from the tents of Korah, Dathan, and Abiram.'"

With that he left the platform walked through the crowd assembled in front of it and turned southward, toward the camps of Kohath and Reuben.

I had to see what happened next. I slipped away from my family and joined others who followed Moses. He stopped near where a crowd was already assembled. Again, he called out, "Depart. Now. Get away from the tents of these wicked men! Touch nothing of theirs lest you be consumed in all their sins."

There was a movement of the crowd as people scrambled away from the named tents. And then I saw Pallu's father Abiram, and a woman beside him, standing at the tent entrance. They were surrounded by children. A baby crawled at the woman's feet. Youngsters, several boys and a girl, stared sullenly. There were adults too. I caught sight of Pallu, looking defiantly at the crowd.

I drank in the sight of him, my heart pounding so hard it felt like it would hammer its way out of my chest. I wanted to shout out, "Get away from there, Pallu!" But the words were only in my head.

Moses moved to the front of the crowd facing the rebels and declared, with deadly seriousness and loudly so all could hear, "By this you shall know that the LORD, has sent me to do all these works; for I have not done them of my own will. If these men die naturally like all men, or if they are visited by the common fate of all men, then the LORD has not sent me.

"But if the LORD creates a new thing, and the earth opens its mouth and swallows them up with all that belongs to them, and they go down alive into the pit, then you will understand that these men have rejected the LORD."

No sooner had he finished talking than there was a rumble, a cracking, and the earth began to shake. I couldn't stay standing—all of us were thrown down. Still I kept my eyes on Pallu and his family.

The shaking opened a crack between the crowd and the cursed tents. I heard their screams and saw Pallu, his arms out as if to keep his balance, his face full of terror. Then, before my eyes, he tumbled into the chasm. They all fell into it. The sounds and sights of that day are seared in my memory forever.

I tried to get up to see into the gulf where they'd been thrown. But the writhing, rippling earth pinned me down. When the shaking finally stopped, the ravine into which Pallu and his family were thrown was no more. The earthquake had knit the seam tight. That was the last thing I can recall of that day.

* * *

The Contest

Korah's 250 approach the fire.
Each puts a coal into his brass censer.

Atop the coal, he lays holy incense.

Tabernacle door is obscured by smoke and incense
Then, from the hand of Yahweh - FIRE!
In conflagration, He shows who He will censor.

Each man is consumed in flames who holds a
censer.
Only Aaron and his sons allowed to offer holy
incense —
Yahweh adjudicates this with fire.

"Now rescue the holy incense censers from the
fire."

* * *

Threnody

All we desired was displace Moses.
"My plan is foolproof, bound to succeed," Korah
told us.

Korah said nothing of any risks
how our men could burn kindling — like desert
tamarisks.

My husband was a tribal leader.
Now we are destitute — my children have no father.

Who will help us pasture goats and sheep,
tell the old stories, sing us songs when we cannot
sleep?

Who will carry water, set up tents?
Such a deadly punishment for one act makes no
sense.

Altar is overlaid with censer brass
while our men are ash. Moses — you deal an unfair

pass.

* * *

Under the Cloud

"You have killed the LORD's people," Israelites complain.
They stand apart from Moses and Aaron as if they have plague.
But look—tabernacle is again covered in a glory cloud.

God speaks to Moses from the shining cloud:
"I will consume these people because they complain."
Aaron—prepare your censer against God's wrath as plague.

In waves people stagger and fall under the plague.
Aaron, runs amongst then, atoning by the light of the cloud.
Still thousands die—mouths stilled can no longer complain.

All defense against plague is lost when you complain under the cloud. [18]

Chapter Eleven

I walked and walked and walked. Would this desert never end?

Suddenly I arrived at a precipice. Unaware, I stepped into air and began falling... falling ... falling ... into blackness. Like Pallu. I was falling into a pit with Pallu.

My feet touched bottom and, with a jerk, I awakened. I opened my eyes. Sebia sat beside me, her face full of concern.

"You're awake," she said. "At last. I feared you might never awaken."

"Why?" I asked. My voice was weak and thin, my mouth parched.

"Here, have a drink." She helped me sit up and brought the flask to my lips, angling it to flow into my mouth. Water came out in a burst, too fast for me to swallow. It caught in my throat, I coughed and it seeped out beside my mouth, onto my face and down my neck. That felt good.

"Lie down now," Sebia said, lowering me back onto the mat. "You've been very sick. The plague took so many. We feared for you and mother."

"Is mother sick too?"

"Yes, but she is on the mend."

As I lay back looking up at the tent top I felt the space around me spinning. I closed my eyes to quell the dizziness but shortly heard the trumpet call, sounding the alarm for us to break camp.

I got up as quickly as I could and began to gather

and pack my things. But I couldn't find the robe I used to bundle my possessions. When I went outside to ask for help, Bezalel and Father called me to assist with finding our goat, which had run away.

I wandered through our encampment and the next, calling his name while the people all around were busily taking down, folding, and loading their tents onto each other's backs and the backs of their beasts.

I simply couldn't find the goat and made my way back to our tent. It was gone. They had left without me! What would I do out here all alone? Hot, sweaty, and terrified, I ran after the multitude, when I awoke again. It was all a dream!

Sebia was still beside me. She bathed my feverish face with cool cloths. "Bad dream?" she asked.

I nodded, feeling exhausted, weak, empty, and sad. Why did I feel so sad? Then it came back to me—the sight of Pallu and his family, swallowed up by the earth. He was gone and all my dreams with him. When Sebia left me, I closed my eyes and turned in bed to face the dark tent wall. I wished I could die too.

* * *

Over the next days, from the conversations around me, I pieced together what had happened while I'd been ill. After the earthquake, fire had consumed the Levites that were with Korah. Plague had broken out among the people immediately after and killed thousands. Mother and I were fortunate to have survived. [19]

Gradually my strength returned. I was awake the morning Grandfather Hur came hurrying into the tent, excited. "Amazing things we saw today," he said. "Yesterday, to finally quiet the arguing about who should serve in the tabernacle, Moses had each tribal head bring him a rod of wood with the tribe's name written on it. Moses put the twelve rods into the holy tent. He told us God said to him, 'The rod of the man whom I choose will blossom.'

"This morning Moses removed the rods. All remained just like they were when they were placed in the tabernacle except for Aaron's rod — the rod of Levi. It not only blossomed but overnight produced ripe almonds."

"That should quiet those who continue to complain about Aaron's leadership," said Bezalel.

"More than that," said Grandfather. "The people who saw what happened today have gone to the other extreme. Now, instead of wanting to be in charge they are terrified of even coming near the tabernacle for fear Yahweh will also slay them.

"But Aaron calmed them. He said Yahweh spoke to him, and told him that he and his sons should take the responsibility for the tabernacle work. All others must stay outside its boundaries, not even come near the furnishings and utensils for fear of Yahweh's wrath." [20]

"I'm glad we're not from the tribe of Levi," Mother said. That's all she said. She didn't grumble about this pronouncement of Yahweh's like she once might have.

I thought of Miriam and how, even though she was part of the Levi tribe, she got leprosy when she tried to share Moses' job. Still, she was indeed once a leader when she led the celebration dance after the Red Sea crossing.

My mind wandered to the aspirations I had had before I came to love Pallu — how I wanted to be like Miriam. Could this be why Pallu was taken from me, because I was destined for a different role? And did I have it in me?

I recalled Miriam's words of blessing: "God bless you and keep you, my daughter. God smile on you and gift you. May God look you full in the face and make you prosper."

I thought of the timbrel Bezalel had given me. I went to the corner of the tent where I had hidden it under some baskets and uncovered it. It was as beautiful as ever. As I lifted the instrument and gave it a shake, the brass zils jingled merrily. Propped against cushions I sat on my mat and tried to remember Miriam's song from that long-ago day. Slowly the words came to me and I sang them, even though my voice still quavered with weakness.

For the first time since Pallu's death I felt a spark of hope. Maybe there was a future for me. Maybe Yahweh had a purpose for me like He did for Bezalel and Aaron and Miriam. Though it was the middle of the day, I felt my eyes begin to droop again and I drifted into a sweet, dreamless sleep, my timbrel clutched in my hand.

* * *

As my energy returned, I began helping with tasks around the tent—tending the fire and preparing the manna. I was not good at that, though. My thoughts easily got muddled and before I knew it, the smell of scorched food reminded me I'd made a mess of things again.

Perhaps it was because, despite my determination to forget him, it wasn't easy to purge from my mind and heart the memory of Pallu. It was as if, in the short while I knew him, he had worked his way into the very fiber of my being.

I dreamed of him often—only to wake to the cold,

empty truth. He was gone. I would never see him again. My thoughts of walking in Miriam's footsteps had a hard time competing with his memory, so the day that Cetura came for a visit was a welcome distraction.

"I heard you were sick," she said, after we'd hugged in greeting. She gave me a searching look. "You are still pale, and thinner."

"But better," I assured her. "And you?"

"Very well. Disappointed—as everyone is about being stuck here now for who knows how long."

"Are you and Paltiel still planning to marry?"

"Yes." Cetura lowered her eyes. Her cheeks bloomed pink under tanned skin. "We've even managed to spend some time together despite that we're only betrothed. He wishes we didn't have to wait for a whole year to marry. He was as distressed as anyone when he heard that our entry into the Promised Land was postponed. But he refuses to side with those who blame Caleb and Joshua for the delay."

"'Blame Caleb and Joshua? Why would they do that?"

"I don't know. I guess they want someone to blame."

This puzzled me but after what had happened lately to those who criticized and questioned Moses, the topic made me uneasy and I changed the subject.

"What is it like, living the life of a wife-to-be?"

"Time passes slowly," Cetura said with a rueful smile, "even though Mother fills my days with lessons on how to spin, weave, mend the tent, cook manna a hundred ways, and care for a home."

We chatted more. It was good to be with Cetura again—to relive memories of Egypt and share her dreams about the future. But after she left, I could honestly say I didn't envy her. I was glad that I had made peace with my state. Somehow, I couldn't see Miriam tending a fire or mending a tent. Hopefully I would never have to become an expert at those things either.

* * *

As I walked back to our tent from the pits this morning, I glanced toward the tabernacle and saw the cloud above it, as still as ever. No move today.

It had been two months since the spies returned, six weeks since the earthquake that swallowed Pallu and his family and forever changed my life. It looked like Moses' prediction was coming true—at least for now. We were not going anywhere. After the upheaval of the last weeks, a morning check of the cloud had become part of my routine. Its unmoving presence was reassuring and comforting.

I entered the tent to find Father, Mother, and Grandfather Hur all sitting in the main room. They looked up as one when I entered, as if they had been waiting for me.

"Sit down, Zamri," Mother said, motioning to a vacant spot beside her. "We have something to talk to you about."

I looked from one to the other. What could this be? They watched in silence as I took a seat. Then Father cleared his throat and his face lit up with a smile as he looked at me. "Good news," he said. "We have received a request for your hand in marriage. "

"What?" I looked from face to face. They were all beaming. "Who?"

"Elah," Mother burst out, as if not able to keep the news inside any longer.

"Elah? Do I know an Elah?"

"Caleb's middle son," Grandfather Hur explained. "It seems he has had his eye on you for some time."

Elah. I searched my memory for who he might be. Someone from our tribe. Someone who had had his eye on me. Had I ever sensed someone watching me, besides Pallu? I recalled Bezalel's wedding. Could Elah be the youth I saw staring at me then? And there had been other times I had sensed watching eyes too.

Everyone was looking at me, to see my reaction. My head was spinning and I could scarcely stay sitting upright.

"Aren't you happy?" Mother asked, breaking the silence as she peered into my face.

Normally this was the happiest day of a girl's life, but I felt only panic. With no warning, I was to be betrothed. And to a stranger. How could that be?

"You should be grateful that someone asked for your hand," Mother went on.

"I don't want to marry, " I whispered.

"I beg pardon." Grandfather Hur sounded incredulous.

I momentarily flicked my gaze up to look at him, Father, and Mother in defiance. "I won't do it," I said, louder.

Father frowned. "Yes, you will," he said, gently but firmly.

I took a deep breath, squelching the urge to throw myself on the tent floor kicking and screaming like I did when I couldn't get my way as a child.

"I know it's a surprise," said Mother, "but you have a whole year to get used to the idea."

The three pairs of watching eyes and the silence in the tent pressed in on me. I needed to get away, out of the tent and into the open. I stood shakily to my feet. "Can I go? Please?"

"Where?" asked Father.

"Just out" I answered, and stumbled toward the tent opening.

I walked aimlessly under the strengthening sun, my thoughts a desperate jumble. I was to be betrothed. I would be a wife to someone I hadn't even met. Was he old or young? If he was the person from Bezalel's wedding, he was young—maybe just a little older than I was. I tried to remember more details but couldn't recall anything else.

I would have to move to his family's tent. I remembered what Cetura said about Caleb and his family. I didn't want to move, especially to the home of a family that was unpopular. I wanted to stay with Mother, Father, Grandfather, Bezalel, and Sebia. Tears blurred my vision while my restless feet carried me on and on. Suddenly I realized that I was thirsty, tired, and wished I were back at home. But I had no idea where that was.

Through blurry eyes I searched for familiar landmarks. I scanned the horizon for Judah's banner, but it was nowhere in sight. Then I saw the cloud hovering above the tabernacle and it oriented me. What a relief! Keeping my eyes on it, I made my weary way back home. But there was no relief for my mind. I did not want to be betrothed. What could I do to change my family's plans?

I knew the contract hadn't been finalized. A formal agreement had to be made. There was a ceremony with washings, exchanging gifts, and other formalities. Perhaps I could get conveniently lost on the day of the ceremony, or hinder it in some way.

"Here she is!" Simeon's clear four-year-old voice announced my arrival back at the encampment.

"Where were you?" Father hurried to me as I trudged toward the tent. "We were worried. Bezalel and Sebia are out looking for you."

"Sorry," I said, "I lost my way." I took a long drink of the water Father offered me and stumbled to my bed. As I lay down, my body landed on something hard. The timbrel. I freed it from the covers and hugged it to myself. In this bad dream of impending betrothal, I would not again forsake my dream of being like Miriam.

Chapter Twelve

I was strong enough to gather manna again. On my first morning, my steps quickened when I saw Cetura, her face properly veiled. She jumped up as I approached and held out her arms. "Zamri, how wonderful to see you out here!"

We hugged and then got to work, chattering as we filled our baskets. She told me the things her mother was teaching her about mending tents and sandals, and how she was enjoying it more than she thought she would. "But here I go, on and on, talking about myself," she said. "What's new with you?"

I was silent for a moment and then reluctantly spilled the news. "My parents have had a betrothal request."

She stopped her work, stared at me wide-eyed, then jumped up and smothered me in another hug. "How wonderful! Congratulations. Who is the lucky man?"

"Elah," I answered. "Caleb's middle son."

"Oh." Her facial expression sobered, as she eased away from me. "I don't envy you. Bad family to be connected to right now." Then, looking at my face, she hastened to add, "At least bad with the other tribes. Not so unpopular with Judah."

I stifled the dismay that I felt rising. "Do you know Elah," I asked, "or anything else about him or his family?"

"Well, as you know, he's Caleb's middle son. Caleb himself is a widower. His wife died when we were still in Egypt."

"Who looks after the meals and oversees the home?"

I asked.

"Elah's older brother Iru is married to Merab. She's just a little older than I am and I've heard she does an excellent job of keeping the tent and making sure everyone is fed."

"And what's Elah like?"

"Oh, I've just seen him from time to time—and at a distance. He seems quiet and shy."

"Is he good-looking?"

"He's not ugly," Cetura said. "But not as handsome as my Paltiel—or as manly."

My heart sank. After Pallu, how could I marry a boy? However, my family had made the decision and custom said that my fate was sealed. Or was it?

*   *   *

Despite my secret resistance, the preparations to formalize the betrothal continued at our tent. Grandfather Hur and Father were resolute. Mother and Sebia were looking forward to hosting Elah and Caleb.

Bezalel caught me alone one day. He opened his hand to reveal a gold ring in his palm. "I made this for you to give Elah at the ceremony."

I looked down at the shining circlet, but said nothing.

"What is it, Zamri?" Bezalel looked at me sharply. "Don't you like it?"

"It's beautiful," I said, still not looking at him. "But..."

He put his hand under my chin, raised my face so that our eyes met. "Little sister, don't be silly. Elah is a fine young man. Grandfather, Father, and Mother want only the best for you."

He dropped his hand from my face, but his eyes still held mine. I looked away. He wouldn't understand why

I couldn't go through with this. He would only try to convince me to change my mind.

* * *

During the next few days, my resistance to my upcoming betrothal only grew stronger. I had to get out of it somehow. But how?

My feelings made me uneasy. No one I knew had defied their parents like I was planning to do. But the sight of my timbrel gave me courage. My family would understand when they saw me take my place as a young Miriam.

"Why are you restless?" Mother asked, as she dressed me in the garment she was preparing for me, telling me to stand motionless while she adjusted the fit.

"I need air. I want to go outside."

"Stay around and help us with the celebration plans."

I couldn't. The bustle around our tent made me want to escape more than ever. On my return from the pits I decided to detour to Sephy's tent. Maybe she would understand. At the very least, talking with her would get my mind off the impending betrothal.

As I made my way through the camp to the tents of Dan I remembered how Pallu and I had met on just such a walk. I shoved the sad thought down. No chance he would ever call out to me again.

Sephy was sitting outside their tent, working on a weaving. "Zamri!" she called out, and jumped up to meet me. "I haven't seen you for so long." There was a sparkle in her eye and a glow on her face.

We hugged and I sat beside her. "I heard you were ill," she said.

"Yes," I answered, and told her of the plague that

struck Mother and me. "And you?" I asked. "How have you fared?"

"I am with child," she said, her face beaming. She patted the rounded stomach under her tunic

"That's wonderful! When?"

"In the spring. Near your birthday. Just think—you'll be seventeen! Isn't it time you were married. I hear Cetura is betrothed."

"Yes, she is and so excited about it. As for me, that's what's on my mind. My parents have been speaking with Caleb and are wanting to arrange a betrothal with his son Elah."

"Why that's great news!" Sephy said. Then, probably noticing my lack of enthusiasm, "But you don't seem happy. What's wrong?"

"I'm nervous about it," I said. "I'm not sure what to expect. Tell me about your betrothal day."

"It was very traditional," Sephy said. "The day started with my ceremonial bath. Later Shoshan and his father came to our tent and my father and his discussed and signed the contract. Then all of us gathered under a canopy my family had set up outside the tent, father spoke a blessing over us, and we sealed our betrothal with a sip of wine from a common cup. Oh yes, and Shoshan gave me this."

Sephy raised her right hand to show the wide band that encircled her first finger.

"It's beautiful," I said, thinking of the ring Bezalel made for me to give Elah. But I didn't dwell on it, for her description had given me an idea. What if I didn't go along with the ceremony she had described and instead ran from the tent? I could surely manage something like that.

We chatted some more about her life and mine, until I noticed that the light had changed. "It's getting late," I said as I rose to go. "I've been here too long. I'd better get home or they'll send a search party. But thank you! I feel much better after what you've told me."

* * *

The big day had arrived. On this day Elah and his father would come and finalize the betrothal. And, one way or another, I planned to refuse him.

My hair was still damp from the washing ceremony when Mother slipped the dress on me that she had been labouring over for the past days. Then Sebia began fussing with my hair. Though I was on the lookout for a moment to get away, Mother and Sebia stuck to me like burrs. Interrupting the ceremony would be my only way out.

Sebia put the final touches on my hair, stood back, and looked me up and down. "You are beautiful," she said.

I didn't feel beautiful. I felt nervous and like a cheater who was allowing my family to pamper me, knowing that before the day was over I would disappoint and embarrass the whole clan. I took a deep breath to gather my resolve. I would stick to my decision.

I heard a commotion outside the tent and unfamiliar male voices. Caleb and Elah must have arrived.

I was deemed ready. Mother and Sebia lifted the tent divider and ushered me into the main room. There they were—four strangers. Caleb, I recognized as Grandfather Hur's friend and one of the twelve spies. He was tall, swarthy, and imposing. Beside him stood another tall, dark man, a younger version of Caleb, and two youths. The one with curly light brown hair looked younger than I. The other, with wavy brown hair and a newly sprouting beard was wearing an ornate robe suitable for the betrothal ceremony of a chieftain's son. He must be Elah.

I couldn't help but compare him to Pallu. There was no comparison. Pallu was dark, manly, and confident. Elah was a mere boy. His ruddy face was flushed. He looked eager, excited, and nervous.

His eyes were on me. I dropped my gaze and felt a pang, knowing that before this day was over he would be crushed and humiliated. Oh well, my future was at stake here too.

Father invited everyone to sit and introduced Caleb's three sons—Iru the tall one was oldest, the one with curly hair was Naam, the youngest, and the middle one in the fancy robe was Elah, as I thought. We took our places on mats on the tent floor, father and Grandfather Hur on either side of Caleb. The three of them studied and discussed the papyrus he had unrolled—the formal betrothal agreement—while the rest of us waited in nervous silence. [21]

I felt eyes on me. My face grew hot. I didn't look up.

At last the discussions were done and it was time to finalize the agreement under the canopy that father had erected outside our tent. The time for me to act was almost here. My heart pounded hard.

We all moved outside. Father directed me to stand under the canopy beside Elah. Standing next to him, I realized he was taller than I thought. Though we did not touch, I felt his body beside me, radiating warmth. And I felt his eyes on me, boring into me, seeming to will me to look at him. I flicked my gaze to his face for a lightning second and saw intensity, adoration, and delight.

Oh no!

The formalities were beginning. Grandfather Hur grasped a cup of precious wine and held it high as he pronounced, "Blessed are You, Yahweh, King of the universe who creates the fruit of the vine. Blessed are You, Lord, our God, King of the universe, who has sanctified us with His commandments, commanded us concerning marriages, and permitted to us those who are married to us by these rites. Blessed are You Lord, who, in this way, sanctifies His people Israel."

When he was finished. He handed the cup to Elah, who took a sip. Again, my eyes were drawn to his, which were watching me the whole time, probing, studying, asking.

Now Grandfather extended the cup toward me. My hands were slick with sweat and my heart pounded in my throat. Now. This was the moment. My last chance. I must push the cup away, refuse to bring it to my lips. Now.

Again, my eyes were pulled toward the hazel ones looking down on me. They were full of cherishing, adoring, loving, and I knew, in that instant, I could not douse the light in them.

The cup was in my hands now. I held it and held it, then tipped it toward my mouth, inhaled its fruity perfume, and, with the tiniest of sips, partook of its sour strength.

Elah's face broke into a big smile.

Grandfather Hur took the cup from me and continued to guide us through the formalities—more blessings and then the placing, by Elah's warm calloused hands, of a golden circlet on the first finger of my right hand. Bezalel was beside me now with the ring he had made for me to give Elah. Somehow, I got it onto Elah's finger.

I felt the warm toughness of his hands long after our guests left in the late afternoon. The unfamiliar bleat of new goats drifted in from outside the tent—Elah's betrothal gift. And next to my robe rested a veil—my outdoor face covering for the next year. What had I done? [22]

Chapter Thirteen

Overnight my status had changed. Claimed and all but married, everyone expected me to be a woman. At sixteen that was not too much to ask. Still, to me it was a burdensome thing.

"Don't forget your veil!" Mother would call out, coming after me holding the head covering whenever I left to collect manna, tend the animals, fetch water, even go to the pits.

There were cooking lessons. Though I had helped Mother preparing food before, now she expected me to duplicate the various ways she made our manna on my own. "How can you manage to get it lumpy?" she cried in puzzlement over the manna gruel I ruined. Manna loaves that came out neatly formed and baked to golden perfection when she made them, turned into dry unappetizing lumps in my hands. I burned the griddle cakes.

I was no better at other tasks. She tried to teach me how to mend rips and patch worn out places in our tent as well as our clothing. I watched her deft hands. She made it look easy. But when I tried to do as she did, I was all clumsiness.

"I can't do it!" I cried, exasperated.

"Oh, but you must learn." Mother answered. "You have a very capable sister-in-law to live up to."

"Why must I learn to do these things when she already does them so well?" I argued.

"Because every woman needs to be able to do them

for her own household. You will not live in Caleb's tent forever."

She would leave me on my own to finish, say, the mending, but the voices of Simeon and Jaffa playing outside the tent were too much to bear. Throwing aside the fabric and yarn I would attach my veil and join them.

"Zamri!" Simeon called out, "can we play with the goats?"

"Sure, let's go!" I grabbed him by one hand, Jaffa took the other, and we headed toward the animals.

Time passed quickly as we spent time with the goats Elah had brought. We petted them, brushed their dark coats to a glossy sheen, and went past the reach of their ropes in search of greenery to feed them.

Suddenly Mother would appear, my unfinished work in her hands, looking thoroughly irritated. "Zamri, you haven't finished this, and it's time to prepare the evening meal."

Yes. Time to return to the tent and wreck some more food. And so it would go.

Beneath all this resistance I knew there was something deeper than simple forgetfulness and irresponsibility. It kept me awake at night as I mulled things over.

How I felt about Elah was so different than how I felt about Pallu. Pallu made my heart race and my face blush. Elah did not. I barely knew him. If I met him outside the burden of this betrothal, we might be friends but I couldn't imagine anything more.

I kept thinking about the look in his eyes during the betrothal ceremony. Why did he look at me that way? He didn't know me. That look would change when he knew me better, of that I was certain.

Moving away from my family was another thing. That thought shadowed me like a dark cloud. But it had all been decided and by sealing the contract I had only myself to blame. So, I must do better, I *would* do better — cooperate with mother's training, live up to the standing I now had with Jaffa and my other young cousins.

Then the morning came with its jobs and expectations, its drudgery and mistakes, and something in me rose up and pushed back. I didn't want to do this. I couldn't do this!

* * *

One of my jobs now was fetching water. It was a job that was never finished. The water jugs were always empty or almost empty.

On this day, I left the tent to help care for the animals, promising I'd get the water later. Simeon and some of his little friends came with me. We tended the goats and in our search for green bits for them came across a great hairy spider which we watched from a safe distance. Then we spotted a lizard and saw how it changed colour as it moved from rock to rock.

Before I knew it, the sun was high in the sky. "I'm thirsty," declared Simeon. "Me too," shouted one of his friends.

"We'd better get back to the tents," I said, remembering then that I hadn't yet fetched our water.

When I got back, though, the water jug was full. Who filled it, I wondered. Mother was not in the main room of the tent but I heard voices coming from Bezalel and Sebia's room. The curtain was drawn but I pulled it back just enough to look in and see Sebia on the mat. She appeared to be crying. Mother was sitting beside her.

"What is it?" I asked. I pulled the curtain back and

entered.

"Sebia insisted on fetching the water for you," Mother said, her eyes flashing recrimination. "It seems the effort of lugging the heavy jug back here was too much for her. She's feeling unwell."

I was puzzled. How could carrying a jug of water make someone who had done this for months, feel ill. Sebia answered the question on my face.

"I am with child," she said, looking at me with tear-filled eyes. "But the effort gave me cramps and now something bad is happening."

I looked down at the mat where Sebia lay and saw the red stains.

Mother attended Sebia for the rest of the day, leaving me responsible for everything else. For once I put my mind to my tasks, full of regret over what had happened as a result of my irresponsibility.

When Bezalel arrived, he went to Sebia and mother joined me at the cooking fire, looking grave. "She lost the baby," she said.

"I'm so sorry," I said. I felt terrible.

When Bezalel joined us later, I couldn't avoid his eyes. They looked at me pointedly with sadness and a glint of blame.

* * *

Ten months of my betrothal had passed. How quickly the time was going. I was now seventeen. Sephy's little boy was born right on time, one day after my birthday. My household disasters were mounting too. I managed to scorch our Passover lamb, and our tent, with my clumsily mended sections, was a standing joke. But I had also taught Jaffa, Simeon, and little Talia a fair bit about the care of goats and kids, ewes and lambs. Though the hours spent in the tent doing women's work had given me some skills, I was still far from proficient. Even so, the day I would become Elah's wife crept ever nearer.

One day, Cetura sent word that her wedding celebration was very close. Since I was to be one of her bridesmaids, I got myself ready. Three days later a messenger from her family came to tell me to come in the evening. Just after sundown, I grabbed my timbrel (there were few enough times to use it—my friend's wedding celebration was surely one) and prepared to leave. Bezalel stopped me. "Sebia and I will walk with you," he said. "We must take good care of our betrothed sister."

Though I'd taken this walk by myself scores of times, his expression of care was comforting. Things had been strained between us since the fateful day Sebia lost her unborn baby. His words now gave me hope that our relationship could be repaired and resemble what it was before that day.

Cetura's encampment buzzed with excitement. I joined three other friends of hers already waiting with the radiant but nervous bride. Cetura's plain face was as beautiful as I'd ever seen it.

A few minutes after I arrived Sephy walked in. The three of us hugged in a happy reunion, then Cetura took us both by the hand to her sleeping mat and showed us the embroidered square of cloth she and her mother had prepared for this day—the bit of fabric that would soon hold proof that Cetura was a virgin and would be a worthy wife.

It hit me then. This was what I would be facing all too soon. I was glad, for once, that Pallu and I got no further than a kiss even though I had dreamed of more.

We returned to the main room of the tent to await Paltiel and his friends—a wait that could take us to sunrise. Despite the lateness of the hour, the excitement in the room drove away any sleepiness.

I studied Sephy. She seemed changed—less willowy and her face was fuller. A closer look at her form confirmed my suspicion. She was with child again! Our eyes met and she grinned big—her face wreathed in happiness.

Two of Cetura's other friends were betrothed like I was, and so the conversation drifted to domestic matters, the activities of the betrothal year, and then questions for Sephy. She filled us in with what it was like to birth little Chaim and how this pregnancy was different from her first.

One of Cetura's single friends from another tribe entertained us with stories of how sought after she was. "Caleb from Judah came to our house one day. He was there to speak to my father about the possibility of me marrying his youngest son, Naam."

My ears perked up. Could this be a future sister-in-law?

"Oh no," said another. "Who would want to be part of Caleb's family? It's because of him we're stuck out here in the wilderness."

"I know," the first girl said. "Father cut that visit very short."

My heart thumped, my face burned. So, this was what I was getting into. I looked up to see Sephy and Cetura both watching me with concern.

The distant sound of timbrels, pipes, flutes, and drums cut into the conversation. We jumped to our feet as one. The groom had arrived! I attached my veil, and joined the happy throng outside the tent.

* * *

Daylight illuminated the surroundings when the party finally broke up at the tent of Paltiel's family. It was a new day but sleep was still far from my eyes as I walked with Cetura's parents back to the tents of Judah.

Scenes from the wedding replayed in my mind. The jingle of my timbrel recalled the band of musicians that accompanied Paltiel and his friends to Cetura's tent, and my timbrel and I were part of the noisy walk after Paltiel claimed his betrothed and took her to their new home.

I heard again Paltiel's joyful shout from the bridal chamber on seeing proof of the purity of his bride. As part of the wedding ceremony, all of us friends of the bride and groom as well as Cetura's mother and father witnessed that soiled cloth. Then we all sat down to the wedding supper, as sumptuous a feast as could be made with manna and milk.

But now my timbrel's joyful jingles mocked me as I again faced my approaching fate. If only I could be anticipating a wedding night with Pallu, the man I had loved, instead of the youthful stranger to whom I was betrothed.

Chapter Fourteen

"What? Have you been crying again?"

Though I had tried to dry my tears and cool my hot cheeks and burning eyes with hands chilled from collecting the day's manna, Mother still saw the evidence.

"What do you have to cry about?" she asked me, taking the basket of food I'd collected. "Betrothed women about to be married don't mourn. They're happy."

"I don't want to leave here, and you" I managed to get out before the tears I'd held back overwhelmed me.

Mother enveloped me in her warm robe. "I don't look forward to you going either," she murmured. I nestled my head under her chin and give vent to the fear and apprehension that had been creeping ever closer with the approach of my soon-coming wedding. "But this is the way of life," she said after my sobbing had calmed. Gently she wiped the tears from my eyes, then, her hands on my shoulders, turned me to face her. There were tears in her eyes too.

"Come now. We can't waste the day in crying. Help me make breakfast and then we need to pack your things."

Yes, the dreaded time had arrived. No matter that I was going to live with a man I scarcely knew, whose face I couldn't even remember, who competed in my thoughts with someone I loved but would never see again. Women had done this since our great-great-grandmother Rebekah left her family for a man she had never even seen. Mother had reminded me of that, countless times.

By day's end my personal possessions were packed in a neat bundle, my wedding dress and veil hung, ready to be put on, and Jaffa was on the alert to fetch Cetura and Sephy the moment word was out that this was the night.

* * *

I had been ready for a week now and still Elah had not come. Could it be that he had changed his mind? The possibility left me with a tiny pebble of regret but mostly a rockslide of relief. Maybe all my fears and worries were for nothing, and life would continue as usual.

Then, this night, one of Bezalel's friends came running to our tent. "The wedding procession has left Caleb's encampment. Elah is on his way!"

My family leapt into action. Bezalel went to find Jaffa and left with her to fetch my attendants. Mother pulled me from the fireside and Grandfather Hur's stories to the women's quarter to help me into my wedding clothes. Sebia was soon there too, her skillful hands arranging my hair, then covering my head with the veil. I was almost ready when I heard the faint sound of timbrels and voices — and then nothing.

"I think I heard them," said Sebia.

Mother cocked her head to listen. "I don't hear anything."

"They've probably silenced the parade to surprise us." No sooner had Sebia said this than I heard the blast of a shofar followed by a shout: "I have come for my bride." Even though I'd heard it just once, I recognized Elah's voice.

Lights flickered through the weave of the tent walls. Then bedlam broke out.

Father called into the tent, "Where is Zamri? Bring her out."

Mother and Sebia finished their last touchups, then stood back and looked me over. They smiled at each other and nodded. I inhaled deeply to calm my pounding heart as Mother on one side, Sebia on the other took my hands and led me from the tent to meet my future.

Elah came to me and took my hand from Sebia's. His hand was warm, its grasp strong. It was also damp. Could he be nervous too?

I felt his eyes on me. His gaze locked with mine through the veil. It was intense—almost frighteningly so—but also tinged with longing and tenderness. It was the same look that had kept me from refusing him on our betrothal day.

I pulled my eyes from his to look around. Our encampment was teaming with people, many of whom I didn't recognize in the flickering torchlight. Then I saw Cetura and Sephy, their faces beaming with happiness and affection.

"Let's be off!" It was Iru, Elah's brother and best man.

The singers, pipers, and timbrel players took up their instruments and now with full joyful volume led the throng through the tents of Judah from my home to Caleb's encampment.

Elah held my hand securely in his the entire way. I felt his eyes on me from time to time but no words passed between us. It would have been almost impossible to talk above the din of the procession in any case. The celebration that accompanied us as we walked the pathways between Judah's tents, felt unearthly, like a dream.

When we got to Caleb's encampment, Elah led me into the family's tent to the huppah that had been prepared for us. Now the nervousness, that had begun to calm during our walk, returned. Again, my heart pounded hard. I took deep breaths to calm its frantic rhythm. I felt a desperate urge to yank my clammy hand from Elah's and run. Mother had told me exactly what to expect on this my wedding night. I couldn't help but feel like a lamb being led to slaughter.

Elah must have noticed my fear, for here in the privacy of our chamber, he drew me to him and lifted the veil off my head. "Don't be afraid little Zamri," he murmured into my hair.

I clung to him, finding unexpected comfort in the warmth and solidity of this youth who was about to become my husband. Then his hand moved down from my back to my waist and below in an intimate caress and I stiffened. Such intimacy was what I dreamed of between Pallu and me, not this stranger. I stood stiff and guarded under his touch that had turned from brother-tenderness to desire.

His movements became urgent as he removed my dress and led me to the sleeping mat on which lay the virginity cloth mother and I had prepared. Thoughts like how did it get there and what if the man beside me were Pallu flitted through my mind as Elah made love to me.

* * *

I woke in the cold tent and pulled the covers close. I opened my eyes and looked around. It was growing light but the place I was in was unfamiliar. Then I remembered — I was married.

I turned over and saw Elah. His eyes were open, studying me. In the dim morning light, I peered back at him. His hair was brown and curled over his forehead, around his ears, and into his neck. His beard looked sparse, partly, perhaps, because it was lighter in colour than his hair, and partly because it hadn't grown in thickly. His eyes were the dark hazel I remembered from our betrothal day. They did not pierce through me like Pallu's did. Still, even in their softness, their intensity made me uncomfortable. I looked away.

"You're awake my little bird," Elah murmured. He drew me close so that my head rested on his chest.

"Do you know why I chose yesterday for our wedding day?" he asked.

I shook my head.

"It was my birthday, my twenty-first birthday," he said. "And now it will be another birthday, the birth of my family, our home." I could hear the thump, thump of his heart—a rhythm that increased as his hands drifted over the hidden parts of me. "You're so lovely," he murmured.

I recalled last night, his delighted shout at finding the stains on the cloth to prove my virginity. Now his desire consumed him once more. Again, I let him take me while my mind wandered to Pallu.

We lay long in bed until the sun's warmth had us throwing off the covers. I looked around the tent and saw my wedding dress in a crumpled heap where it fell last night. In another corner was the bundle of my belongings. Someone from my home must have carried it with them in the wedding procession.

I got out of bed, went over to it, unknotted its cover to reveal my familiar things—undergarments, tunics, and robes that smelled of home. I chose clothes and begin to get dressed.

Elah, who had been watching me, came over. "Do you have to?" he asked. I resisted his trying to take off my clothes but he began tickling me and soon had me in his arms again. As he led me to the mat, I recalled my wonderment at why the bridal celebration included seven days of huppah seclusion for the bride and groom. Now I was beginning to understand. If only these seven days could have been spent with Pallu.

Part Two: Summer

Chapter Fifteen

All too soon our wedding week was done and I faced the challenge of taking my place in Caleb's family. I dreaded meeting the capable Merab for the first time. Her first words to us, as we joined the family for breakfast, were not promising. "I hope food tastes as good sitting up as lying in bed." Her voice was loaded with sarcasm.

I felt my face flush. I stole a glance at Elah but he didn't seem bothered. Instead, he grinned as Iru chuckled. When Father Caleb joined us, silence descended. In his authoritative voice he blessed the food, then took up the basket of manna cakes Merab had prepared. When it got to me I chose one, held the golden round for a moment, sniffed the sweet smell of it, and took a bite. Its crunchy crust gave way to a soft sweet centre, done to perfection. I quickly finished one and reached for another. These were good — better than mother's.

Merab, who had been sitting with her toddler, a girl named Aliyah, on her lap, thrust her onto Iru and bolted from the tent. A minute later I heard coughing — and retching?

I exchanged puzzled looks with Elah. Iru noticed. "Merab is with child," he told us. "This is how she was with Aliyah too — sick and nauseous every morning and often through the day. We were hoping Zamri could help with Aliyah and other tasks around the tent.

"Yes. Of course she will," Elah answered, without so

much as a look my way.

* * *

I was back to gathering manna every morning, fetching water, stoking the fire, preparing the food, and keeping an eye on two-year-old Aliyah on days when Merab felt ill—which was pretty well every day.

It was a lot like my betrothal year, when Mother tried to teach me how to be a good wife. But it was different too. For Merab, despite how sick she felt, still seemed to have the time and energy to watch my every move. "No, the baskets are stored there," she corrected me, and "You're boiling the manna too long," and "The bed coverings need to be refolded—evenly this time," and "Aliyah's tunic is on backward." On and on it went. I thought of Sebia as a new bride in our home and how she must have felt when mother kept correcting her.

I escaped from the tent whenever I could. Often, I took Aliyah with me to go for slow walks around the camp so she could practice her newfound ability to walk and then run. We wandered outside the camp, scrambled over small boulders, and looked under rocks to uncover bugs and spiders. We watched lizards, spotted rock hiraxes, and visited Elah and the flock.

Sometimes I took my timbrel and sang to Aliyah, the songs I remembered as a little girl. Then I taught them to her. Our singing attracted more children and I led them all in Miriam's Red Sea song. [23]

On such days, I lost track of time. More than once, when Aliyah and I got back, we found Merab, pale but busy, readying the fire for the manna she had prepared to cook for the late meal.

"Mommy, Mommy!" Aliyah would shout, running to her and flinging herself into Merab's arms. Merab would hug her but peer suspiciously at me. "You two have been gone long enough. Where have you been?" There was never a whisper of appreciation or thanks from this thin-faced, wary-eyed sister-in-law.

* * *

Merab's time was approaching. I had tried my best to please her but, if anything, she grew more critical and demanding. "This manna meal has lumps in it... The cooking area is always a mess after you finish with it," and so it went.

One day her mother, who had worked as a midwife, arrived. Heaven help me, she was an older version of her daughter. That day after I finished my chores I left the tent to find Elah. He was not Pallu but he was all I had in this family. As I approached the place where he grazed his flock, he looked my way and I saw his face light up. Then he turned his attention again to the ewe he was tending.

I came up beside him and watched as he comforted the animal. She seemed to be in distress, snuffling at the ground, moving in circles, bleating and digging at the earth with her snout.

"What's wrong with her?" I asked.

"Nothing's wrong," Elah said, with a chuckle. "She's about to give birth." He grabbed my hand as we watched the ewe lie down, then get up again and root around in circles, bleating the whole time. Then I saw a sack appear from below her tail. The sack grew ever larger until, plop. It dropped to the ground.

"Her lamb?" Though my father had kept sheep for as long as I could remember, I'd never watched a lambing. "What do we do now?"

"Nothing," Elah said. "If everything goes well, she'll

know just what to do."

The ewe turned around, sniffed the small wet creature, then began to lick and nibble it clean. Under her ministrations, a darling lamb appeared.

Meanwhile, another parcel had dropped from her behind. She turned her attention to it while the first born tried to scramble to its feet. It fell, then tried again, finally getting onto all fours. It managed a step or two on long shaky legs before it collapsed once more.

The drama before us continued till both lambs were on their feet. The first one seemed to know just what to do. It found the ewe's teat and was soon making greedy sucking sounds. But the second appeared confused.

Elah approached it and guided it toward the ewe. It sniffed at its mother but then wandered away, wobbling on newborn legs and falling.

"Maybe we should take it home and feed it there," I suggested. "I had a lamb once that I fed when its mother died."

"No," Elah replied with uncharacteristic firmness. "I won't have that. The sheep in my flock are not pets. They must learn to survive on their own."

"I know how to care for sheep too, you know," I said, surprised by Elah's instant rejection of my idea.

"I know how to take care of my flock," Elah said, his voice softening. "Trust me."

* * *

Merab had her baby—another girl. They named her Haviva, "well loved," though I'm sure another girl was a disappointment, especially to Iru who had had his hopes set on a son. I didn't get much of a chance to get acquainted with the little one. Merab acted as if she was the only person who could care for her baby properly.

When her mother went home, my work increased again. This was not because Merab thought I was capable. She was always making snide remarks about the food. Elah came to my defense, though I wondered if I embarrassed even him.

Aliyah was my bright spot. She had just turned three and we went out every day after my chores were done. I showed her the lambs. We secretly named them Pebble and Rock, and sometimes we brought them treats, even though Elah didn't approve of our making pets of them.

We clambered around on the rocks, in search of rare desert flowers. Sometimes we explored life under the boulders. I loved to see the beetles and ants scurry away at the lifting of their housetops.

This day I was preoccupied with watching such a scene when I heard Aliyah's loud and sudden cry. I looked around. She had been right beside me a minute ago. Where had she wandered?

I followed the sharp sound of her screams to see her a short distance away, on the ground. Had she been bitten by a snake or scorpion? I raced to her. "What is it?"

A bump was rising on her head and there was a small gash which oozed blood. She must have fallen on the rocks. I lifted her gently onto my lap, blotted the blood with the bottom of my robe, then cuddled and comforted her till her crying subsided. "What happened?"

"I fall," she said, still sniffing back tears.

"Let's go home to Mommy." I set her on her feet to walk but she cried out in pain as she put weight on her foot. I saw it was swollen and becoming discoloured, so I scooped her in my arms and carried her back to the tent.

There, Merab was nursing Haviva. I placed the still tearful Aliyah next to her and began to explain what had happened. But I don't think Merab heard anything I said after seeing the injuries.

"Oh darling," she crooned, pulling Aliyah close to her. She looked up at me, her eyes flashing sparks. "What were you thinking, leaving her unattended? Can't you do anything right?"

"I'm so sorry. I didn't mean for something like this to happen."

She answered me with a "Humph," then turned her attention back to Aliyah. Feeling dismissed, I went to our room of the tent. Would I ever fit into this family?

* * *

Over the next days, Aliyah's injuries healed nicely, unlike the injury my carelessness had done to my relationship with Merab. One evening after the meal, Aliyah came to me, pulled on my hand, and urged me up. "Out, out."

"You want to go out?" I asked, smiling. Her little hand still pulling on mine, I scrambled to my feet. "I'll take you for a walk," I said. I looked at Merab for permission. "I won't take my eyes off her."

Merab responded with a cold stare. Then her gaze shifted to Iru. No words passed between them but the communication was clear. Iru got up, walked over to us, detached Aliyah's hand from mine and took it in his own. "Papa will take you for a walk."

I felt as if I'd been slapped. I wondered if there was more to Merab's reaction than just fear of Aliyah's safety. I recalled her eyes boring into us at other times when we were together. Could she be jealous?

Unwelcome tears flooded my eyes. I clenched my

teeth to keep my emotions hidden as I left the tent to join Elah and Caleb who were sitting near the fire.

Naam emerged from the tent a moment later. With his long strides, he soon caught up to me. It seemed he had heard and seen all that had just happened. "Don't let her get to you," he said. "That's just her way."

"Thanks," I said, feeling a glimmer of hope. Maybe Elah wasn't the only one on my side in this family.

Naam and I joined Elah and Caleb by the fire. They were sitting in uncharacteristic silence.

I took my place beside Elah who sat, elbows on his knees, face cradled in his hands, staring at the flames, looking unusually dejected.

Across the fire pit in the flickering light sat Caleb. I recalled how intimidating he appeared the day he returned from Canaan with the eleven other spies. I remembered, too, his unshakeable insistence that we could take the land despite walled cities and giants. From that day on his piercing gaze and strength of will had frightened me, though he had been nothing but kind in the few times we had anything to do with each other.

Now I studied his face. Even when he was relaxed, his eyes bored into things, though right now as he looked at Elah, the intensity of his gaze was softened by concern.

"What's on your mind son?" he asked, breaking the silence.

"Oh, not much," Elah replied, not looking up.

"Yes, there is. Tell me. What is it?"

"Something that happened in the field today."

"What happened?"

"Shepherds from Reuben blocked me from watering my flock for a good while."

"Why? Did you do something to anger them?"

"It's not what I did, but who I am." Elah looked up now and there was a hint of accusation in his voice as he continued. "They've been taunting me for weeks. They say it's all your fault that we're stuck in the wilderness instead of entering Canaan. Today for the first time they went beyond words."

This was the first I'd heard of Elah's trouble. Sympathy rose in me. I knew how much he loved his flock. I watched Caleb's face to see his reaction. Surprisingly, instead of sympathy or outrage his eyes twinkled and a smile warmed his face. "I get the same kinds of comments," he said. "Don't let their pettiness affect you. It reminds me of the attitude of most of the spies on our mission who saw only obstacles and problems. They forgot how Yahweh brought us out of Egypt, parted the Red Sea, and helped us defeat the Amalekites.

"If you have done nothing wrong, son, don't let their words or actions intimidate you. Put your trust in Yahweh alone, not the good opinion or approval of others. That is what I have had to do ever since I returned from Canaan. Keep the long view in mind, son. Remember, we're not here forever."

"Moses said forty years. Only a few have passed since you returned," Elah replied.

"Time passes more quickly than you think. And remember Moses' words to me — Yahweh's promise to our family: 'Surely the land where your foot has trodden shall be your inheritance and your children's forever because you wholly follow the Lord my God.' You will survive and when we get to Canaan, we'll have whole cities as our own."

"I don't want cities," Elah muttered, "just enough land to graze my own flock."

"Someday, like Iru, you'll come to love the excitement of cities too."

Elah didn't reply but kept staring into the fire. [24]

Chapter Sixteen

Naam was in love. The day he comforted me about being kept from Aliyah, we became friends and allies. Often Elah, Naam, and I sat by the fire in the evening talking. He told us he had had his eye on a girl from the tribe of Reuben (I shivered when I heard that name).

"Cherut is beautiful, with curly hair and green eyes. I'm working on Dad to start negotiations."

So far, Caleb had resisted. "She's from Reuben," he said. "Too many rebels have come from that tribe. I have an uneasy feeling about becoming aligned with it."

I wondered what he would think if he knew that I had loved a Reubenite, would willingly have married him, and still couldn't help but compare Elah to him. My secret must never come out.

Naam was insistent, persistent, and as the youngest he often got his way where others wouldn't. One evening a little while later he was all excitement as he announced, "Tomorrow Father and I go to talk to Cherut's parents."

Shortly after that Naam was betrothed. Then began the year to ready our home for another woman. Merab seemed less than thrilled with the responsibility of enlarging the tent in addition to taking care of her little ones. And since there was no one else, I took responsibility for it, even though I was sure my skill at spinning and weaving didn't begin to measure up to hers.

I enlisted Elah and Naam to help me collect goat hair for the project and then worked for hours each day, spinning it into yarn. I decided to ask Mother to come and help me figure out how wide to make the weaving for the walls and get it started.

The day she came to help me, I introduced her to Merab. who greeted her with a cool polite smile. "Actually, I've met your mother before, on your wedding day." She spoke to me like I was a young child.

"I've asked her to come and help me with the new room of the tent."

"Oh, I could have done that," Merab said.

"I didn't want to trouble you."

As mother and I worked, I thought back to the gatherings at our home when we enlarged the tent for Bezalel and Sebia. I remembered how all the women in our clan pitched in to help. I was thankful now that I learned as much as I had then. After mother left for home, I realized how much I missed the comradeship of the women in my family. So far, those in Caleb's encampment had taken their cues from Merab and avoided me.

What would it be like to have another woman around, I wondered. Would she be another joyless critic like Merab? When I hinted at my concerns to Naam, he laughed. "Cherut is not a bit like Merab," he said. "She's lively, quick, and loves to laugh."

* * *

As I helped Naam prepare for his bride, the days trekked by in numbing sameness. After going out in the early mornings to collect manna, fetch water, and help Merab prepare the morning meal, it was endless spinning and weaving. I was glad I had many months for this project.

Though Merab didn't raise a finger to help, I sensed

her disapproval when she examined my work. Once I overheard her say to Iru, "The weave in Zamri's panels is far too loose. Those walls will let in wind and sand." After that I made an extra effort to tighten the weave as I worked alone at this seemingly endless task.

Sometimes Aliyah came to watch. She was full of three-year-old questions: "What are you doing? Why? When will you be finished? Can you play with me?"

Merab would appear right about then. "You mustn't bother auntie," she would say.

"Oh, she's no bother," I'd reply. But it was no use, for Merab would take Aliyah by the hand, lead her out, and I would be left staring at their disappearing backs.

"Why does Merab keep Aliyah from me?" I asked Elah, in the privacy of our room. "Surely it's not still because I neglected her for a few minutes that day many moons ago."

"Who knows," he said. "She has always been a hard one to figure out. But why does it bother you? Aliyah is just a child."

"She's good company. I miss her."

"Well," he replied, drawing me to him, "perhaps we can remedy that by having a little Aliyah of our own."

He was asleep now after he had made love to me. But I was wide awake as I thought back to our conversation. It was not the first time he had alluded to us having a child.

I studied him in the dim light. His chest rose and lowered in the slow, steady rhythm of breathing. His face looked peaceful and young. I saw in it the face of an innocent boy and I realized, I liked him, even loved him in a way, like one does a brother or friend. But he had never kindled in me the passion or the fire that Pallu did.

Could my divided love be the reason I was not yet with child?

* * *

On the day of my nineteenth birthday Elah asked if there was anything I wanted. Yes, there was. I wanted a break from this everlasting spinning and weaving and the gloomy, heavy presence of Merab.

"Could we go visit Sephy and Shoshan?

Elah readily agreed so that was where we were off to, the next day.

I had another reason for wanting to visit Sephy. Two reasons, actually. Elah and I had discussed what wedding gift we might give Naam and Cherut. My idea was to ask Sephy to do one of her weavings for them to use as a cover for their bed or a tent divider. And today, the day after my birthday, was the birthday of their firstborn Chaim. He turned two today so I brought my timbrel with me. Maybe we'd get a chance to celebrate with a little song and dance. We took the long walk to their tent in the late afternoon, after the sun had lost its midday strength.

When we got there Sephy greeted me with a hug. "You've come just in time for our party!"

We joined Shoshan and his parents under the canopy outside the tent and were soon drinking tea and eating manna cakes. After being kept from Aliyah for so long, I couldn't take my eyes off Sephy's beautiful little boy.

"Come," I said, holding out my arms to Chaim. But he was shy, burrowing his face in his mother's clothes, then peering out at me warily.

"Go," Sephy urged.

"See what I have here," I said, pulling out the

timbrel. "We'll sing a song."

He came to me hesitantly, I pulled him gently into my lap, and began to sing a song my mother had taught me when we were still in Egypt, keeping the rhythm with the timbrel. Quickly he forgot his shyness and reached for the instrument. He tried to grab it but it was too heavy so I took his hand and helped him tap the rhythm while I sang.

A baby's cry told us that Matan, Sephy's second son, had awakened. Sephy fetched him while Chaim and I continued to make music. After Sephy had nursed him she handed the baby to me. He was warm, solid, and content, his round face flushed from feeding.

While I cuddled the little one, Chaim managed to pick up the timbrel, jingle it and pull it toward his mouth. Shoshan's mother came over, sat Chaim into her lap and, taking the timbrel from his hand, crooned my favourite song—Miriam's song.

I rose and still holding little Matan, danced around, stepping in time to the music. Then Sephy, her mother, and Chaim joined me as went weaving around the encampment in a dance that recalled the morning after the Red Sea crossing.

"I haven't had so much fun since Cetura's wedding party," said Sephy, laughing and out of breath as we found our way back to the shelter where the men were still in sober conversation.

Elah caught my eye and raised his eyebrows in unspoken communication. Could it be time to go home already? The visit had passed so quickly. I hadn't even talked to Sephy about why I came.

"I have a request of you," I said. "Elah's brother is betrothed, his betrothal year is coming to an end, and all

I'm finding time to do is enlarge the tent. We still have no gift for them. Would you make a weaving for us?"

"I'd love to," she replied without any hesitation. "Any idea of what you want as a design?"

I glanced over at Elah. We hadn't discussed this.

"We were thinking... I was thinking perhaps you could weave into it something in honour of Father Caleb's family—-something with the lion crest of Judah?" I glanced over at Elah. He looked surprised and pleased.

* * *

The tent panels were woven. It was time to see how the enlargement would fit. But I needed help attaching the new panels to the main tent.

Merab had been extra irritable the last few days. Elah and Naam might be willing, but I felt embarrassed asking them to help with women's work. I decided to get Mother to help me again. This time I went by myself to fetch her.

With the distance between our encampments, I hadn't been there for weeks. It was so good to see father and Grandfather Hur. The tent still felt like home.

Mother and Sebia both agreed to come back with me. As we walked, Mother gave the latest news of the aunties and cousins while Sebia walked in silence. I looked over at her. She appeared to understand my unspoken question about any news from her, and shook her head. Did I see a glisten of tears in her eyes? I felt overwhelmed with regret as I recalled the day she lost her unborn child and my part in it.

On arrival Mother examined the tent walls I had woven. "You did these?" she asked.

"Yes."

"They're beautifully done."

"Tight enough?"

"Oh yes. One rainfall, even the moisture of night dew will swell the weave and make it impenetrable."

Mother, Sebia, and I worked at attaching the tent walls to the poles I had collected. And though one section didn't fit as tightly as the others, mother assured me that it would be quite sufficient.

When we were all done, I served tea and manna cakes before Mother and Sebia set out for home, leaving me with a satisfied feeling. I had completed a daunting task.

After the evening meal and still feeling euphoric, I slipped away from the others at the fire and went to our room. I lifted the flap to the outside to let in the moonlight, then found my tambourine and sang over myself Miriam's victory song to the jingling rhythm of my instrument.

* * *

I was collecting manna the next morning when I heard the trumpet blast—the signal to move. I glanced toward the tabernacle and noticed that, indeed, the cloud had lifted.

I finished the job and rushed back to the encampment, which had become a hive of activity. Merab was directing the camp takedown.

"Hurry, prepare food," she ordered me. Then she turned to the others who were disassembling the tent. "No, Naam, it's folded this way." She demonstrated how to pack the tent walls, only to be interrupted by a crying Haviva.

"Where's the cooking pan?" I asked when I didn't find it in its usual place.

"Someone must have packed it," Merab muttered. "We'll have to eat our manna uncooked today."

"Then I'll go fetch water," I said. On the way, I passed other encampments packing up. I recalled the orderly takedown of my home campsite — something I had never appreciated before.

I returned to find our things mostly packed, though everyone was in a bad mood and only a small serving of manna was left for me.

As we left our old campsite, I accompanied Elah and his flock. After the impatience and irritability of Merab, it was a pleasure to travel in his calm presence. I couldn't help but notice the glow in his eye when I caught him looking at me. Though he didn't excite me like Pallu did, I liked to be near him.

We had been walking for half a day when a frantic Merab, holding a squalling Haviva, jogged toward us.

"Is Aliyah with you?" she asked.

"No," Elah answered. "We haven't seen her since we left and she was with you."

"She's missing. I can't find her anywhere!"

Her words set my heart to beating hard. Aliyah lost and alone? Unthinkable. "I'll help you search." I accompanied her as she went from family to family describing her little girl and calling out "Aliyah. Aliyah."

"Let's separate," I said. "We'll cover more territory that way. I'll go back and retrace our steps. Maybe she fell along the way."

I jogged back, past family units, calling Aliyah's name, careful, as well, to scan the boulders and scraggly growth all around for any sign of her

At last I came to where my family travelled. "We've lost Aliyah," I told them breathless.

"I'm here," a little voice announced, and there was our little stray, holding tight to Sebia's hand.

"Oh, thank God!" I dropped to my knees beside her and engulfed her in a big hug.

"She was wandering off by herself," Sebia told me. "We recognized her and convinced her to come with us."

"Thank you!" I felt weak with relief as I grabbed Aliyah's other hand. "Darling you don't know how you scared us."

We walked along slowly while I regained my breath. "I'd better get her back to her mother," I said. "She's frantic."

Merab's reaction at being reunited with her little girl was every bit as ecstatic as I expected. And then something wonderful happened. After smothering little Aliyah in hugs of joy, Merab looked at me with tears in her eyes. "Thank you," she said. "I've been possessive and jealous. Aliyah loves you but I've kept her from you. No more. I'd be very grateful if you could help me with her, especially as we travel."

"I'm only too happy to do that," I assured her. For the first time I'd known her, she reached out and gave me a real hug. Then I took Aliyah by the hand. "Come. Let's get a drink of water and find Uncle Elah and the animals."

Chapter Seventeen

We traveled for days and days. I was tired of being thirsty, hot, dusty, and bone weary. But I tried not to complain, especially when Aliyah was around.

One day what looked like an oasis appeared in the distance. I told myself not to get hopes up as it was probably a mirage. But it wasn't. We camped that night under palms, our thirst quenched with fresh cool water.

Next morning when collecting manna, I saw that the cloud had settled on top of the tabernacle. Maybe this would be more than a one-night stop.

When I returned to camp we hurried with our meal in case the trumpet sounded to signal another day's travel. But it never did. Would we be here for days, a week, weeks? Only the cloud could tell.

Once we had rested from traveling, Naam voiced his impatience. The weeks of travel had stretched the time of his betrothal to over a year. He was eager to bring his bride home and begin married life.

The groom's family had responsibilities for this celebration. I recalled how mother and I had worked to prepare for Bezalel's wedding. That meant Merab and I would need to get busy. Merab's attitude, since I found Aliyah, had softened toward me and I decided to discuss it with her.

"What do we need to do for Naam's special day?"

"I suggest we do the bare minimum," Merab said, folding her arms in front of her, as she did when she had made up her mind about something.

"But Caleb is a leader. We must put on a feast and

celebration that does his position justice."

Merab's forehead furrowed and she chewed on her bottom lip as she thought and then offered reasons why we should make it the simplest day possible. Naam was the youngest and the youngest never got a big party. Desert life made it hard to celebrate even simply, let alone extravagantly. Planning for a celebration was likely to be wasted because we'd probably have to move in the middle of everything. Anyway, she wouldn't have the time or energy to put into a celebration. After a lot of discussion, we came to a compromise, which had me doing most of the work.

I set my attention toward planning manna variations and making extra torches so our campsite would have a festive look. At least we had Sephy's weaving, delivered just before we left on our travels, to decorate the bridal chamber.

* * *

The big event took place a week later. At the wedding celebration, I caught only a glimpse of Cherut, veiled and in her bridal clothes. Only a glimpse, that is, until I happened to look over and caught her momentarily lifting her veil and scanning the crowd that had gathered.

For a second our eyes locked. There was a merry glint in hers. I smiled back—even gave her a wink, after which she quickly dropped the veil in place again.

The next morning I was eager to meet her. It was their wedding week, though, and they wouldn't be joining us for meals. Still, they needed to eat. Midmorning after I heard voices and Cherut's laughter, I assembled food and drink, took it to the entranceway of their huppah, and announced its presence.

"You can come in," Naam said, lifting the curtain. I glanced around their room, beyond the clothes strewn about, to its occupant—a slim girl with wide greenish-hazel eyes set in a delicate face framed by the most luxurious auburn hair I had ever seen.

She smiled and I recognized her face from the day before.

Naam made the formal introduction. "Zamri, meet Cherut. Cherut, this is Zamri."

I smiled back, set my basket and pitcher on the floor and the two of us embraced. Then I held her at arm's length and give her a big smile. "Welcome to the family."

* * *

All week I brought food to the newlyweds at mealtimes. As I did, I grew ever more comfortable with Cherut and the fact that she would soon be joining us in our everyday tasks.

We talked briefly when Naam wasn't around. She asked me about the various family members, whom Naam had obviously told her about, for she knew them by name.

One day I caught sight of a beautiful Egyptian necklace among her things. I recognized it immediately—a menat.

The sight brought back a flood of memories. Even though five years had passed since I had seen them, I vividly recalled the processions that had made their way along the canals of Goshen—the plaintive wail of pipes and flutes, the clacking of menats and sistrums, and the brightly dressed women dancing in a frenzy. I recalled too Grandfather Hur's stern response to my questions of what the celebration was about and could I join in.

"The Egyptians don't worship the one true God Yahweh. We don't carry on like they do, pray to the Pharaoh and idols, or wear amulets and other magic objects. I don't want you lingering on the fringes of their processions to watch."

I wondered what he'd say about Cherut's menat.

* * *

Cherut and Naam's wedding week was at an end. Now we could officially welcome her into the family. I was happy to familiarize her with our household, which Merab seemed content for me to do.

Though Cherut liked to sleep in the morning as much as I did, I got her up to gather manna with me. After our sleepiness was dispelled by the warmth of the sun, we talked.

"Tell me about your family," I said, hoping that just maybe they had had some connection with Pallu's.

"I am the youngest of five," Cherut told me. "Mother was a slave to a high class Egyptian woman. When I turned twelve and for two years until we left Egypt, I worked in her home too. This is from her."

Cherut pulled on the neck of her tunic to show what she wore beneath it — the menat I had caught sight of the other day. "It is very lucky. Mistress gave it to us the night of the Passover when everyone was begging us to leave. Mother told me to keep it and wear it. It has special powers"

"What are they?" I asked.

"It helps to get one with child and preserve the baby till it's born."

My ears perked up but I didn't ask any more questions, remembering Grandfather's warning.

Cherut and I grew to be friends as we worked

together. I told her about my family, my strict Grandfather Hur, my capable mother and steady father, my sister-in-law Sebia, and my gifted brother Bezalel who Moses had put in charge of building tabernacle and supervising all the other craftspeople.

One day after a couple of weeks I gathered up my courage and asked what I had been wondering about since I found out that Cherut came from Reuben. "Did you know Abiram's family? The one that was swallowed by the earthquake?"

"Oh yes, I knew them well," she said. "My older sister was fascinated with their son Pallu. He seemed to like her a lot too. But nothing came of it. Rumour was that he planned to marry someone else.

"Many in Reuben still blame their death on Moses, our father-in-law Caleb, and Joshua and their stubbornness," Cherut went on. "I was surprised when my father consented to Naam's request to marry me."

The time passed quickly as Cherut and I worked and talked. Her coming had given me a woman friend at last and was opening my mind to many things.

* * *

Merab was another story. The way she acted toward Cherut reminded me of how she treated me when I first came. Often, I noticed her in the shadows, watching us work, her arms folded tightly in front of her, her brow furrowed, chewing on her bottom lip. When Cherut's mistakes got too much for her, she interjected. "The baskets don't go there ... can't you stack the kindling evenly... fill the water jugs more, so we don't have to take so many trips. Do it like Zamri does."

I ignored Merab's not-so-subtle attempts to get me on her side. And I couldn't help but laugh when Cherut mimicked Merab behind her back, arms folded tightly, chewing her bottom lip, her face scrunched in the most fearful frown. She had a lot more nerve, as a newcomer, than I'd had.

* * *

Cherut and I spent many hours together. One day I confided to her, "Elah really wants to start a family. But I'm not getting pregnant."

Instead of the sympathy I expected, Cherut gives me a sly smile. "That will never happen to me," she said.

"How do you know?" I asked

"Because I possess magic. Come, I'll show you."

She took me to their huppah and from the tangle of clothes and bed coverings pulled out a linen parcel tied with string. Carefully she untied it and folded back the layers of cloth to reveal two figurines.

"This is Bastet," she said, holding up a cat-like figure suspended on a chain. "She wields powerful magic for women. Mistress also gave her to us on leaving. She told us Bastet has power to cause babies to be born."

The second figurine was made of clay, a small but ugly dwarf statue. "My Bes," Cherut said, holding the figure close. "With him I'll never lose any babies."

Despite myself, I felt a shudder go through me. I could only imagine what Grandfather Hur would say about these things.

"Does anyone else know about these?" I asked. "Has Naam seen them?"

Cherut gave me a conspiratorial grin as she re-wrapped and tied them into their linen covering. "No. And I'm not going to tell him. You won't either, will you? Because if they're taken away, it will be very bad for me — for all of us. These charms have power to hurt as well as help."

I didn't know what to say. I felt uneasy knowing these things were in our camp but I didn't want Cherut to get into trouble.

Noticing my prolonged silence, Cherut looked at me with alarm. "You must not say anything. Please."

"No, I'll keep your secret," I said at last, as she tucked the parcel out of sight.

Chapter Eighteen

The second anniversary of our wedding day, and Elah's twenty-third birthday, began like any other. I got up sometime after he had left to be with his flock, dressed, then went to awaken Cherut.

Lately she had been harder and harder to rouse. She told me one day that I shouldn't waken her suddenly in the morning because of some tale she had heard about sudden waking and how that put one's soul in danger of separating from the body. She sure had a collection of convenient beliefs at her beck and call!

This morning she slept more soundly than ever so I gave up, took all our baskets for gathering manna, and left by myself. As I worked, I thought about the two years since I'd become Elah's wife and come to live at Caleb's encampment. They'd passed quickly, yet I could scarcely remember my life before them.

Merab and I had made peace in that she no longer hovered over everything I did. Cherut was her object now. And she continued to allow me to play with Aliyah and Haviva.

I wasn't sure how Caleb felt about me. I often suspected he disapproved, as he seemed to of Cherut. Sometimes he quizzed her on her home and family. But he stopped short of asking her about specifics and he didn't pry into their quarters. I didn't think anyone else knew the secret of her Egyptian charms. They certainly hadn't heard it from me.

And then there was Elah. Though I felt no passion for him, I knew he was a good man and I should be happy... which I was for the most part, except that I was still childless.

As my mind wandered, my hands were busy, filling our baskets. I was almost finished and beginning to wonder how I would carry all of them home by myself when Cherut arrived. "Sorry," she said breathlessly. "I just couldn't get up this morning. I don't know what's wrong with me but lately I'm so tired."

We sat down to eat our morning meal shortly after we got back but Cherut, instead of partaking with her usual zest, grew pale, excused herself, and a minute later I heard coughing. I found her outside, at the back of our tent, obviously sick. She looked up at me pale-faced and shaken. "I feel awful."

Merab joined us. We helped Cherut to her feet, walked her to her room, and helped her lie down. "Hopefully it's not the plague to sicken us all," I said to Merab.

She grinned. "I don't think we'll catch this," she said. "I suspect Cherut is with child."

Of course! How could I not have realized this?

If Cherut was indeed with child, I was happy for Naam and her. It was wonderful for them to have a little one on the way and so soon after their wedding day. It was the news every bride wanted. But it didn't seem fair for them have a baby before Elah and I, who had been wed for two years. For the remainder of the day I wrestled with my confused feelings.

Dwelling on these things wearied me. I was tired of desiring what I couldn't have, of straining after something that was beyond my grasp. At times like this I wished I were back in my home with father, mother, and Grandpa Hur, not burdened any more with being a good wife and wanting a child—this thing that was out of my power to make happen.

It didn't help when, that evening after he loved me tenderly, Elah unwittingly rubbed salt on my already raw spirit by whispering his dreams of the sons and daughters we would have someday.

* * *

Now that Cherut was with child, Merab took her under her wing. Together they established an approximate date when the little one would arrive. Merab, having gone through two confinements, was full of sympathy and advice while I could only look on in silence.

When they talked about Cherut's coming motherhood, I left to spend time with Aliyah and Haviva. We collected dried grasses, I tied off sections to form heads and hands, then wrapped the straw figures in scraps of fabric—little dolls for them to play with. I remembered the doll Bezalel made me when I was a just a little older than Aliyah. I thought of asking him to make them such toys the next time I went home.

Playing with the girls like this, it was easy to imagine they were my daughters. If only they were!

* * *

As Cherut's belly grew, her slim frame thickened— all proofs that she was indeed with child. Her extreme sickness soon passed, though she tired easily and I was again left alone to gather manna in the mornings. Thankfully, someone always came to help me carry the baskets home.

Today it was Cherut herself. She was talkative and in good spirits. "Isn't it a beautiful morning? I'm so glad

I feel well again and can enjoy these things. Don't you just love the way the light reflects on the hills?"

For the first time since meeting her, I felt irritated by her perkiness and preoccupation with herself. When I didn't reply, she looked at me sharply. "Are you angry?" she asked. "Upset that I don't help you like I did before?"

"No. You couldn't help feeling sick."

"Then what is it?

I felt emotion rise inside me. If I confided to Cherut what was really bothering me, I feared I would cry, and I didn't want to do that in front of her.

Meanwhile, we arrived at the tent, and together began preparing the meal. But Cherut didn't let the matter rest. "You haven't answered me. Tell me, why are you upset? Is it because you're not yet with child yourself?"

My eyes, brimming with tears, I nodded dumbly.

She grabbed my hand. "I thought so," she said. "Maybe you need some help." Her voice fell to a whisper, "the help of the gods. I could lend you my amulets and charms, my Bastet and my Bes."

* * *

Cherut's offer haunted me. It seemed like an easy solution. At the same time, I feared to take her charms and amulets into my possession.

"What other things did Egyptian women do to get with child?" I asked her when we were alone.

"My mistress had a lot of wisdom about this. She did rituals with dates and garlic. Sometimes she smeared blood on her legs and belly. And she ate great amounts of lettuce. Of course, she had her charms too. With all these, she birthed many sons."

The things that Cherut had mentioned — the garlic,

dates, and lettuce—were not available to us here in the desert. Smearing blood on myself didn't appeal to me in the least. The very thought brought back scenes from the night we left Egypt with its bloody door frames, as well as the bloody tabernacle rituals. Hanging onto a few amulets was a lot simpler. Still I put off accepting them from her, hoping that one of these days I would find I was with child without having had to resort to these measures.

Chapter Nineteen

"Tell us about your time of spying Canaan," Naam urged his father one evening as we sat gathered around the fire. "Cherut hasn't heard the stories."

Father Caleb didn't need a second invitation.

"We left Kadesh Barnea and trekked through desert till we came to the land of the Amalekites. Remember them? They were the people that came out against us shortly after we left Egypt. The people who Joshua and our army defeated while Moses prayed to Yahweh with his arms raised. [25]

"From there we came to the hill country. The Anak live there, huge men as tall as this." Father Caleb stood and reached his arm above his head. He was not short and I couldn't imagine people the height he indicated. Beside me Cherut shuddered then put her head in her hands as if not wishing to see even Father Caleb's demonstration.

Father went on. "Following a river, we passed through fields of wonderful crops and large tracts of grazing land. In that area, we passed through a valley, called Eshcol, which was lush with vineyards. The grapes were still not ripe but we could see there would soon be a mighty crop.

"We also passed by many towns—Arad, Hebron, Bethel, Shechem, and Beth-Shan. Finally, we came to a beautiful large lake where we bathed ourselves and enjoyed fish. Then we went on to find the cities of Hazor and Rehod. All these cities were large with thick walls and lookout towers, very well fortified."

"How did the people of the land treat you?" Iru asked.

"We avoided them as much as possible—traveled by night and stayed discreet by day. Even so we had many close calls, where people noticed us and pointed us out. We did look different from them with our faded, dusty clothes. Somehow, we always managed to elude them and stay away from interactions."

"Tell what happened after Rehod," Naam said.

"From Rehod we retraced our steps, past the towns we had seen before. One, named Hebron, captured my imagination." Caleb's face lit up. "In my heart, I laid claim that day to that city or as some call it, Kirjath Arba. Kirjath Arba is the name of the mightiest Anakim of them all, the giant Arba himself. Someday it will be mine!"

Father Caleb paused. The fire sputtered gently into the silence. The dying flames licked the charred branches that glowed pink into the dark, faintly illuminating our circle of faces. From somewhere nearby I heard the spooky call of a desert owl.

Beside me Cherut stiffened. Her eyes grew large. She looked terrified. [26]

* * *

Cherut grew larger with child every day, while nothing changed for me. My way of women was as regular as the coming and going of the moon. More and more I thought of accepting Cherut's offer. Would there be any harm in me having just one of her charms in my possession? I wouldn't pray to it, of course, just have it close—a harmless object with immense benefits should it work.

One day, while I was preparing food and again preoccupied with this, Cherut joined me. With her sharp intuition, she picked up on the source of my mood. "Are you still fretting about not getting pregnant?" she asked.

I nodded

Her voice fell to a whisper. "Take one of my charms. It *will* help you."

"Don't you need them for yourself?"

"Oh, I have more. Come. I'll show you. I have just the one for you.

We went to Naam and Cherut's room and from under a pile of covers Cherut drew the tied and wrapped cloth she had showed me before and spilled out her trinkets—Bastet, Bes, and a lovely turquoise stone, oval with soft rounded edges, which I hadn't seen. She picked it up and proffered it to me. "This represents the most powerful Egyptian goddess for women, Hathor herself. With her help, you'll surely be with child soon."

I examined it. It glowed in the dim light of the tent. Surely there could be no harm in such a lovely thing. And because it wasn't carved into any likeness, its presence among my belongings would probably not even raise any questions or bring any trouble. I took a deep breath, reached my hand toward Cherut's and she dropped the stone into it.

* * *

Over the next weeks, I quelled any concerns that I felt over the Egyptian charm that was now hidden amongst my things. I was sure I'd soon be with child and as soon as I was, I promised myself, I would return the stone to Cherut.

The cloud hadn't moved us for many days and our lives fell into an easy, relaxed rhythm. When the day's work was done, we had time and energy for leisure. One evening, Elah and I visited my old encampment.

We arrived to find the whole family together, about to sit down for the evening meal. Though we had eaten before we left, we joined the family in partaking of Mother's manna cakes. I had forgotten what a good cook she was. Hopefully Elah wouldn't get the idea that I should be able to duplicate these.

After the meal, mother and I served tea. I watched how my family took to Elah. I liked how Grandfather Hur leaned toward him and included him in conversation. Elah, as usual on such visits, was mostly quiet but I could tell Grandfather thought a great deal of him.

Mother, Sebia, and I visited in the inner room. Mother filled me in on the news of the relatives—who was in poor health, who was soon to be wed and, of course, news of babies on the way or newly born.

Sebia was quiet—unusually so. When Mother went to replenish the tea, I asked her about herself.

"Nothing's changed," she said with a small resigned smile. "No babies on the way here."

"Neither with me," I said, and then spilled what was on my mind. "But that may change soon. Cherut has given me a remedy."

"What?" Sebia was all attention.

"A stone. She says it represents the most powerful Egyptian goddess for women—Hathor."

I saw puzzlement in Sebia's eyes.

"I don't worship or pray or sacrifice to the stone," I reassured her. "I just have it nearby in case it will help me. Cherut has more of these and she became pregnant mere months after their wedding day."

I realized, then, with a pang, that I had said too much. I had broken my promise of secrecy to Cherut. If only I could stuff the words back into my mouth.

Meanwhile, Sebia, looking surprised even disapproving, said nothing but shook her head.

"Well, I had to do something," I defended myself. "Elah speaks so often of wanting sons and daughters..."

Just then Mother reentered the room.

It was not till Elah and I were walking home later that I realized I had forgotten to pledge Sebia to silence over Cherut's secret — which was mine too.

* * *

"Father Caleb wants to see you," Merab announced to me one morning when I returned from a walk with Aliyah and Haviva.

He had never requested to see just me before. What could it be? Had I done something wrong?

I joined him in our tent's main room where he motioned me to sit across from him. I sneaked a look at his face. His expression was serious but not angry.

"Zamri, you've lived with us for over two years now. How are things with you?"

His voice was gentle and reassuring, and I relaxed somewhat.

"Pretty good."

"How are the three of you, Merab, Cherut, and you, getting along?"

"Fine," I said, wondering where this was going.

"I have heard rumours about Cherut," he said. I felt shivers all over my body. "I heard that she has in her possession some trinkets and charms from Egypt. Is this so?"

Caleb knew! How did he find out? I didn't know

what to say. Caleb, with his piercing eyes that seemed to see into my very being, scared me. I dared not lie to him. I cast about for what to say.

"Doesn't everyone?" I answered. "Didn't the Egyptians press us to take all kinds of trinkets, jewelry, and ornaments?"

"Yes, they did," Caleb replied. "But there is a difference between having them with us for the purpose of putting them to use in a constructive way and trusting in their power.

"You spend a lot of time with Cherut," he went on. "If she is trusting too much in the things of Egypt, I would like you to help her see the danger of her ways. You come from a good family. Your grandfather is one of the elders in Judah and your brother the tabernacle's chief craftsman. You have a good foundation in the things of Yahweh and I see in you qualities of a strong, wise woman. What about it?"

What he said surprised me. I met his gaze, then quickly looked down for fear something in my eyes or my face would give me away. "I'll see what I can do."

* * *

For the next days, Cherut's stone together with Caleb's request consumed my thoughts. Who was I to question Cherut about putting confidence in her Egyptian charms when I was trusting in one myself? I often considered returning it. But then the thought of how it could help me argued back. As soon as I was with child, I promised myself, I would return the Hathor stone and never again touch another one of Cherut's Egyptian trinkets.

Neither did I know how to bring up the subject with Cherut. And then one morning when we were collecting manna and out of earshot from other members of the family she asked, "Why does Naam's father dislike me?"

"What makes you think that?"

"The way he looks at me when he watches me. He looks disapproving, and he never smiles when he addresses me, like he smiles at you and Merab."

"I hadn't noticed," I said to her and realized this was the opening I'd been waiting for. "He did ask me about you once though—about your Egyptian charms."

Fear leapt into Cherut's eyes. "Did you tell him?"

"No. I said we'd all been offered such things when we left Egypt. He didn't press me further about what you had."

"I wonder how he found out."

"I don't know. Maybe Merab overheard us talking? Or someone found them with your things? He did ask me to talk to you about not trusting in them." I gave her a rueful smile. "I guess his advice applies to both of us."

"That explains it," Cherut said, her face full of apprehension. Her hand went, as it often did lately, to her pregnant belly and she stroked it tenderly. "I won't let him take them away from me. I can only imagine what would happen to me or my baby should I be forced to give them up."

Chapter Twenty

Cherut made light of her clumsiness now and pointed out how her pregnant belly filled out even her most generous clothes. But her carefree attitude was only an act. Privately she told me she was terrified to birth a child. Her hand strayed to the neck of her tunic to touch the menat hidden under her clothes. One day when we were by ourselves gathering manna and she was unusually quiet, I asked, "Is something wrong?"

"I've been thinking about making a request of you, but I don't know how to do it."

"What? Ask."

"You won't be angry?"

"Of course not."

Cherut looked at me searchingly. "Can I have my Hathor stone back? I know it hasn't worked for you yet and I'll give it back to you as soon as my baby is born. I just feel I need it with me now."

"Of course, you can have it back," I said. I was almost relieved to get rid of it. Yet I also felt a tinge of disappointment. I had had such high hopes this charm would help me bear a child.

* * *

Cherut's time grew near. She sent Naam to the tents of Reuben to fetch her mother. They returned and with them brought bundles of supplies. I remembered Cherut's mother from the wedding — a tiny, wiry bird of a woman with Cherut's red hair, only on her it was fading.

I took her to Cherut and Naam's room where for the

last few hours Merab and I had taken turns trying to ease Cherut's fears. Merab, with her experience, had helped her get more comfortable. Cherut had gone from reclining on her mat to sitting on cushions with her back against the tent wall, to pacing the small space.

She was up and pacing when her mother came in. She stopped long enough to greet her, then with a groan resumed her walk.

"Where do you plan to birth this child?" her mother asked.

Cherut gave a small cry as a cramp overcame her. "In here," she said when the pain eased.

"You can't have the baby in here," her mother said. "We need a special arbor, like we had in Egypt." Turning to Naam she gave orders to erect a tent enclosure a short distance from the tent. "And hurry!" she said. "I think her time is near."

I asked Cherut's mother if there was anything I could do. She told me to unpack massage oil from her things, warm some water, and collect swaddling bands for the newborn, which Cherut dumbly pointed out to me among her things. I collected the cloths, found the oil, and went to heat the water.

* * *

Cherut labored in the hastily constructed birth arbor for hours. I brought the things I had gathered when her mother moved her there and after the evening meal carried over food and drink for them.

When I entered, I found Cherut sitting on bricks similar to what the Egyptians used. Her mother must have brought them, as we certainly didn't have any. She sat behind Cherut supporting her back.

"Can you take my place?" she asked when I entered.

"I need to see what's happening below."

I put down the basket of food and took her mother's place, my feet spread on either side of Cherut. Her back against my stomach radiated warmth, her shoulders glistened with sweat, and her hair curled in damp tendrils around her face.

Meanwhile Merab joined us.

"The baby's head is showing," Cherit's mother said excitedly. To Cherut, "Next time you feel the urge, give a big push."

Cherut relaxed with a whimper only to tense up again a few seconds later. Her body grew rigid with effort and a loud groan came from deep inside her. Below, at her legs I saw a motion as a slippery pink being slid out, onto the bricks.

Merab picked up the baby. "It's a boy!" she announced.

"A boy?" Cherut asked, looking up into my eyes. Her face that had just been furrowed in anguish softened into a smile.

Cherut's mother handed me a damp cloth and with it I cooled her sweaty face and shoulders. When all had been delivered, we settled her on a mat with cushions to support her.

Merab, who had been tending the infant, now handed him to Cherut. She dropped what she had been clutching—the tiny grotesque figure of Bes—to receive and cuddle her son.

Later I helped her mother and Merab tidy the arbour. In the process I saw, at close range, the bricks on which Cherut had birthed her baby. Painted on them was an Egyptian queen-like figure with blue hair that I recognized as the goddess Hathor.

* * *

When Cherut's mother returned home, life in our encampment got back to normal—a new normal to be sure with another baby in the family. Cherut and Naam named him Raanan: "green and flourishing." And flourish is what he did.

This new little life meant one less set of hands to share the workload, as Cherut was now often busy with her baby. Sometimes, though, she swaddled him close to her and carried him with her as she resumed some tasks.

She was not as possessive of him as Merab was with her girls. "Can you hold him for me?" she asked often throughout the day, handing him to me after he had been fed.

I loved cradling him, singing to him till he fell asleep, feeling his soft warm weight in my arms, content and completely trusting. But spending time with him was a mixed blessing. This bundle of new life—sometimes cooing, sometimes squalling—reminded me over and over of my own lack.

I sensed that Elah felt it too. I saw the look in his eyes when he held little Raanan. His eyes met mine and I recognized longing, though he no longer made comments about us having a family after I broke down in tears one day over another reference he made about us having children.

Cherut picked up on my feelings. One day after I'd spent some time with Raanan she whispered, "I don't need my charms now. You can have my Hathor stone back and borrow any others that you'd like."

Her unexpected offer made me hot all over. I had been considering this possibility, half hoping Cherut would remember her promise, half wishing she'd forget it so that I wouldn't be faced with this decision. "Thank you," I said finally. "Let me think about it."

"What is there to think about?" she asked, looking a little peeved. "You want a child. My charms will help you get one."

Her words were tempting; I did so want a child. But the Hathor stone hadn't worked last time and the thought of hiding this secret from everyone again didn't appeal to me either. I shook my head. Cherut gave a little snort, as if to say, "have it your way."

Chapter Twenty-one

"I request that everyone be present at our evening meal tonight," Father Caleb said one morning as we were finishing breakfast. Puzzlement and anticipation grew throughout the day as we pondered and discussed what his request could mean.

"Perhaps Moses has given him a special job," Merab suggested.

"Or he wants to change who does what around here," I said.

Cherut didn't say anything, but I saw apprehension in her eyes.

That afternoon Merab, Cherut, and I put extra effort into the meal. In the cool of early evening we gathered in the big room of the tent to share it. All, that is, except for Caleb. He had asked us to assemble, but where was he?

Aliyah and Haviva grew restless so Merab began to feed them while the rest of us continued to wait.

Then suddenly the tent opening lifted and Father entered. But he was not alone. He had someone with him—a woman. All eyes went to them and conversation stopped.

Father Caleb smiled big and happy into our questioning faces. He drew his companion gently forward, looked at her reassuringly, and then at us. "Thank you for coming together like this," he said. "I have something to tell you. Today I announce to you our intention to marry. This is Devora who will soon be my wife. She is the widow of my friend Sethur from the tribe of Asher, a fellow spy to the land of Canaan. [27] We'll be wed after the required 30 days of betrothal." [28]

Our stunned silence was broken by Iru, who jumped up. "Congratulations Father!" he said, going over to Caleb and thumping him on the back. Elah and Naam followed him as the room erupted into exclamations and questions.

"What did Grandfather say?" Aliyah asked Merab.

"Did you know this was in the works?" Cherut asked me.

I shook my head, my attention on Devora. Another woman in our household. What would that be like? Would we get along?

I studied her. She looked a few years older than Merab with dark hair tucked beneath a beautifully embroidered head covering. Her face, with its slightly prominent nose, was tanned, smooth, and unlined. She was not beautiful but looked pleasant enough.

She and Father Caleb took seats in Father's customary spot and we all grew quiet. After he pronounced a blessing on the food we passed around the manna loaf and cakes we had prepared.

Caleb was soon in conversation with his sons while Devora ate in silence. Her gaze lifted, her eyes met mine, and her face relaxed in a tentative smile.

Meanwhile Haviva wandered over to her, lifted her arms and begged, in her two-year-old way, "Up? Up?" Devora looked at her and then at us as if to inquire who her mother was and would it be okay to hold her.

Merab jumped up, took the few steps to Devora, swooped Haviva into her arms and carried her off muttering "Don't bother the lady."

"She was not a bother," Devora said, her voice low and calm. But her face had flushed crimson.

"Did you know your father was planning this?" I asked Elah that night as we prepared for bed.

"No. But I'm not surprised. He has had many sad, lonely moments since mother died. Then I noticed his mood pick up a few weeks ago."

"What do you make of Devora?" I asked.

"She's fine," Elah answered, then drew me close. "But she's not as beautiful as you, my little wife, mother-to-be of our children."

I stiffened and pulled away.

"Sorry," he whispered, and drew me gently to him again. "I'm sorry. I forgot. And I want you to know, you please me, children or not."

I stared into the dark long after I heard Elah's steady slow breath of sleep, my thoughts going around and around. I must find a way to bear this man a child.

* * *

"How will we prepare for Father Caleb's wedding?" I introduced the subject with Merab and Cherut the next morning. "We don't have much time. It's just weeks away."

"Thankfully the tent doesn't need to be enlarged," Merab said. "Father already has his own room."

"But we do need to contact musicians, prepare food and extra torches for the celebration," I said.

"I will do all I can when this little one lets me," Cherut said. At that moment, little Raanan awoke and let out a hearty squall.

"Let's keep this as simple as possible." Merab's response was what I expected. "This is, after all, a second wedding for both of them."

"But he's a leader in our tribe and it's an important day for him," I countered. "Let's make it as special as we can. As well, Devora will be joining us in managing our encampment. It would be good thing to gain her favour from the start."

Merab shrugged. "The way I see it, Devora will need to adjust to us, not us to her. But do what you like. I'll help where I can but I have little ones too."

I mulled over what Merab had said. Time would tell how another woman would fit into our household. Meanwhile, Merab's reminder of the fact that I was the only one with no child broke down my resolve to refuse Cherut's charms.

When Merab left shortly to tend Haviva I sidled up to Cherut and whispered, "I've thought a lot about the charms. I'll take whichever of them you can give me."

"I knew you would change your mind," she said with a grin.

She led me to her room and I left with the Bastet image on its fine gold chain. I would never wear it, I promised myself, but would keep it near me, hidden with my things until I got pregnant. Surely no one would blame me for doing all I could. And I would make sure that no one but Cherut would ever know.

* * *

I was eager to share the news of Caleb's betrothal with my clan. Elah and I made the trek to their encampment a few days later. Sebia's face lit up when I told of the arrival of Raanan. And the news of Caleb's upcoming marriage interested everyone—everyone that is, except Bezalel. He seemed preoccupied and looked at me strangely.

After we had eaten, he motioned for me to join him

and we went outside. Darkness had fallen and the air was chilly. The moon hung orange and beautiful just above the rocky outcrops that boke the horizon, illuminating our surroundings.

As Bezalel took my arm I looked up at him questioningly. We walked some distance from the tent where he stopped and turned to me. "I need to talk to you about what you said to Sebia on your last visit."

Mentally I went back over that visit. Oh no!

"You told her that Cherut had offered you Egyptian magic to help you bear a child, and that you accepted."

"It was just a stone," I said defensively, "which I returned to her soon after." I didn't mention that it was she who asked for the trinket back and, since then, I had another in my possession.

Bezalel gently turned me. He placed a hand on each shoulder and peered into my face. "Little sister, don't have anything to do with those things," he said earnestly. "Remember the commands Moses brought down from Sinai, especially the one: 'You shall have no other gods before Me'?"

"I was never worshiping the stone Cherut gave me. I just kept it with my things."

"I don't know if you remember, but I once wore an amulet," Bezalel said, "a gold pendant with the image of Ptah. Its power was to make me a skillful artisan in Khafra's shop. Grandfather objected to it and we argued about it when I came home. Remember that?"

I did remember. I nodded.

"Then came the night of blackness" Bezalel continued, "the night of plague when Shoshan and I were trapped by the dark in our craftsman's encampment. I sensed, at that time, that the dark was not only physical but a blackness of the spirit and that I would never escape it as long as I held onto anything that belonged to it. [29]

"I remembered Grandfather's words that Yahweh was the only one to serve. It was a battle. Finally, though, the darkness frightened me so deeply that I tore the amulet from my neck. That was the moment I felt really free.

"So, I beg you, don't have anything to do with Cherut's amulets or any of her Egyptian things. They will bring only darkness and fear. And whatever you do, don't ever bring one of them here."

Bezalel's story frightened me. It brought back the discussions we used to have in our home about Egyptian magic. I realized they were the source of the mixed feelings I had been struggling with.

"Promise me you won't have anything to do with those things?" Bezalel asked, looking at me searchingly.

I couldn't tell him the truth. Still, I wanted him to think well of me. Looking down from his penetrating gaze I gave the slightest nod of my head.

* * *

It was less than a week before we had planned to celebrate Father Caleb's wedding when the cloud lifted from the tabernacle. Shortly after, the trumpet blasted, signaling it was time to move on.

"As soon as we're settled again we'll have the wedding celebration," Caleb told us as we began packing.

Travel days were the familiar blur of walking, with accompanying dust, thirst, tired feet, and crying children. When conversation lagged, my mind went to Bezalel's warning. I felt torn. On the one hand, I would

170

love to be free of Cherut's charm. My possession of it weighed on my conscience and I was constantly worried that someone would find it. On the other, it was my only hope for bearing Elah the child he so badly wanted.

To distract me from these restless thoughts, I helped Merab and Cherut with their little ones whenever possible. Often Aliyah joined Elah, me, and our flock.

Being with Elah calmed me. I loved to watch him with his ewes and lambs. He talked to them gently and lovingly, and they responded, gathering around him, butting each other out of the way to get as close as they could.

On travel days, I gathered manna alone again—a big job. One morning Aliyah awakened early and asked to join me. Though she was only five, she turned out to be a bigger help than I expected. She even carried the small basket back to the encampment by herself.

A week of plodding on over rocks and sand through heat and cold brought us to another oasis. As we set up our camp, I saw that the cloud had settled on the top of the tabernacle, giving me hope that we might stay here longer than overnight.

"Make sure the walls are taut and tight—no slack places." This day Father Caleb was more interested in the tent setup than ever before.

"If the cloud stays in place, tomorrow will be the big day," he informed us at the evening meal.

Merab, Cherut, and I exchanged worried glances. There was much to do and we were weary from traveling. But Father Caleb was determined.

* * *

Father Caleb's wedding day dawned clear and cold, like all the others. Collecting extra manna to make food

171

for our guests was the first task on my list. I forced myself out of the warmth of our bed, collected all our household's baskets, and left on this chore, only to be joined a few minutes later by Elah.

"The sheep and goats can wait for me this morning," he said. "I know it's a busy day for you and you need help."

When we arrived back at the encampment with our loads of food, the rest of the family was up. With so much to do, Elah fetched the water for me. After breakfast, when both Merab and Cherut were occupied with their little ones, I worked alone on the cakes for our guests. I was beginning to wonder how I would get everything done when I realized that Aliyah was shadowing me.

"Can I help?"

"Sure." I showed her how to form the manna softened by goat milk into cakes so I could begin browning them slowly over the fire. We worked together on the food for hours then tidied our encampment and prepared extra torches. When Cherut and Merab were finally free to help, there was little left to do.

Excitement mounted as evening approached. "Let's go!" Caleb called to his sons as the sun dipped below the horizon. Family members from nearby encampments playing pipes, lyres, and timbrels joined the men as the wedding procession moved through Judah to Asher to fetch Devora.

In the lull that followed, I changed into fresh clothes, fixed my hair, then dug out my timbrel. This was a celebration I had earned!

* * *

I emerged from our room onto the courtyard of our encampment and viewed it with satisfaction. It was neat and tidy, the torches for extra light lay in a pile nearby, ready to be lit. I listened for the sound of the wedding party returning, but still heard only silence.

In the big room of our tent I checked the baskets of food for our guests and viewed the stacks of cushions and mats (many borrowed) that would make our tent comfortable for soon-to-be-arriving guests.

I was about to go outside again when Merab entered. She didn't look happy.

"I think everything is ready," I said to her, hoping she would be reassured.

"Well, you spent enough time on this." Her voice was heavy with sarcasm.

"What do you mean? I just did what needed to be done."

"I could have done it in a fraction of the time. You've prepared too much food. Remember, whatever isn't eaten will only have to be thrown out. And I hope you're not thinking since I let you take charge of this, that now you're the boss around here."

"What are you talking about?" I asked, honestly puzzled. "I just wanted to make sure Father Caleb's wedding celebration was worthy of his position. You yourself said you were too busy to do it."

"Just so you know, nothing's going to change around here," Merab said.

"But it will," I reminded her. "As wife of Father Caleb, the head of our clan, Devora will be taking charge."

"How can she? She doesn't know anything about us or our household."

I heard the faint sound of instruments and singers. The wedding party was coming and I wanted to join them. "I'm sure it will work out somehow," I said. "I hear the wedding party. I'm going to join them. You coming?"

"No. I'll stay here with my sleeping girls."

"Bring them too."

Merab shook her head, her furrowed brow testimony to her persistent worries.

Timbrel in hand I ran down the pathways of Judah, following the sound of music to where the procession was making its way to our tent. When I reached it, I, with my timbrel, walked along with the musicians. Then Elah was beside me, looking happy and excited. He took my free hand and we led the party to our encampment.

The children, wakened by the noise, came out and joined us in the celebration. I handed my timbrel by turns to each of them, and they took part in the music-making.

I stole a glance at Father Caleb. He looked light-hearted and happier than I'd ever seen him as he walked arm-in-arm with his veiled bride, leading her to his room, their huppah. It was time for me to get to work again.

"Where are you going?" Elah asked, as I slipped away.

"To serve our guests," I said, and headed toward the tent, tied back its opening and fetched baskets of food to pass around.

Much later, when the party was well underway, I realized I hadn't seen Cherut all evening. I found her in her and Naam's room. Baby Raanan was contentedly asleep in her arms but she looked sad.

"Why aren't you at the party?" I asked. "You're

missing all the fun. Here, let me hold Raanan and you go."

Cherut shook her head.

"Why not?"

"They don't like me."

"What? Why do you say that?"

"Father Caleb has always been cool toward me. And the day he introduced Devora, the way she looked at me told me she felt the same way." There were tears in Cherut's eyes.

"Oh Cherut, I think you're reading far too much into this. I'm sure they don't dislike you. You'll see."

"You go back to the guests," Cherut said. "I'm too tired to be any fun anyway. I'll just go to bed myself."

"No. Please come."

But Cherut shook her head and I saw she was determined. I left, realizing, perhaps the misgivings I'd had about Devora's coming weren't only mine and would inevitably have to be faced, rooted, as they were, in who we were, not who she was.

Chapter Twenty-two

I anticipated and dreaded the time Devora would join us for everyday activities in the kitchen. I went out to gather manna by myself the day after their wedding week was done, wondering what I would find when I got back. What actually confronted me was a total surprise.

Nothing!

No fire had been lit. The water that was left from yesterday was not warming. Aliyah and Haviva were up and chasing each other around the campsite in a childish game, but there was no sign of an adult anywhere.

I placed my baskets of food where we made meal preparations and was about to return to the manna field to fetch our third basket, when Merab emerged from their room. She looked sullen.

"Where's everyone?" I asked. "Why is there no fire?"

"I don't know. I'm not in charge. Iru told me to let Devora take her place as mistress. I'm just following orders."

Just then Devora entered. The look on her face told me she had heard what Merab has just said.

"I'm sorry," she said with quiet dignity. "We should have discussed this earlier. But now we must get to work. Zamri, could you start the fire? Merab, you know where to go to fetch water, could you do that please? When Cherut is up, she can help me to prepare the manna."

Merab, looking disgusted, shook her head as she gathered the jugs. She had not done this job for a very long time.

I went out to start the fire only to be interrupted by Devora asking where we kept our cooking pans. Once the fire was going, I went back to retrieve our third basket of manna. On my return, I saw that Cherut had not yet appeared so I joined Devora in making the meal. She was preparing the manna in a way we'd never done it.

"So, how are you this morning, Zamri?" she asked.

"Fine," I replied. "Tired."

"Are you the one who gets up early to collect the manna?"

"Yes."

"Is that always your job?"

"Pretty much."

Merab arrived with the water and Devora asked her to fill the large pot and heat it. I heard a big sigh from her as she followed Devora's instructions.

Somehow, despite the late start, we managed to get the food prepared so that when the men come from tending their flocks, they had only a short wait. And the new manna dish, which was really tasty, earned Father Caleb's compliments, so no one would dare offer any criticism, even if they had it.

As we served the food in the tent's big room, I heard Merab mutter from inside, "What a mess!"

She had a point. Devora was definitely not as organized or tidy as Merab was. But even the chaos in our work area couldn't destroy a certain atmosphere of calm Devora's presence had already brought to our home.

* * *

"After we've eaten and the chores are done, we need to have a talk," Devora said, looking at Merab, Cherut, and me in turn. And so, after the food and utensils had been tidied away, the courtyard swept, and the nighttime cushions and blankets folded and stored, the four of us gathered in the tent's main room, three of us apprehensive about what Devora had planned for us.

"I'd like to start off in the right way," Devora said. "I know you've run this home very well up till now and I don't want to change what's working. So, who does what?

After a moment of uncomfortable silence, Merab volunteered, "We all help with everything."

I exchanged glances with Cherut. That was not the way it seemed to us. Devora noticed.

"You don't agree?" she asked, looking at me.

"Well, we do help each other. But in the years that I've lived here, I can't remember Merab ever once going to collect manna or fetch water — until this morning that is."

"Well I have little ones to look after, "Merab said. "It's pretty hard to do those things and tend to the girls as well. I've been busy keeping things organized in the tent."

"It looks like you're doing that very well," Devora said. "On top of that you did a wonderful job of hosting our wedding. Thank you!"

"Oh," Cherut said, "Merab didn't work on that. Zamri did."

"Really?" Devora looked at me with new respect. "You've been a busy lady."

"But she has no little ones," Merab interjected. "And we all helped with it."

I grinned and shook my head. "Little Aliyah helped me more than you did," I reminded her.

Devora looked thoughtfully from me, to Merab and back to me. "I said I didn't want to change what was working," she said. "But I sense that the way things have been has not been working all that well. I'd like us to try something different.

"You'll all take your turn at doing every job. When you're out, we'll make sure your little ones are cared for. I will join you wherever I can. I'd like to make sure things are fair.

"We'll start with the evening meal. Merab, I'll work with you on that."

Merab scowled her answer.

* * *

True to her word, Devora divided our tasks and, in turn, spent time with each of us. One morning she went with me outside the camp to gather our food for the day. She soon got past small talk. "Do you like this job?" she asked.

I hadn't thought for a long time about how I felt. "I suppose," I said. "I used to hate it when we first had to do it after leaving Egypt. Not so much anymore."

"What do you like about it?"

"It's quiet and peaceful out here. I can do it without paying much attention so it's a good time to think."

"You've been part of Caleb's family for how long?"

"Almost three years."

"How has that been for you?" Somehow Devora's questions, though personal, didn't offend me. I got the sense that she really did want to get to know me. In short order, I was spilling to her my difficulties with Merab when I first arrived, how Merab kept Aliyah from me, how that was solved, and how Cherut's coming had given me a friend.

"I see you and Elah have no children. Is that on purpose?"

This question caught me off-guard and I felt my throat thicken as my emotion rose. The silence lengthened and Devora looked at me pointedly. 'I'm sorry," she said. "I've always been curious—and outspoken. It's just that watching you with Aliyah, Haviva, and Raanan makes me see what a marvelous mother you'd make. I loved it when you took out your timbrel on our wedding night and shared it with the children."

"Thank you. My timbrel is special to me. My brother Bezalel made it and gave it to me just before his wedding. It's a reminder of our special brother-sister bond."

"When you play it, I'm taken back to Miriam and how she led us women in that victory dance."

A shiver went through me at the mention of Miriam and I was soon confiding to Devora what I hadn't ever told anyone else. "She was my hero before I married Elah. I wanted to be just like her and someday lead in worship and dance like she did. That was before I came here and found I was no leader at all."

Devora looked at me, surprise on her face. "I wouldn't say that," she said. "I see you leading all the time. You were the one who led the preparation for our wedding. You're the one who leads the children in discovery and play. And you have a lot of influence over Merab and Cherut."

I thought, in that instant, of Cherut's amulet hidden with my things. Some leader! I would need to keep that little tidbit quiet to preserve Devora's good opinion of me.

Our baskets were full.

"You understand, I'm sure," Devora said, as we headed for home, "that leadership comes out in many ways. Women lead in a way that suits the moment and the situation. Think of Moses' mother Jochebed. She is famous to us now but was unknown when she was training little Moses in the ways of Yahweh, planting within him the fear of God even before he was weaned. It was her leadership that set him on the path to become our great leader." [30]

As we entered the tent and handed our baskets to Merab and Cherut, I realized Devora had found out a great deal more about me than I had about her.

* * *

A few days later Devora asked Merab and me to be responsible for the morning chores while she and Cherut gathered manna. I entered the inner room of our tent to find Merab already in a flurry of tidying.

"She always leaves a mess," she muttered. "It's impossible to find anything in this clutter."

Devora was untidy to be sure, but I wanted to defend her. "She's a good cook though."

"When she finally gets around to serving the food. I've never met anyone so distractible. She stops and talks to everyone."

"She likes people," I said. "She listens to them, to us, even the little ones like Aliyah and Haviva. People want to be with her and talk to her."

A squall from Raanan, who had been asleep when Cherut left, cut into our conversation. I picked up the infant, cuddled, soothed, and freshened him, then bound him to me and went to fetch the kindling and water.

In these moments, I pretended that I was his mother and thought how life was almost perfect with our tasks now distributed more fairly in the kinder gentler atmosphere Devora had brought to our encampment.

I was starting the fire when Devora and Cherut returned with the manna. They were in mid-conversation. I caught Cherut's words as they approached.

"The Egyptian gods helped me like they helped my mistress in Egypt."

"But Yahweh has forbidden us to worship the Egyptian deities," Devora answered.

As they passed me, their pace slowed and then they stopped as Devora spoke intently to Cherut. "Remember the tablets that Moses read to us. 'You shall have no other gods besides Me.' We are not to go after these gods of the Egyptians. Don't you recall what happened to the people who worshipped the golden calf?" [31]

I lowered my gaze and busied myself with tending the fire and shielding little Raanan's face from the smoke. But my mind was on what I'd just overheard. Had Cherut told Devora about her charms? Did Devora know that I was hiding one with my things?

I took the baskets of manna from Cherut and Devora, but didn't let my eyes meet Devora's for fear of what she'd read on my face. Cherut took Raanan from me and I continued to help Merab prepare the food. When we gathered to eat a little later, I tried to keep from showing my nervousness by teasing Aliyah, getting a drink for Haviva, and busying myself with the cleanup.

Later, I found Cherut by herself. "What did you and Devora talk about this morning?" I asked. "I couldn't help but overhear part of your conversation."

Cherut looked down, not meeting my gaze. But the flush on her cheeks was the answer I feared. "You told her about your charms, didn't you?" I said.

"She came right out and asked me. My answer slipped out before I thought."

"Did you tell her that you lent one to me?"

"It might have come up," Cherut said, still avoiding my eyes.

Now I dreaded my next meeting with Devora.

* * *

I had a hard time getting to sleep that night, thinking of Devora, wondering what she knew, and what she had told Father Caleb. I finally fell asleep and slept so soundly, I failed to hear Elah rise to tend the animals, finally awakening to Devora's touch on my shoulder, her gentle voice. "Zamri. Time to get to work. We need to collect extra today for Sabbath."

I scrambled from under the warm covers, pulled on my clothes and tied my robe close against the chill morning air, forgetting for an instant what I had dreaded for the past hours. But it all came back to me as we walked in silence to the borders of the camp.

There many were already at work. I squatted down near other women, hoping that their presence would keep Devora from bringing up personal matters. She set to work nearby.

We worked in silence for a good while and I was further relieved when some wives of Father Caleb's friends come over to meet Devora and chat with her. I worked quickly, filling the usual baskets and starting on the extra ones. I was almost done when Devora rejoined me. "My you've done well," she said. "I got talking and haven't collected much."

"That's okay. We don't have much more to do," I said to her, hoping my diligence had earned her favour.

We worked together in silence again and I started to relax. Maybe she wouldn't bring up the subject of Cherut's charms after all. Maybe Cherut hadn't said as much as I feared.

And then, when we were done and ready to head for home Devora stopped and looked at me intently. "Zamri, I found out something from Cherut yesterday that concerns me." She paused. I waited for her to go on but when she didn't, I looked into her face. She didn't look angry, just serious. "Do you know what I'm talking about?"

"What?" I asked.

"You do know, don't you?"

I didn't answer, afraid that if I said something about the charm and she was referring to something else, I'd get myself in more trouble than necessary.

Devora waited for my answer but when I said nothing she continued. "It's Cherut's connection to the idols of Egypt. She admitted to trusting in them for her child. And then she told me something I found hard to believe—that she had lent one of her charms to you, to help you get pregnant."

As she talked, my face grew hot and my heart pounded.

"Is that true?" she continued.

I nodded dumbly.

"Why?"

I took a deep breath and swallowed hard to make the lump in my throat go away. "Elah so wants a child," I whispered, "and I'm not conceiving. Cherut was with child mere weeks after wedding Naam. It's not fair. She says the charms helped her and she offered them to me."

Devora gave me a long searching look, and then drew me close in a hug. "I know," she said. "It's hard. I too was childless in my marriage to Sethur. It is a natural and good thing to want children. But in this we must follow our mothers Sarah, Rebekah, and Rachel. They also had trouble conceiving. They and their husbands prayed, but to Yahweh who alone has power to open and close wombs. Not to the Egyptian gods who Yahweh has forbidden us to worship. These Egyptian idols, charms, and amulets bring with them a curse, not a blessing, as Moses reminded us when the people worshipped the golden calf." [32]

Bezalel's story of his amulet and the plague of darkness came back to me and I realized the presence of Cherut's amulet had been bothering me more than I admitted, even to myself. "What should I do?" I asked tearfully.

"What do you think you should do?"

"Give Cherut her charm back?"

"I was thinking of something even more drastic. I believe we should destroy the charm she gave you and all the others she has. By doing that we will free you, her, and our tent from their defilement."

As we made our way back to the tent, I could only begin to imagine Cherut's reaction to such a suggestion.

Chapter Twenty-three

Mid-afternoon of the next day, Sabbath, a messenger came to fetch Father Caleb for a special meeting of leaders. He returned in time to join us for the evening meal.

"What did Moses want with you?" Iru asked.

"An unusual thing," Father Caleb replied. "A man was brought to Moses. He was found gathering kindling, a job we all know is forbidden on this day. Apparently even though his family and neighbours warned him, he ignored them and continued. Moses asked us to meet to discuss what should be done with him."

"What did you decide?"

"Moses will inquire of Yahweh while the lawbreaker is under guard."

I found this news alarming. Not that I'd ever been tempted to gather manna or fetch water or kindling on our day of rest. I was happy for the break. But this fuss over such a seemingly small violation of Yahweh's law brought to mind yesterday's talk with Devora about that law, how we needed to keep it, and how I myself was breaking it with the charm that was still hidden amongst my clothes.

The next morning I was barely back from fetching water when the messenger arrived and announced that at the sound of the trumpet we were to gather. Moses would deliver Yahweh's verdict on the Sabbath-breaker.

We hurried with our meal and left our tent in its morning disarray to join the crowds streaming to the meeting place. We arrived to see a man, head bent, arms and feet bound, standing before Moses.

"Silence, to hear the judgement of Yahweh," Moses called out. A hush fell over the multitude. Moses' words rang out again. "The LORD has said, 'The man must surely be put to death; all the congregation shall stone him with stones.'"

There was stunned silence, which was broken at last by the clatter of rocks as people began picking up stones, and then a thump, as the first stone hit its mark. I looked at their target and saw terror in his eyes. As more and more people heaved stones. I closed my eyes and put my hands over my ears. When the deed was done, we returned to our tent in sober silence.

For the rest of the day I couldn't get what I'd seen and heard out of my mind. I kept recalling the fear in the man's eyes, hearing the sound of the stones, the man's shrieks, and then the silence.

And I kept thinking of my mother's words: "This God of Moses's makes no sense. Yahweh's punishments are too harsh." [33]

The stoning of the lawbreaker affected us all. Elah brought up the topic at the evening meal, asking what had been on my mind all day. "What have we seen today, Father? It troubles me."

"It troubles me too," Father Caleb said. "It's a reminder that Yahweh is serious about His commands. It's our responsibility to learn from these times when Yahweh demonstrates His displeasure. We learn from today to obey all Yahweh's commands, even the small ones. Similarly, we learned about following Him precisely when Aaron's sons were burned for offering strange fire, and learned about not grumbling when God sent quail that satisfied our cravings but made us sick, and about accepting Moses as our leader when God sent fire on the rebels at Taberah."

I had struggled with critical thoughts all day. Now words that I'd heard my mother say tumbled from my mouth. "But His punishments are too harsh. They don't match the crimes."

Caleb fixed me with his penetrating gaze. "It's not how trivial the infraction, but the attitude behind the breaking of the law that offends Yahweh. Such attitudes often start small, with seemingly small sins but if unchecked grow into a rebelliousness that infects entire families. In this case, the man's family was fortunate to have escaped stoning as well."

"Like the families of Dathan and Abiram were destroyed," Iru said.

"Right," said Father Caleb. "Yahweh was justified in wiping out that entire rebellious clan. They deserved what they got." [34]

His words knocked the breath out of me. How could he say that? He didn't know them! Inside my head I was screaming, *No! They didn't deserve it!* I clenched my jaw and bit my teeth together to keep from shouting out. But emotion overcame me anyway. I rose and hurried from the room.

My face still felt swollen, my tears scarcely dry when Elah joined me in our room. "What is it Zamri?" he asked. "Why did you leave so suddenly? Why are you crying?"

I shook my head. I couldn't tell him. I must never tell him. He might put me away if he knew I had loved someone before him—that this man still held a part of my heart.

"Tell me," he begged. "I can't comfort you if I don't

know what it is. Is it Merab, or Cherut, or Devora? Is it your barrenness?"

I only shook my head dumbly.

* * *

I dreaded Devora asking me about my sudden departure, which I knew she would. I made an extra effort to avoid her but couldn't do it for long. Four days later when we were in the tent making morning preparations while Merab and Cherut were out, she confronted me in her typical gentle yet persistent manner.

"I noticed you left the evening meal hurriedly a few days ago and seemed troubled," she said.

"It was nothing."

"No, it was not nothing. What troubled you? The talk was of Abiram's family. Did you know them? Was someone among them your acquaintance, or a friend?

How did she know? I nodded but said nothing.

"Tell me about it," she said. "Your words will be safe with me."

Should I tell her? It would be a great relief to speak to someone of this, to not hold it so tightly within. But I dared not for fear others, like Elah, would find out.

"I won't tell anyone. I promise. Your secret will be safe with me," Devora said, as if reading my mind.

The temptation to spill my story was too great. "I had a friend in that family," I said at last, not daring to meet Devora's eyes. "His name was Pallu. We wanted to marry. His father Abiram even asked my father. But Father and Grandfather Hur refused him."

"You cared for him?" Devora asked.

I nodded and looked up at her through tears. "I saw Yahweh's judgement of them. I witnessed the earth swallowing them, swallowing Pallu. It was horrible. They didn't deserve it, as Father Caleb said."

Devora reached out and placed her warm hand over mine. "I think I understand," she said. "My first husband Sethur also died under Yahweh's harsh hand. He was chosen to spy out the land for our tribe. I cared for him a great deal, was so proud of him, and felt overjoyed when he returned safely. We hadn't yet been reunited when the spies gave their report to Moses. He sided with the others against Caleb and Joshua, advising the people not to go into the land. And there, before my eyes, I saw him die of plague." [35]

I had never thought of how the families of these men must have suffered. I gave Devora's hand a squeeze

"For the longest time, I was heartbroken and angry at Moses and Yahweh for my husband's death. I prayed that I would either understand some purpose in this, or that I too would die. I didn't die. Instead, in the weeks and months that followed, as I thought about and remembered Yahweh's ways and miracles, I began to understand. Yes, He is harsh but also kind. Think how He spared our firstborn sons and brought us all out of Egypt. He provides food and water, even though not always when we'd like it. And He only punishes disobedience against His laws."

"But why so suddenly and with no warnings or second chances?"

"If you recall, there were warnings and second chances. When the spies returned, at any time these faithless ones, including my Sethur, could have turned and sided with Joshua and Caleb in trying to convince the people to believe Yahweh's promises. By voicing their fears, they implied Yahweh's help was not to be trusted, even though they had witnessed it at other times against the Egyptians and the Amalekites.

"Then Caleb came into my life and I experienced Yahweh's care in a whole new way. I tell you, Zamri, trust Yahweh. For everything. He has given you a wonderful man in Elah. By the way, does Elah know about Pallu?"

I shook my head.

"You might want to tell him. It is not wise to keep secrets like that from your husband. Take my advice as someone who has been there. Don't spoil your relationship with a living man by dreaming about someone who has died. And trust Yahweh for children as well, instead of trusting in Egyptian idols. You have destroyed Cherut's charm, haven't you?

What could I say? I hadn't. I looked down, not answering. As the silence stretched between us I felt Devora's eyes boring into me. Finally, she spoke again.

"Zamri, hanging onto it is also disobedience and it's dangerous. It is as dangerous as the spies' refusal to trust Yahweh to bring us into the Promised Land. As dangerous as that man gathering sticks on the Sabbath. Don't try Him in this way."

* * *

Devora's warning shook me. I had never thought of having Cherut's charm as dangerous. How could that be as serious as defying Moses, like the spies had, or outright rebellion? Yet neither would I have considered gathering a little kindling on the Sabbath serious enough for stoning.

After the morning meal, I went to our room, hurried to put all in order, then dug through the garments in which I had hidden the golden Bastet amulet. I pulled it out and look at it closely. The cat's eyes looked mysterious and sly. The gold that had always had a warm gleam now appeared malicious. No longer did it seem like a beautiful and innocent trinket. I knew what I must do.

But in my head, I heard: *What about Bastet's power to help you have a child? You're throwing away your last chance.* I paused. Was I? Devora had just told me how she asked Yahweh to help her after her husband's death. He did. Yahweh helped her to let go of her anger and see the wisdom in His ways. He even brought another husband to her. Maybe He would help me too. I had never spoken to Him before, yet now felt a strong urge to do it.

"Great Yahweh," I whispered. "I will put away this Egyptian charm and in doing so, I entrust myself to You for a child. "

Now the trinket felt like it was burning a hole in my hand and I couldn't wait to get rid of it. I grabbed a small shovel on my way to bury it outside the camp.

* * *

"I got rid of the charm," I told Devora the next time we were alone together.

"God be thanked!" she said. "We don't want to tempt His patience. I have talked to Cherut about doing the same but she resists me. Perhaps you can help persuade her."

"I'll try," I said, though I dreaded bringing up the subject. I knew how attached she was to these objects and how upset she would be that I got rid of one, let alone would dare ask her to do the same.

My opportunity came a few days later as we went together to fetch water.

"I have something to tell you," I said and then

hesitated, not sure how to go on.

"What?" I detected suspicion in her sharp eyes.

"You know that Bastet you lent me? I threw it away."

"You what?"

"I got rid of the Bastet charm."

"How?"

"I dug it into the sand outside the camp."

Her face paled and she stopped. "You've been speaking with Devora, haven't you? Why? And where 'outside the camp'?"

"I can't tell you where," I said to her. "Yes, Devora and I had a talk. She explained to me how hanging onto these Egyptian charms is dangerous, how they invite Yahweh's judgement, like it fell on the man who broke the Sabbath by gathering sticks."

Cherut's face closed and her mouth became a stubborn line.

"I think you should get rid of yours too," I finished. There. I'd said it.

Instead of the anger I expected, Cherut's face crumbled with emotion and tears flooded her eyes. "I can't," she choked out. "I want Raanan to survive and I want more sons."

"Devora says we can trust Yahweh for that, like our foremothers did." I put my arm around sobbing Cherut's trembling shoulders, but she shrugged me off.

"I can't see Yahweh," she blurted out. "He covers Himself in clouds and fire, and is frightening. What does He care about me and my children?"

"Perhaps more than you think. But don't you see that you need to consider others besides yourself? You know how Yahweh's judgement comes down, not only on lawbreakers but also their families. Devora thinks your

Egyptian idols are endangering our whole encampment. What if you're found out, like the man collecting sticks was, and we all get punished? Devora may decide to find and destroy them on her own if you don't willingly give them up."

Cherut's face was set and unreadable as we waited in line for our turn at the spring, then filled our jugs and returned to the tent. But the next day she came to me with a bulky parcel in hand, a sullen look on her face. "Here, take this. This is what you asked for. Do what you like with them."

Chapter Twenty-four

The camaraderie between Cherut and me was gone. She avoided me now. When I entered our women's quarters where she and Merab were at work, their conversation silenced, as if they didn't want me to hear. Both of them shunned Devora as well. It was two against two.

When I mentioned the tension to Elah, he shook his head. "You women," he said, grinning.

"It might not seem like anything to you," I said, "but it's pretty awkward to live with those you feel are criticizing your every move."

"What started it?" he asked, now serious.

"Devora discovered Cherut was hanging onto some Egyptian charms," I told him, and explained the situation without mentioning my part in it.

"She'll get over it soon," Elah assured me when I came to the end of my tale.

But not that soon, it seemed. The tension in our household dragged on. I welcomed the chance to get away that came with an invitation from Sephy and Shoshan to celebrate Chaim's birthday. The anticipation even erased the hurt that came the day before his party, when no one but Elah remembered that it was my birthday — that I was twenty-one.

* * *

"Shalom!" Sephy ran to meet us as we neared the family's tent. "Cetura is here too. We'll have a good old reunion!"

Elah and I joined Shoshan's parents, Shoshan,

Chaim, their three-year-old son Matan, along with Cetura, Paltiel, and their little son Yaron, already toddling around.

Always before when I'd come to visit, I had made a point of playing with the children. Now Chaim came running over. I gave him a hug, wished him a happy birthday but he stuck close.

"He's been looking forward to you coming all day," Sephy said. "He was hoping you'd bring your timbrel."

"And that I did," I said, taking it from the folds of my robe.

"Can we sing? Can we march and dance?" Chaim asked, jumping around.

I looked over at Sephy who nodded her assent. I took the children a short distance away, gathered them around me and began to sing the songs my mother had taught me. The children took turns playing my timbrel as we re-enacted the Red Sea crossing and the Amalekite battle, until all of us were tired.

I shooed the children off to play. The men were in conversation under the canopy. I joined my friends and Shoshan's mother in the women's room where Sephy and Cetura were immersed in comparing their mothering experiences. Cetura, who was pregnant again, described her latest aches and pains along with questions of what to do with her willful two-year-old. At a lull in the conversation, Sephy turned to me. "And what about you?" she asked. "How have you been? And what's new in your family?"

I told them about Caleb's marriage to Devora and the changes that brought about in our encampment. "Of course, the main share of the work still falls to Devora and me, as we have no little ones to care for."

"And when are you going to change that?" Cetura asked playfully.

I felt my face flush and a lump form in my throat. I looked down and managed to mutter, "One of these days — I hope."

Sephy grasped the situation. She looked at me with sympathy. "I'm sorry," she said. "It's just that you're so good with the children, we're hoping you soon have a couple of your own. But enough of this. Come. Mother has prepared food and a special treat for not only Chaim, but someone else who has just had a birthday."

She took my hand, drew me up, and we went to join the others outside the tent where Chaim and I were seated together in the place of honour.

* * *

The sadness that came over me at the party lingered into the next morning.

"Why so quiet?" Devora asked as we tackled the cleanup in the tent after the morning meal. "You seem upset."

"I'm okay."

But in typical Devora fashion, she didn't let it go at that. "Did something happen at your friend's place last night?"

It was useless to try to keep secrets from her, I knew, as she wouldn't let things rest. So, I told her about the lovely evening with its distressing undertone. "My friends have children — Sephy two, Cetura one with another on the way. Why can't I get pregnant?"

Devora stopped mid-task to listen to me, then came over, put her arm around my shoulder and gave it a squeeze. "I know," she whispered. "It's hard. All I can say is, do all you can and keep trusting Yahweh."

Her words, 'Do all you can,' echoed in my mind throughout the day. Had I done all I could? I recalled her earlier advice that I needed to share with Elah my first love for Pallu. That was still a secret between us. Could Yahweh be keeping motherhood from me because I was hiding this from him?

* * *

I struggled with the thought of telling Elah about Pallu. I imagined how he might react and my mind became a battlefield. What if he got so angry he wanted a divorce and brought me to Moses to be judged? What if my revelation put a barrier between us so that Elah no longer trusted me, began treating me cruelly, or even took another wife? Or could I perhaps be making too much of this? Was I erecting obstacles in my imagination that were simply excuses to not tell him?

Maybe none of the things I imagined would happen and life would go on as usual or even get better—he'd trust me more because I'd been honest with him and told him my secret. Maybe my secret really was the obstacle to me conceiving a child, and telling him would open my womb.

I dwelt on this for weeks, rehearsing what I could say, how he might respond, what would happen next. My preoccupation began to affect my day-to-day tasks. Cherut laughed when she found me talking to myself. Merab became annoyed when she discovered the baskets stacked on the wrong shelf and the bed coverings piled in odd places.

* * *

"What's on your mind, Zamri?" Elah probed one night as we were getting ready for bed. "You've not been yourself for a while now. What is it?"

Could this be the opening I had waited for? My palms grew sweaty and my heart began to pound.

"I need to tell you something," I said, not daring to look up.

He was instantly all attention. I felt his eyes boring into me. "What?"

"It's about the time before I knew you," I said, mouthing the words I'd repeated in my head a hundred times. "Someone else wanted to marry me and I cared for him..."

"Did he know you in an intimate way?" Elah broke in.

I shook my head. "No," I whispered. "I was a virgin on our wedding night, as all witnessed. You are the only one who has known me."

"Then why are you telling me this?"

"Because in my heart I've found it hard to stop caring for him. Devora suggested I come clean with you — be completely honest, and that because of my honesty, I will finally conceive a child."

"Who is he?" Elah asked, his voice rising, anger sparking from his eyes. "Do you still see him?"

"No," I said. "He is dead.

"But who? You still care for him? I'm competing with a dead man?" Elah's face was flushed, his hands clenched. I slipped closer to him, sensing his hurt and confusion. I put my hand over his, but he flipped it off.

"Who are you?" he said, looking at me coldly, in a way he had never looked at me before. "What kind of lie have you been living — have we been living?"

Things were going badly just as I feared and my resolve to do this calmly without emotion was swept away by the tears that blurred my sight.

After our argument, Elah wrapped himself in his robe and turned away from me. The peaceful rise and fall of his breathing mocked the storm inside me. He knew that had I loved someone else, but I couldn't bear to tell him more. As it was, I wondered what had I done? Wrecked our marriage and our home? Made the chances I would have a child even worse? I knew I had tarnished forever the image that Elah had had of me. What would happen now?

At last I fell into sleep, troubled by dreams where I was dragged before Moses by Elah while his shocked family looked on. I startled awake to find it was morning and Elah had already left to tend his animals.

* * *

A week passed. Since I had revealed my secret to Elah, nothing really terrible had happened except that for the first time in our marriage, Elah held himself aloof from me. It made me sad. I longed for what I had had before and realized I had taken him for granted.

I was lonelier than ever, for Cherut too avoided me—and I would never be close to Merab. Devora saw that I was troubled and guessed why. "I suppose you told all to Elah," she said when the two of us were gathering manna that morning.

"How do you know?" I asked.

"Because both of you are not yourselves. How did he take it?"

"Not well. After his anger died down he hasn't brought it up again. Do you suppose he's considering putting me away, even bringing me before Moses?"

"Somehow, I don't think he'd do that," Devora said. "I've watched him when you're around and he still has eyes for no one but you. Be confident you did the right thing. Deceit is destructive to any relationship. In the end, I believe this will make your marriage stronger."

I was not convinced. Worry continued to gnaw at me.

* * *

Cherut was with child again. That became clear at the morning meal a few days later when she was sick and I realized this wasn't the first time this had happened lately. All day I fought envious thoughts. How was it fair that she was pregnant for the second time while I still waited for my first child?

But, I told myself, perhaps the fact that she had conceived without the help of her charms would also open the door to renew our friendship.

"You are with child, aren't you?" I said as we worked together, preparing the evening meal.

She gave me a little smile and nodded.

"Congratulations!" I said. "See, you didn't need your charms to make it happen. Things will be fine without them."

But instead of opening the door, my comment seemed to close it, for immediately Cherut's expression became guarded and the small glimmer of warmth was gone.

"For how long have you known?" I asked, seeking to ease the tension. But Cherut ignored me and the rift between us remained.

When the day's tasks were done, I slipped away to our room where I vented my frustration and hurt. Elah found me there a little later. "What's wrong?" he said, coming over to where I was scrunched up in tears. He squatted down beside me and put his hand in my back with a tenderness he hadn't shown since the night I confided in him.

"I can't do anything right," I blubbered and spilled out what had just happened between Cherut and me.

"I guess my attitude for the last while hasn't helped either," he said as he drew me close. "I've been thinking a lot about what you told me, and how I reacted. I think I figured it out.

"I've always felt third best in our family — to father especially. Iru is most like him — driving, ambitious, positive. And who can help but love Naam, the baby of the family? I, on the other hand, have sensed that father disapproved of me for some reason.

"Then you came along and for once I believed I was first in someone's heart. It was a shock to find that I was also second-best for you."

His revelation opened within me a tenderness toward him I hadn't felt before. But I also knew that I couldn't deny what I had told him about me and my past. And so, there were no words. Instead, I reached for his hand and held it in both of mine.

For a long while we sat in peaceful silence. "Maybe I shouldn't have told you," I said at last. "But Devora encouraged me to, insisting that our relationship would grow stronger if it was built on truth."

"And it will," Elah said. "I'm sorry for the way I reacted. It just took me a while to get used to the idea that you had cared for someone else when all along I thought I was the only one."

"You are the only one now," I murmured into his chest.

"I'm glad for that," Elah whispered into my ear as the thumb of his hand began to move in a tender caress of mine.

* * *

I was so certain my honesty with Elah would bring about conception that I was shocked when my way of women came at the usual time. I was often teary at this time of month but this day I was particularly on edge. And so, when the morning's tasks were done, I did what I hadn't done for a long time—went for a walk by myself.

As I walked, I whispered a simple prayer. "Yahweh—why? I have done all I know to do. Why have I not conceived?"

My gaze was drawn to the cloud that rested over the tabernacle. Were my eyes playing tricks on me, or did I see movement in it? I stopped and stared at it transfixed. Yes, there was motion—a billowing as when a mist rises from boiling water. I was sure I'd never seen such movement in the stationary cloud before.

I stood there for a long time watching, with the strong feeling that Yahweh saw me and heard my prayer. When I finally turned and headed for home, it was with a lighter heart.

Chapter Twenty-five

Four years passed. In spite of the reassurance I had received under Yahweh's cloud that I would conceive, there was still no child.

Caleb's family continued to grow, though. Cherut and Naam had their second child a girl, Enat, followed by another son, Lavi. After his birth, Cherut appeared to have finally forgiven me, for she was friendly again.

With the growing squeeze in the tent, Iru, Merab, Aliyah, and Haviva moved into their own tent next to ours. This eased kitchen tensions greatly. Merab happily took responsibility for her own household and Devora was free to run ours in her easygoing manner.

We kept moving on during these years as the cloud went before us from one camping place to another. One day we had just set up camp after being on the move for a week. Normally the weariness of travel and setup overcame me by this time, but not this day. For I had discovered, while on our trek, that Sebia was with child. This was the best news I could get. As soon as our camp was settled, Elah and I went to visit my family.

When we arrived at my home encampment, we found things in unusual disarray. They had barely set up their tent and there was much still to do of organizing the sleeping quarters and cooking the evening meal.

"Your mother isn't well," Sebia said. "I've been keeping her comfortable."

Mother lay in restless sleep on a pallet under a hastily erected canopy. She opened her eyes when I greeted her but seemed not to recognize me.

"I'll get a bed ready for her," I said and busied myself in the tent, returning to fetch her. She was so weak, she couldn't even stand so it wasn't until Father, Bezalel, and Elah came to help us that we transferred her to the cool tent.

Much later, when we were finally gathered together around the evening meal, I got the opportunity to talk about the news.

"We hear you are with child!"

"Yes," Sebia said, her face glowing.

We discussed when the baby was due and how she had been feeling. It turned out not well. She had been plagued with the sickness and weakness I had seen in Merab and Cherut. On top of that, Bezalel was being extra protective, ensuring that she didn't overexert herself. With mother so sick, it became clear there would be a problem.

"You could use some extra help around here until mother gets better," I said. "Can I stay behind and help out?" Elah readily gave his assent. And so, that night and many more, I slept in my girlhood home.

* * *

How different it felt to be doing household tasks for my family now. Before I married and left home I questioned every duty and tried to avoid work whenever I could. Now I simply did these homely chores as a matter of course, even as I sensed love pouring through me to the ones I served.

Mother improved slowly. After I had been there for a week, she rose from her mat and joined us in the women's quarters where Sebia and I were preparing the meal. I felt her eyes on me, but my fear that she disapproved of what she saw was soon allayed. "You're a much better worker than you were before you married," she said.

I laughed in surprised delight. "I had to be a good worker with a perfectionist like Merab in charge," I said. "And Father Caleb's household is big and busy. So many mouths to feed and more all the time—though the number has gone down since Iru's family moved."

Grandfather Hur still clung to his old habit of sitting at the entrance of the tent, observing, thinking, and meditating. I loved the feeling of being under his protective gaze as he watched me come and go.

One day after the morning chores were done, he motioned for me to take a seat beside him. "You're too busy," he said. "Come and talk with me a while."

I sat down beside him.

"How are you faring with Caleb's family?" he asked. "Are you happy?"

"Oh yes," I said, wondering where this conversation was going.

"Elah, is he good to you?"

"Yes, he's good to me. He's a good man."

"Have you forgiven me for refusing to allow your betrothal to Pallu?"

That was it? Had my attitude then been bothering him all these years? "Oh yes," I said. "It all worked out for the good, though I was pretty upset at the time."

"I know," Grandfather said. "I just wanted to make sure you no longer held that against me."

"Oh no, Grandpa." I reached out to take his gnarled veined hand, that felt rough and warm.

"And the others? Who else lives with you?"

I told him about the family, about Merab with whom I had had such difficulty getting along at first but whose standards had helped me improve as a worker. I talked about Cherut and her carefree ways that masked superstitions and fears. And I went on and on about Devora who, I realized, had become like a second mother to me.

"Devora helps me see Yahweh's ways differently," I told Grandfather. "She too has felt His harsh judgement after the death of her first husband, one of the spies. But she overcame her bitterness about that and has a new respect for Yahweh — for His holiness and how we must know and follow His commandments. When we do, we have nothing to fear."

"Yahweh be praised!" Grandfather said, his face glowing. "I have prayed for you that you would come to that realization."

We sat in silence for a time and then Grandfather asked, almost hesitantly, "You and Elah... are you planning to have children of your own someday?"

His question caught me by surprise and I let go of his hand. For a minute, I couldn't even look him in the eye as I struggled with a wave of emotion. Finally I managed to whisper, "We've tried. For years." Then I told him what I hadn't told anyone else, even Elah. "I've prayed to Yahweh about this and thought I saw a sign in the cloud that He had heard. But that was years ago now, and still no child."

Grandfather reached for my hand and held it within both of his. "Don't give up," he said. "I have also prayed for you to have a child — a son, on whom I may lay hands and bless before I die. I believe Yahweh will yet answer your prayer."

After three weeks, mother was well again and I could return home. Elah came to fetch me. "Don't hesitate to ask for more help if you need it," I said to my family as we took our leave. "And when the baby is due, I'll happily return to help."

I couldn't stop talking on the way home, happy to be back with Elah. Yet I sensed that this time with my family had been significant.

* * *

Sebia was nearing the time of her confinement. Thankfully I could say that in the intervening months I had come to a measure of peace about my own barrenness. I was weary of wishing and hoping for something I couldn't have, and so I resigned myself to being the one who filled in the gaps around the campsite when the mothers were busy with their little ones. I got used to being only an aunt, the one to play with, entertain, and look after the children when parents needed a break. In spite of my resignation, seeing Elah's eyes, full of wistfulness as they followed the antics of his brothers' children, still brought up feelings of sadness and inadequacy.

However, the hope of Bezalel and Sebia's little one soon to arrive filled me with joy — almost as much joy as if it were my own. Maybe it was the lifting of the responsibility I had felt for Sebia losing her child all those years ago that played a part in this.

I arranged for Bezalel to send for me when Sebia began labouring, but an entire week passed after the midwife had set for her confinement before a messenger arrived at our home. He came with the news that the baby was about to be delivered.

An excited and nervous Bezalel greeted us when we got to the encampment. He pointed me to their room of the tent. I pulled back the curtain and entered. It was filled with women. Mother, two aunts, and the midwife were all focused on Sebia, who was in the throes of heavy labour. I watched as mother, despite the midwife's presence and her own recent frailty, seemed to have taken charge. She suggested to Sebia how to change her position to make herself more comfortable, asked for cold compresses for her sweating brow, and rubbed her back in between the sharp pains.

Those became more intense and frequent until Sebia gave a gasp that was almost a yell and a dark head emerged from between her splayed legs, followed by, a moment later, a shiny pink body, caught in the midwife's waiting hands. It was a girl. As the newborn's cry filled the tent, Sebia's face changed from a grimace to a joyful smile.

A few minutes later, Mother handed her the washed and swaddled newborn. "Welcome little Ari," Sebia murmured as she nuzzled the baby's twizzle of hair. Bezalel, who must have entered the room after he heard the baby's cry, stood beside her, his eyes full of wonder at the sight of their infant daughter.

I was amazed at the pure joy I felt, without a hint of envy or self-pity.

* * *

I stayed on at my parents' encampment after Sebia birthed her child. This proved to be a good decision as Mother, who had been all energy and efficiency to help Sebia, was overcome with fatigue. It seemed she was paying for her expenditure of energy.

Grandfather Hur was not his usual self either. Instead of rising at the normal time, he stayed long in bed, walked haltingly, always with his walking stick, and spent very little time in his customary seat at the door of the tent.

I discussed these things with Bezalel. The changes in Mother and Grandfather hadn't appeared as obvious to him, since they had occurred gradually before his eyes. But he admitted that both were weakening.

The baby, though, was wonderful. I cuddled her whenever Sebia handed her to me and when she was busy with her, I did all I could to help with household chores.

Sebia was soon on her feet again. She bundled little Ari to her and joined me in gathering the family's manna. Mother, too, revived. When a week had passed, I knew it was time to return to my own family and pick up my ordinary life.

* * *

Ordinary life as I knew it before Ari's birth never happened, though. Shortly after getting home, it occurred to me that my monthly bleed was late. It never came. Instead my nose and stomach become exquisitely sensitive to smells that I had never noticed before. Was I ill?

One morning I had to quickly leave the cooking fire to get away from the smoke and odor of food. Well away from the heat, I took deep breaths of cold, clean air to settle my stomach.

Cherut noticed and came over to where I was sitting. She squatted down beside me touching me gently on the shoulder. "What's wrong?" she asked.

I couldn't answer for the lump of sickness that had risen in my throat, so I just shook my head. Cherut looked at me closely and rubbed my back. "Perhaps you are with child?"

"Perhaps," I whispered.

Cherut jumped up, clapped her hands and did a little dance. Despite how ill I felt, I couldn't help but laugh.

Elah was beyond delighted. I caught him looking at me with new wonder in his eyes. "I can hardly believe it," he said when we were alone. "Could there really be a little one within?"

Though my body didn't show any changes, I felt different. I was always tired and developed a new relationship with food—ravenous for it, yet repulsed by it at the same time. Now I understood poor Cherut and why she had had such a hard time rising in the morning and often claiming she was too weary to help with chores.

When we broke the news to Merab, she too was thrilled and full of tips on how to handle my altered state. "Get something in your stomach first thing in the morning," she advised. "Rise from sitting or squatting slowly, and in the morning drink water cooled by the night air." I tried these things but didn't know if they make any difference. It felt like my body was in a strange river with its own rapids and currents that I must now swim through as best I could.

* * *

Over weeks, the nausea and great weariness lessened, replaced by visible changes, as my belly grew. I talked to my little one when I was alone. "Good morning, darling. How are you today? I can hardly wait to meet you."

I imagined visiting my family and telling them the news. I was back to gathering the morning manna and while I gathered it, I told my little one about my people and how happy they would be to hear that he or she was on the way.

"Mother will probably be the first person you meet," I said, imagining her at my side during the birth like she was with Sebia. "And what will you be like? Maybe you will have the gifts of Bezalel, who is a great artist. I hope you have the kindness of your father and my father, and the wisdom of your great grandfather Hur, though you could do without his stubbornness."

I imagined Grandfather Hur pronouncing a blessing on my child, and then remembered how frail he looked last time we visited. Death must not take him till he had seen this answer to his prayers!

I happened to glance up and my attention was caught by the cloud over the tabernacle. As I studied it, I was sure I saw it glow brighter, even pulsate like it did those years ago when I prayed. Yahweh's presence was in that cloud, I reminded myself. He saw me still and was watching over me.

"Thank You!" I murmured, and in that moment, I felt a flutter within, different from the usual feelings of my stomach at work. Had my baby just moved?

* * *

A few days later and feeling much better, I was eager to share the news of our expected baby with my family. The afternoon Elah and I went to my family's encampment we were met by Cousin Reisa's daughter Jaffa playing with a baby near the tent opening. We greeted her and Bezalel came out of the tent on hearing our voices.

"This isn't little Ari, is it?" I asked, hardly believing that the infant who had so recently been born could already be sitting up.

"It is," said Bezalel, joined a moment later by Sebia.

"She grows as fast as the Nile reeds."

They invited us into the front room of the tent and offered us tea.

"Where is mother?" I asked.

"Not well," Sebia said. She's weakening again. But she'll want to see you."

I went with Sebia into the dim inner compartment where Mother lay on her mat. She tried to sit up when I entered but fell back heavily. I sat beside her mat and took her hand. "I have news," I said. "I want you to be the first to know. I am with child."

Her eyes opened wide in surprise, she pressed my hand, and said, feebly but with a glint in her eye, "Well, it's about time."

I ignored her good-natured dig and went on. "So, you have to get better. I want you to be with me at baby's birth."

"I'll try," she said.

"What wonderful news!" Sebia, who had remained with us, broke in. She grabbed my hand. "Let's go tell the others!"

Joy filled the house as word got around. Even Grandfather Hur roused.

"We need you and mother to grow strong so you can meet our child," I said to him. "Our little one needs your blessing, Grandfather."

"I would love nothing better," he assured me.

When it was time to go, Elah and I walked home in the moonlight hand in hand. I felt thoughtful, my joy at the new life within dimmed by the cloud of illness that hovered over those I loved.

* * *

A messenger sent by my family arrived just days

later. Mother's condition had worsened. I needed to come at once.

Elah couldn't leave his flock so Devora went with me. We arrived to find the family gathered around mother's mat. Her eyes were closed and her slow breaths rattled in her chest. I knelt beside her and took her hand in mine. Her eyes didn't open, though I saw an ever-so-slight quiver of her eyelids.

"How long has she been like this?" I asked.

"Since this morning," Sebia said. "She refused food last night, just seemed to want to sleep, and this morning we haven't been able to rouse her.

I watched her breathing, her mouth open, lips cracked and parched.

"Here is a cloth soaked in water," Sebia said, handing me a dripping cloth. "I have been dampening her mouth."

I took the cloth and squeezed droplets of water into mother's mouth, but even to this she made no response.

As we sat around her mat, I remembered a song she sang to me when I was little and I begin to hum it. That started us singing the old songs to comfort ourselves as much as her. The songs were interspersed with incidents we remembered from her life. Meanwhile Devora found the manna, collected by someone that morning. She baked it in her customary way and served us cakes.

Mother took her last breath as the sun set. Word quickly got around that she had passed. The sounds of wailing soon filled the air giving voice to the sadness I felt. If only she could have lived a few months longer.

By the light of torches, I helped Sebia wash and wrap her dear stiff body. Then the whole family in procession, my grieving father directing the others, carried her body outside the camp and buried it in the sand.

Devora and I spent the night in my old home encampment. In the chill morning, we trekked back home. As we walked, I couldn't help but look toward the place we had laid mother's body. Already in the sky above, vultures circled.

Chapter Twenty-six

A trumpet blast roused us early. We would be moving again this day—the day before my twenty-seventh birthday. I pulled myself out of bed to start packing.

Six months had passed since my mother's death. They were months of sadness. We had travelled far away from her desert grave, but I was still getting used to the fact that she was gone and that I could no longer ask her for advice or tell her this or that.

But these months were also a time of anticipation. I was old to be having a first child. Since Mother's passing I'd grown heavy, clumsy, and found movement cumbersome. That meant being excused from gathering manna. Merab and Iru's eleven-year-old Aliyah and eight-year-old Haviva now had that job for all of us.

We had not moved for weeks and in my changed condition I found travel particularly trying. My body tired quickly with walking and in the heat my feet became swollen so that my sandal straps left deep indentations. Then, sometime in the early afternoon, the ache in my back tightened into cramps, light and fleeting at first, but persistent and growing in intensity and frequency.

"I don't feel well?" I said to Elah, who walked beside me keeping a close eye on me as well as his flock. "This couldn't be the baby coming, could it? It shouldn't be for another few weeks."

Elah raised his eyes to the cloud, which led us ever onward. "Just try to hold on a little longer, he urged. "Hopefully we will stop soon."

The time dragged as I forced myself to take another step, and another, and another. At last we stopped. I sat on our pile of bedding while Father Caleb, Elah, and Naam set up camp. When our room was ready, Elah helped me stand and Cherut fetched the bedding.

I felt a warm trickle going down my leg, a trickle that turned into a gush.

"I think my time is here," I said to Elah as he helped me to my mat.

* * *

The next hours were a blur. I remember riding waves of pain, alternating with periods of such weariness I drifted momentarily into sleep. From these I was abruptly and rudely awakened by another pain.

At some point I was aware that a midwife had come. She fussed over me, getting me to change position as she kept an eye on how the birth was progressing. As if from a far distance, I heard her say to Cherut, "I think the babe is facing the wrong way."

What she attempted, of manipulations and massages, didn't make any difference and my agony stretched on through the night and to the next day. I wished for nothing more than my mother or if not her, Devora.

People came and went as I drifted in and out of alertness. At one point, it seemed I saw Cherut holding the Bes figurine in one hand and waving something over me with the other as she chanted unintelligible words. Thinking about it later, I was sure it was a dream. After all, Cherut had destroyed all her Egyptian artifacts years ago.

Finally, Devora arrived. She came to my mat full of apology and concern. "I'm sorry, we were delayed," she said. She bathed my forehead with cool water and propped me up to give me a drink. As she cared for me, I heard her murmuring words that sounded like a prayer and a wave of peace descended over me.

A moment later another clenching cramp possessed my body. But the sensation was different now, as if something had given way.

"The babe has turned!" the midwife exclaimed from where she was crouched to see the baby's progress.

With the next cramp, I pushed with all my might and felt something slip out below. A baby's lusty cry filled the tent. I had birthed my child. We had a son!

* * *

After the birth of our baby (we named him Kenaz, "this possession" — a good sturdy traditional name in Caleb's clan[36]), life quickly got back to normal for everyone but me. Or perhaps more truthfully, I had to get used to a new normal.

Now I was at the beck and call of little Kenaz's constant needs and demands. No sooner was he freshened and fed than his little bottom was soiled again and he was crying with hunger.

When his crying filled our encampment and I couldn't settle him, Cherut and Merab came with suggestions. "Soak a little manna in water and let him suck it from your fingers," Merab said. "That always comforted Haviva."

"Swaddle him tightly," Cherut offered.

"My mother always loosened the blankets of her little ones, and then let them cry themselves to weariness" Devora said. Everyone seemed to know what to do for him but I. I often wondered if I would ever feel at ease in this new role.

But then there were the days when he smiled, cooed, and seemed completely contented. As the weight of him, swaddled tightly to me, grew greater each day and Father Caleb commented about what a happy, contented child he was, I felt reassured that I was doing something right.

* * *

I reminded Elah often in those first days that I wished for us to visit my old home for Kenaz to get Grandfather Hur's blessing. The way Grandfather looked at the last visit I felt we must do this soon.

We walked there one afternoon, after my days of purification were complete and when Elah could get someone to look after his flock.

As we approached our encampment, I saw it wasn't Grandfather Hur but Father who sat at the door of the tent. He rose to greet us.

"Where is Grandfather?" I asked. "He is not ill, is he?"

"He is well but asleep right now," Father assured us. "I know he'll be delighted to see his newest great-grandchild."

Everyone was eager to get acquainted with the new baby. After Kenaz had passed Bezalel's, Sebia's, and little Ari's inspection, Bezalel took Elah to show him his latest project, Sebia left to make tea while Kenaz and I sat with Father.

He reached for Kenaz, took the baby in his arms and gazed at him fondly. "You look to be doing a great job, Zamri," he said, smiling at me. "And you are happy and have regained your strength?"

"Yes. I am well, and very happy,"

"You have forgiven Father and me for refusing to betroth you to Pallu?"

Surprised that he too brought this up, I hastened to assure him. "Yes. I'm very happy. But why do you mention this now?"

"It troubled me greatly back then, to sense the estrangement between you and us over this. Father and I talked about it. He was sure that when Elah and you had a child, any feelings of bitterness toward us would dissolve."

Then placing his right hand on Kenaz's head, he spoke: "Little son of Judah, he whom his brothers praised, you are an offspring of a lion. The scepter shall not depart from Judah, nor a lawgiver from between his feet. To Judah and his offspring shall the gathering of the people be. Carry on the responsibility, privilege, and blessing of your forefather well." [37]

Little Kenaz, who had been asleep when Father took him, awakened. He looked up into Father's face but didn't cry. It was almost as if he understood the sacredness of the moment.

Sebia arrived with tea and manna refreshments then, ending our moment. Bezalel and Elah soon joined us. Father handed Kenaz back to me and left. We were just finishing our tea when Father rejoined us. "Father Hur is awake now and wants to see you.

* * *

We entered the dim tent and crowded around Grandfather's mat. Father had propped him up with cushions. He looked at us and smiled feebly.

Reaching Kenaz toward him, I said, "Grandfather, this is our new baby."

He looked at me quizzically as if he didn't understand.

"You need to speak louder," Sebia said. "His hearing

is very bad now."

I squatted down and spoke loudly into his ear. "This is your new grandson Kenaz. We have brought him to you today to get your blessing."

Understanding flooded Grandfather's face and it lit up in a smile. "Yahweh be praised," he said, then held out his trembling arms.

I placed little Kenaz into them, and in a surprisingly clear and strong voice, he spoke.

"The Lord bless you and keep you;
The Lord make His face shine upon you
And be gracious to you;
The Lord lift up His countenance upon you
     And give you peace." [38]

Perhaps it was no wonder that after the double blessing, Kenaz slept contentedly all the way home.

* * *

The day Grandfather Hur blessed Kenaz was the last time I saw him alive. A week later word came that he had died. Father Caleb and Devora joined Elah, Kenaz, and me to mourn his death.

When we arrived at our family's tent, we saw that many had gathered to grieve and comfort our family. Even Moses came, arriving shortly after we did. A hush swept over the crowd in his presence, like children hush when a strict parent enters the room. After greeting Father and Bezalel he turned to those assembled and, visibly moved, said, "Hur was my friend. He held up my arms to help defeat the Amalekites and was always loyal. Through the years, I could always depend on him to support me with obedience and respect." His voice cracked with emotion. "Today Israel has lost a great man." [39]

More of Grandfather's friends spoke after Moses, and all of them talked highly of him, telling stories that I had never heard. It made me proud to be part of his family and sad that I didn't know these things sooner.

As a procession of mourners, we bore Grandfather Hur's bound body outside the camp. Then Father Caleb, Devora, and our little family made our way home.

"Another friend gone," Father Caleb said, breaking the sober silence of our walk. "And I fear it won't be the last. Whenever there is another death, I remember Moses' words when he condemned us to wandering—that every man of war counted at the first census would die before we enter the Promised Land." [40]

A shiver went through me as I recalled that Bezalel had also been one numbered at that time.

Chapter Twenty-seven

The day Kenaz spent his first full day with his father, caring for the sheep, was one I would not forget. I shared my mixed feelings about this new stage of my child's independence with Devora while we were at work on the evening meal. After I'd finished talking, she put her hand on my arm to stop me in my work and said, with a big smile on her face, "I have something to tell you too."

"You're not...?" I replied, guessing what she was about to tell me, but afraid to say it for fear I might be wrong.

"Yes, I am with child!"

Our household dynamic changed again over the next weeks as the physical realities of Devora's pregnancy soon made her too tired to carry on with her share of the work as before. My responsibilities increased even more a month later when Cherut announced that she was also with child.

When I told Elah how weary I was from rising early to collect manna every morning as well as fetch water, and spend time at the cooking fires on top of looking after Kenaz, he suggested that I get Cherut and Naam's children to help.

Raanan, their oldest, at seven, was keen to help gather the daily manna. But when five-year-old Enat discovered I planned to take him with me in the morning, she fussed until I promised to take her too — this despite concerns I had. Would they get along? I had heard them fighting often. The morning ended up being a trial to my patience but enlightening too.

"Let's see who can fill their basket the fastest," Raanan challenged when he had picked up the gist of what the task involved. A few minutes later I heard him cry out in protest, "Enat is stealing manna from me!"

When I stepped over to them to see what was happening, I caught Enat in the act of scooping a handful of the white rounds from his basket into hers. She looked up at me and giggled wickedly but Raanan, not amused, struck her hand. She lost her grip and the manna scattered onto the ground.

Her mirth quickly turned to anger and tears. "He did it!" she said, looking up at me for support.

"But you took it from his basket," I said evenly, trying to calm the fight. However, this only made Enat angrier. She stood up, propped her little fists on her hips, then stepped determinedly toward Raanan's basket and gave it a kick, sending the contents far and wide.

Raanan jumped to his feet and leaped at her, but the nimble five-year-old dashed away. Raanan gave chase, calling out, "You will be sorry. Mother will sacrifice you to the gods. You will burn in the arms of Moloch."

Raanan's words chilled me even more than the angry interaction I was witnessing. Where had they heard about child sacrifice? Who had been threatening them with talk of Moloch, the god of the Ammonites?

In the next weeks, I kept my eyes and ears open as I got to know the children better. It turned out they had more fears than just being sacrificed to an idol. They also tormented each other with stories of giants, the Anakim of Canaan, and seemed to have a special reverence for the sun, moon, and stars.

"But you don't need to fear any of those things," I told them. "We have a protector, our God Yahweh. He is nearby, in the glory cloud that covers the tabernacle."

"I don't like that cloud," Raanan announced. "It makes us move and walk a long way so that we get very hungry and thirsty."

"But it is much more than that," I told the children. "Through it God protects us from the hot sun and gives us light to travel in the nighttime. Once Yahweh even protected us from the Egyptians using the cloud. Let me tell you that story."

I told them about how the cloud separated the Egyptian army from us the night we crossed the Red Sea. "So, don't be afraid of the giants that you can't see," I concluded, "or the sun and moon who never hurt us. Instead, trust in Yahweh, the God of the cloud." [41]

* * *

After several weeks of spending time with her children and seeing abundant evidence of their fears, I decided to talk to Cherut. "Your children are terrified of being sacrificed to Moloch and captured by the Anakim," I said to her one day when we were alone. "Why?"

A wary look came into her eyes. "I may have mentioned something about these things but they hear them from their friends too," she said, her eyes downcast, refusing to meet mine.

"Do you still have fears about these things yourself?" I asked, putting my hand on her shoulder.

For a moment, her guarded expression softened and she looked at me with big eyes. "I can't help it," she said. "These gods of Canaan are real. I feel their presence even here within the camp. The sun and moon seem to command my reverence.

"As for the children, Raanan and Enat fight so often,

the only way I can make them stop is by scaring them with the worst fate I can think of."

"O Cherut," I said, "Yahweh of the cloud watches over us. You don't need to hang onto your fears of the Canaanite gods, their giants, or the sun and moon."

Then another idea struck me, as I recalled Bezalel's story of the fearful night of darkness in Egypt, where it wasn't until he took off his amulet that his fear left him. "You did get rid of all your Egyptian trinkets, didn't you?"

Cherut's eyes drifted from mine again, but her answer was instant and unequivocal. "Yes, I did."

* * *

Things were going well between Devora and Cherut until one morning when the children and I returned from gathering manna. As we entered the encampment I heard Devora's voice, calling out, with uncharacteristic sharpness, "Leave at once! And take that vile thing with you!"

I rushed into the tent in time to see the divider to Cherut and Naam's room move, as if someone had just entered.

I peeked into Devora and Caleb's room. Devora was there, lying on her mat visibly agitated and upset.

"Can I come in?" I asked. "What is it?"

Devora pointed a trembling finger toward Cherut and Naam's room. "She came in here with one of her vile Egyptian charms and started rattling it and chanting over me."

"What?"

"I asked her for her help, and what I should do because..." at this, the usually strong Devora burst into tears, "...this morning there was blood on the covers.

That is not a good sign when one is with child."

"And her response was to get one of her charms?" I asked, trying to reconstruct what happened.

"Yes," sobbed Devora. "I thought she had rid herself of all those things."

"So did I. In fact, she told me that she had. But back to you, how are you feeling now?"

"I have no pain," Devora said. "I feel fine besides being fearful that I will lose my child."

"Let's keep you still," I said, remembering how Sebia lost her little one after heavy exertion. "You will rest until the cloud moves us on. No work for you. And let's petition Yahweh to preserve your baby."

I knelt beside her, placed my hand on her rounded abdomen, closed my eyes, and whispered, "Great Yahweh, whose glory fills the cloud, please preserve this little life."

Cherut didn't join us for breakfast. After the morning chores were done, I went to her room and peeked inside. "May I come in?"

When she didn't answer, I slipped inside regardless and found her staring into space, her slim face red and puffy.

"What happened there?" I asked gently.

Cherut burst into tears. "I was only trying to help," she sobbed. "I didn't want Devora to lose her child so I did the best thing I knew."

"What did you do?"

"I charmed the room with this." Cherut looked at me defiantly as she reached for an object on the bed—an Egyptian artifact, shaped like an ankh, on a short pole. The arms of the ankh were held apart by metal rods on which were strung disks that rattled when moved. I recognized it as a sistrum, another object the Egyptians used in their religious celebrations.

"Where did you get that?" I asked. "How long have you had it? You told me just a few days ago that you had destroyed all your Egyptian charms!" My mind flashed back to the vague memory of Cherut coming into my room with something while I was in labour with Kenaz. Could it have been this?

"My mother gave it to me after you made me destroy everything else," Cherut said. "It's really hers."

"Cherut," I said firmly, "you can't keep this. We must rid our tent of it. Undoubtedly it is what keeps you and your children bound with premonitions and fears."

Terror filled Cherut's eyes as my words sunk in. "No," she said. "I must keep it until my child is born."

* * *

Later that day I told Elah what I had discovered and asked him what to do. "I can't bear the thought of that object in our tent," I said. "But neither do I want to sneak into Cherut's room and destroy it secretly."

He agreed. "We should tell Naam," he said. "If he doesn't know about this, he should. Perhaps he can talk her into getting rid of it or do the deed himself."

Elah told Naam, and a week later Naam assured him that the sistrum had been disposed of.

Thankfully Devora recovered. Her bleeding stopped and she cautiously resumed her former activities. But things didn't go so well with Cherut. A few days after Naam told us the fate of the sistrum, she failed to show up for the morning meal. When I checked on her, she was huddled on her mat.

"Something's not right," she said. "My back aches so much, as does my stomach."

I brought her food but she refused to eat, instead growing more restless as the day wore on.

"I have cramps like at my time of the month," she whimpered. "Where is my charm."

"It isn't here," said Naam, who had entered the room to be with her.

"What? It is. Under my clothes."

"No," Naam replied. "I ... I destroyed it."

"You what!" Cherut's eyes blazed at him, then she turned her back toward all of us in a curled-up ball of misery.

We called the midwife. Devora and I went in and out throughout the day to check on her. Late in the afternoon her cramps begin in earnest. That evening, just after the sun went down, she delivered a very tiny, lifeless little girl.

* * *

The six months that followed were filled with blessed hope for Devora and all of us as the child within her continued to grow. One morning she called me into her room. "I think my time of delivery is very near," she said.

That was expected, for she had carried her little one through all the moons of our calculations, and her belly looked like a seed pod about to burst.

"Shall I call the midwife?" I asked.

"No, not yet. But I'd like you to stay close. Your presence is so calming."

I pondered what she had said as I went about my tasks. Who would have thought that I could be a help and comfort to someone as wise as Devora? I remembered back to how I struggled as a new wife and again as a mother. How naïve was my girlhood ambition to be a leader of women like Miriam! It was difficult enough to lead my one little boy, and I'd failed miserably with Cherut, who remained cold and distant after her miscarriage. As for Merab, she was obviously above me in every category and would never be moved by anything I said or did. In the light of all this, Devora's words meant a lot to me.

Devora's instincts proved right. By midday she asked for the midwife and before sundown the cries of baby Achsah, "Adored," filled the tent. [42]

Late that night, the whole family shared the meal I had prepared, as Caleb's sons come to welcome their new baby sister. There was joy and laughter. "I believe we live with another Abraham and Sarah," Iru teased his father. Caleb, for his part, couldn't stop smiling.

Chapter Twenty-eight

Wandering

We were the last slave generation.
Set free from Egypt we wandered the wilderness.
Led by Moses and a cloud
that hid us from Pharaoh, who wanted us back in
his land,
God opened the sea — we passed His first test
of many that revealed the state of our hearts.

Hunger and thirst fatigued the hearts
of even our work-tough generation.
Trekking through barren wastes another test.
Wailed "Where is food and drink in this
wilderness?"
while dreaming of the leeks and garlics of Nile's
delta land,
a change from manna, no more demands of the
cloud.

Led to bitter Mara water by the cloud
We wailed the discontent of our restive hearts.
"Oh, for sweet water, the fruits and meats of Egypt
land!"
Yahweh sent quail — a whole generation
till we grew sick of meat in that wilderness
(every circumstance another test).

Then to Sinai, the test of all tests
where thunder rolled, lightning flashed from the
cloud.

Moses seemed to abandon us in this wilderness,
and Egypt again claimed the hearts
of our fickle generation
on that endless road to our own land.

Many died, never to see that land.
They failed the test.
We trekked on to Kadesh — our rebellious
generation
still following Moses and the cloud
with daily manna and water for our needs, but
hearts
that grumbled and complained in the wilderness.

Moses sent leaders from the wilderness
To spy out rich Canaan land.
They saw it full of people too huge and fierce for
our hearts.
Frozen with fear at this test
We refused to go in even with Yahweh's cloud
and so, doomed an entire generation.

Ruled by fearful hearts that failed faith's tests
we wandered behind the cloud in this barren land
until an entire generation had left bones in the
wilderness. [43]

Long Enough

You have skirted this mountain long enough
Led by day with a cloudy pillar
By night with a pillar of fire
On the road which you should travel.

Led by day with a cloudy pillar
God carried you as a man carries his son
On the road which you should travel

But you complained in your tents.

God carried you as a man carries his son
Through this land of deserts and pits.
But you complained in your tents
Of the drought and the shadow of death.

Through this land of deserts and pits
Where no one lives
Through drought and the shadow of death
In this wilderness that no one crosses

Where no one lives
I will bring you to a place I searched out for you.
Through this wilderness that no one crosses.
To a land flowing with milk and honey.

I will bring you to a place I searched out for you,
By night with a pillar of fire
To a land flowing with milk and honey
For you have skirted this mountain long enough. [44]

Part Three: Autumn

Chapter Twenty-nine

(Twenty years later)

Scouts had recognized landmarks. Word filtered back at the end of a long day of trekking on another one of our many moves. It seemed the cloud was leading us back to Kadesh Barnea.

The name stirred memories. It was there many years ago that Pallu pursued me, and I fell in love. There his family rebelled and the earth devoured them. There I fell ill and nearly died.

I scanned the surroundings as we trudged on. Would I recognize this place? Yes. There in the distance was the prominent rocky outcrop that characterized Kadesh. A chill went through me. The closer we got, the more I sensed that I had been here before.

The cloud halted over the place we had camped at the time of my youth. As we set up camp, memories of Pallu flooded back. I remembered how I met him in the manna fields and how he pursued me. I thought of the first time he kissed me and the short time we looked forward to setting up a home together in Canaan. The strength of my feelings, stirred up by these memories, surprised me.

* * *

A messenger came with news while we were eating breakfast the next morning. Miriam had died.

"She was ancient. How old was she?" Achsah, Caleb and Devora's daughter, now a beautiful young woman of twenty, asked.

"Around one hundred and thirty," Caleb said. "What a woman!"

Yes, what a woman, I thought, as I recalled the first time I saw her. Already past ninety, she had been full of zest, energy, and joy, as she led us woman with her timbrel in celebrating the Egyptian defeat in the Red Sea.

I remembered the day I had approached her — leprous and isolated — outside the camp. Even there she was dignified. I recalled again her words of blessing: "Yahweh bless you and keep you, my daughter. Yahweh smile on you and gift you. Yahweh look you full in the face and make you prosper."

How many times had I repeated those words to myself, wondering, would they come true? I recalled, with a rueful smile, how I had dreamed I would be gifted with Miriam's own spirit. Of course, that had never happened, for I had lived my whole life in oblivion, as a daughter, wife, mother, and aunt (not a grandmother yet, though Kenaz was old enough to wed). My timbrel had comforted only me and been a mere prop in telling the old stories to the little ones in our family — not a badge of leadership, like Miriam's was.

Somehow, she, with her fearless spirit, never seemed old to me. She was self-assured and unmoved by what others thought or said about her. How I admired her dignified air of conviction and aura of leadership. I had secretly hoped I would meet her again, even dreamed of getting to know her better. With her death that dream died too.

Now the sound of mourning filled the air as news of

Miriam's death spread through the camp. I joined the mourners to express the sadness I felt. [45]

* * *

"We need the water jugs refilled," I told Basmat the next morning as I worked at preparing the morning meal. (Basmat was the daughter-in-law of Naam and Cherut, the wife of their eldest son Raanan.)

"She'era fetched what she could yesterday," Basmat replied. (She'era was the wife of Lavi, Naam and Cherut's younger son.) "She said the springs are almost completely dried up."

"Yes," Cherut said. "Kadesh has changed since we were here last. Now there are just trickles where formerly there were springs. Even those grow less every day."

I had been so preoccupied reliving old memories that I hadn't noticed the changes Cherut and her daughters-in-law spoke of.

A short while later a messenger came by and interrupted our breakfast. "The people are gathering before Moses to deal with the water shortage."

We hurried to finish our meal, then joined the discontented crowd that milled around Moses and Aaron. The mood was ugly as people flung their dissatisfactions at our leaders.

"We're thirsty! The Kadesh streams have all dried up."

"Why are we here anyway? We'd been better off if we and our animals had died in the wilderness."

"Where are the grains and figs, the grapes and pomegranates you promised us? There isn't even water!"

Moses and Aaron listened to it all but instead of replying, headed toward the tabernacle and when they got there, entered the sacred space. The crowd that surged after them was stopped from physically accosting them only by the fence that separated the courtyard of the holy tent from the congregation.

Meanwhile, Moses and Aaron stood before the tabernacle entryway, and then I lost sight of them because of the crowd.

"What are they doing?" I asked Elah, who was standing on a rock from which he had a view above the masses.

"They are on their faces," he said. Even as he said it, I saw the cloud, that rested above the tabernacle, begin to glow.

I remembered the time, years ago, when it glowed at me, in answer to my prayer for a child. Now, though, its brightness far exceeded anything I'd seen in it for years as it moved from its place above the tabernacle to rest above where Moses and Aaron lay. Thunder rolled and stuttered from it.

At the thunder, people near the fence fell backward so that the crowd around us pressed even tighter. The glow of the cloud became so bright I could no longer look and closed my eyes against the light while the thunder grew louder. And then I heard from it words I could understand.

"Speak to the rock and it will give water. There will be water enough for the people and their animals."

The thunder stopped. Even though my eyes were closed, I sensed the brightness was dimming. When I opened my eyes, I saw that the cloud had returned to its customary spot above the tabernacle, and Moses and Aaron were back on their feet.

With his rod in hand, Moses left the tabernacle

enclosure. He strode toward the Kadesh rock. Elah grabbed my hand and we joined the crowd that followed close behind.

"Did you hear words?" I asked Elah."

"I think so," he said. "Something like, 'Speak to the rock and it will yield water.'"

"Me too. Will water come from the rock at Moses' command?"

"We'll have to wait and see," Elah said.

The crowd was thick around Moses and Aaron and we couldn't get much closer, so Elah helped me clamber to a rocky ledge from where we got a better view. More and more people gathered around. Then Moses addressed the crowd.

"Hear now, you rebels! Must we bring water for you out of this rock?" Then he turned and struck it with his rod.

Elah turned to me abruptly with a question on his face. I understood his confusion. Had we not heard the voice say he was to *speak* to the rock?

Meanwhile, water rushed out—a massive gush of it. People near the rock screamed and whooped. They scooped water with their hands, brought it to their mouths, and slurped it thirstily while it ran down their arms, onto their feet, making rivulets in the dusty earth.

A change in the light drew my attention back to the cloud. It had moved again and came to rest between Aaron and Moses, and the crowd. Again, thunder rumbled from its bright fiery centre. Yahweh? Speaking again?

I strained my ears to make out words in the rumbles, but this time I didn't understand. I looked up at Elah but he shook his head.

As we hurried home to fetch jugs to fill with water, I mulled over the sight of Moses striking the rock instead of speaking to it, as the voice had instructed him.

The river of water that erupted from the rock that day, came to be called Meribah—the Waters of Contention. [46]

* * *

We had been in Kadesh a couple of weeks when word came from Bezalel that father was not well. I fetched Elah and Kenaz and we rushed to his side.

I couldn't believe how weak and old he looked as he lay motionless, a still, bony figure under a blanket on his sleeping mat. He had managed just fine all these years since mother died, but now he appeared to be fading fast.

We surrounded his mat, Bezalel, Sebia and their grown children, Elah, Kenaz and I, helplessly watching him struggle for breath. His breathing grew more and more shallow as time passed. And then, surprisingly, he opened his eyes and looked up into all our faces. A smile lit his face, he raised his weathered, gnarled hands, and in a surprisingly strong voice said, "Yahweh bless you and keep you, Yahweh make His face shine upon you and give you rest."

His hands fell to the covers then, he closed his eyes again, took one more shuddering breath—and was gone.

* * *

Caleb joined Elah and me at the fire the next day in the evening. It had been a stressful, sad day of mourning, burying father, and helping Bezalel and Sebia host all the mourners who came to comfort us. Now I felt exhausted and sad.

For a long while we all sat in silence. At last Caleb said, "He was a good man, a supporter of Moses. Still he had to die." Looking at me, he reminded me again of Moses' prophecy. "You are not alone in experiencing the death of someone you love. Have you noticed how many have been dying lately? When we returned from spying the land, those many years ago, Yahweh told Moses that all the warriors counted in the census before we left Sinai would die before we entered the Promised Land. The many deaths mean that our time of entering Canaan is drawing near!"

* * *

A few days later Caleb came home with news.

"Moses has sent messengers to the king of Edom to get permission for us to pass through his kingdom. That will bring us to within a short distance from Canaan."

"How soon will they return?" Devora asked.

"It shouldn't be long. And I expect they'll be successful. The Edomites are our distant relatives, after all—descendants of Esau the twin brother of our patriarch Jacob.

But a week later, Caleb returned home, looking disturbed.

"The king of Edom has turned us down," he said. "Even after Moses offered to pay for every bit of food and water we consume. He's asking again, though. We discussed what to do at the council. Someone suggested we promise to stick to the road as well as pay for all we use. Hopefully that will reassure him."

* * *

I began daydreaming of Canaan again—a much different dream than I had had all those years ago, when

Moses sent out the spies. Then my dream was all about Pallu. Now it was more realistic. It included a farm and grazing pastures for Elah's enlarged flock and a house big enough for Kenaz, the wife we hoped to find for him, and all their children.

I was mending the tent and preoccupied with my sweet imaginings a few days later, when I heard a ruckus. I peeked outside to see a messenger run past. He shouted out as he ran, "To your tents. We're being attacked!"

A few minutes later She'era arrived with all the children in tow, and then Basmat came with laundry still dripping.

"What is it, do you suppose?" I asked Cherut, who stood watch at the tent opening.

The sound of angry voices and the clanging of armour grew ever louder, and then I heard the nearby tramp of many footsteps. Cherut hastily pulled the tent opening tight and shrank back. "Warriors. Foreigners. They're pursuing the messenger!"

The sounds soon grew fainter and I took a deep breath. We spent the remainder of the afternoon huddled in the tent, waiting for news. "Do you think the men are okay?" Cherut asked anxiously.

"I hear no sound of battle," Devora reassured her.

Elah was the first of our household's men to return. "Edom refused to let us travel through their land— again. And to make it really clear, their king sent fighters to support his decision."

Caleb, who entered while Elah was talking, continued the story. "They confronted Moses and he reassured them we would not pass through Edom."

"Where will we go, then?" asked Devora, who was

anticipating the thought of a settled home along with the rest of us.

"Yahweh will lead us another way," Caleb assured her.

How much longer would that take, I wondered. [47]

* * *

"I expect we may break camp soon," Caleb announced the next morning. "I'm sure we'll be moving toward the Promised Land shortly, using another route."

Caleb's words reminded me that I still hadn't done what I felt I needed to do — find the place where Pallu and his family were buried, say goodbye, and put that part of my life behind me forever. If we'd be moving soon, I'd better not delay.

After the chores were done and the tent tidied, I gave in to the tug in my heart to find the spot where Pallu had died.

Achsah, restless and eager for any diversion, sidled up to me as I left the encampment. "Can I join you, Zamri?" At any other time, I would have welcomed her company but not today. I smiled at her, but shook my head. For once she didn't argue.

I wandered the outskirts of the camp, to a place with a bluff, where I recalled the tents of Reuben had been pitched. And then it hit me. I was on the exact spot where I had stood and watched the horrific scene those many years ago. I scrambled down to the valley below where I had seen the earth cover Pallu and his family, and sank to my knees under the heavy thought that Pallu's bones were somewhere below where I knelt.

A rush of grief flooded my eyes. "Oh Pallu," I murmured, and wept soundlessly, ignoring the tears that ran down my face, dropping from my chin onto the dry earth. I lost track of time as I relived my relationship with him and let grief have its way.

Then I heard the chittering of disturbed rocks and the pad of footsteps. A minute later Elah was by my side.

"What are you doing here?" he asked. Then, seeing my tear-stained face, "Are you alright?"

"Yes," I said, as he gave me his hand to help me to my feet. "I was just remembering something from when we last camped here."

"Here? What is this place?" Elah looked around, puzzled. "This was part of our camp," he recalled. "But Judah's tents weren't here. This would have been the site of the Levites, or Reuben." Then looking hard at me, "What did you have to do with this place?"

"I don't want to talk about it," I said. "Let's go home."

"But I want to know," Elah said, grabbing my hand.

I didn't want to tell him specifics about Pallu. I feared they would upset him even more than the shortened version I had told him years earlier. But he kept insisting. "We don't go back till you've told me what's troubling you."

Seeing no way out, I finally told him everything—how it was Pallu, son of Abiram of Reuben who pursued me and won my heart, asked for my hand in betrothal, was turned down by my parents, then swallowed by the earth with his family.

"Did you care for him?" Elah asked.

I was silent. "Well, did you?" Elah asked again.

"Yes," I whispered.

He looked shattered. I hastened to add, "Not in the way I care for you, but I did love him in my 16-year-old way."

Elah didn't say anything to that, just released my

hand. Without another word, we started toward our tent. How would this change things between us, I wondered? Knowing him, I was sure it would.

* * *

The trumpet sounded its signal to move on the next morning just as the family gathered around the morning meal. Like we had scores of times before, each one of us had to abandon any plans we had made. I had hoped to finish mending the tent. That would have to wait till later.

We hurried with our meal then began to pack. As I supervised the kitchen take-down, I kept an eye out for Elah. When he arrived with his flock, he glanced at me but when our eyes met he quickly looked away. No customary wink or even encouraging grin this morning. The way he avoided me confirmed that my revelations from yesterday had put up a wall between us. So much for Devora's assurances that my total honesty would improve things.

I walked with Devora and Cherut as we began our trek, not wanting to face Elah's cold silence.

* * *

One long day's walk brought us to a mountainous area. The cloud stopped over one peak. "This is Mount Hor," Father Caleb told us. "We passed by it years ago on our spy journey."

As the men set up the tent, Elah studiously avoided me. It irked me how troubled I was by this. We were mature adults, after all, old enough to be grandparents. How could a relationship, that had weathered so many years, change overnight?

The morning after we arrived at Mount Hor, a

trumpet blast called us to an assembly. We hurried through our morning routine and shortly joined the crowd that was making its way to Moses.

He stood at the camp's edge on a flat elevation at the foot of the mountain together with Aaron who was dressed in his finest priestly robes. Aaron's son Eleazar stood with them.

"Yahweh has spoken," Moses called out. A hush fell over the crowd. "He has told us to go up the mountain in view of you, the congregation. Stay here till we return."

Then Moses, Aaron, and Eleazar began to climb a footpath up the mountain.

I found myself beside Elah. "What will he do?" I asked.

"I don't know," he answered curtly, then turned away, ending the conversation.

I left his side to find Devora and the other women of our household and wait with them. One hour passed, and then another as the crowd lingered, with amazing patience, at the spot where Moses had left us. Then someone called out, "They're returning."

I strained my eyes to see but counted only two men picking their way down the steep path. There was Moses and one priest who looked like Aaron. But as they came closer, I saw that the man wearing the high priest's clothes was not Aaron but his son Eleazar. What had they done with Aaron?

Moses and Eleazar ascended the rocky ledge again. This time Moses didn't have to hush the crowd or ask for their attention, for all eyes were on him and the priest at his side.

"Yahweh told me to take Aaron and Eleazar up

Mount Hor this morning and there clothe Eleazar with his father's garments. I took the priestly robe off Aaron and put them on his son. No sooner had we done that than he collapsed, his breath left him, and he died."

From somewhere the keening and wailing began. I joined my family on the walk back to our tent, feeling sobered and saddened by another death. [48]

Chapter Thirty

A trumpet blast pierced the cool morning. It was a summons for the army to gather. Achsah, who was helping me prepare the meal asked, "What's that?"

"It's the signal for the men to gather for battle," I said. "I can't remember the last time I've heard that sound — it's been so long."

A few minutes later, Naam, Raanan, Lavi, Elah, and Kenaz, along with Father Caleb were bolting their food. Father Caleb looked excited at the prospect of action. It had been a long thirty days of respectful mourning the death of Aaron. Inaction was foreign to his nature.

I watched Elah, willing him to look at me and smile reassurance in the way he formerly did. But he avoided my gaze. When he went to our room to fetch his battle gear, I followed him, watching as he rummaged for his belt and sword. "You take care of yourself," I said, grasping his arm and giving it a squeeze as he went by.

"I will," he said. His eyes met mine ever so briefly but there was no softness in them.

After the men left, we settled down to wait. The tent felt crowded with the children underfoot, but we dared not let them play outside as usual for we had no idea what the threat was or how nearby it might be. I took my spinning shuttle and the bag of collected goat hair and began spinning it into yarn. Devora joined me.

"What do you think it is?" I asked.

"Could be any number of things," she replied. "I vaguely recall the last time we were here, how the Canaanites and Amalekites attacked. My memory is clouded, though, shocked as I was by my husband's death.

"Yahweh was not with our army, then, though, as I recall" she continued. "It was after the spies turned the congregation against Moses. When they refused to go into the land and Moses told them they would be wandering for many years they changed their minds and decided to go and fight after all. Remember?"

Her memories transported me back to that tumultuous time—the days after father turned down Pallu. I recalled how he met me in the manna field and told me that the people were going out to fight after all. Then our army was utterly defeated. Would this battle turn out the same way? [49]

* * *

Several hours later, our men returned. Father Caleb explained the situation. The Canaanite King Arad had attacked our camp and taken men captive. Moses wasn't sure what to do. He was seeking Yahweh's mind. The command to the army was to be prepared for battle if that was what Yahweh commanded. All the men of fighting age were to be on the alert and ready.

"Do you have to go?" Devora asked Caleb. "Aren't you past the age of conscription?"

Caleb looked at her, his eyes big with surprise. "What? Miss this? Never! I have been waiting many years to conquer these peoples."

"Will you volunteer?" I asked Elah that night when we were preparing for bed.

"Oh yes," he said.

"What about your animals?" I asked. "Who will care for them?"

"You know what to do for them," he said.

I voiced the concern that weighed heavily on my mind. "What if you are hurt or killed?"

"You will get along just fine," he said. There was a cold edge to his voice.

* * *

No one was surprised by the battle summons next morning. Our men joined their fellow shepherds-turned-warriors streaming through the camp to the army's meeting place.

In the days that followed we went through our routines of caring for the animals, gathering manna, fetching water, minding the children, and waiting for news. Often, I scanned the distant horizon. Were our men successful or routed again?

At sundown three days later a messenger arrived. Our army had triumphed! They had completely destroyed the Canaanite settlements in the area, as Yahweh told them to. And not one of our men was hurt or killed.

When Caleb arrived back the next day, he was ecstatic over the strength of Israel's novice fighters. "Most of them are so young. Only a few of these soldiers have survived from former battles. Most have never been to war, yet they fight like trained soldiers. It is a miracle!" [50]

* * *

We moved again, trekking over sand and through thorny wasteland, finding pathways between jagged outcrops.

"I thought you said we were near the Promised Land, " Achsah complained to her father. "It seems like we're traveling away from it."

"The King of Edom refused to let us cut through their territory," Father Caleb reminded her. "And since we've fought King Arad, the people of the land are more fearful of us than ever. We will get to the Promised Land eventually, even if it is in a roundabout way."

"I'm so tired," I heard She'era whimper. Poor thing, she was with child so I walked beside her, letting her lean on me for support as we trudged on, and on, and on.

Even mealtimes were a trial.

"I'm sick of manna cakes," Cherut muttered. "I was so looking forward to the grains and fruits of Canaan. I wish I never saw another manna cake again."

As main cook for our household now, her complaints annoyed me. "Do you have a better way to prepare it? You're welcome to take over the cooking," I said.

Day after day the tone of the camp deteriorated. All of us were under a pall of discouragement and dissatisfaction. Complaining was everywhere.

"Yahweh is against us."

"We need a leader to replace Moses."

"Oh, for an end to this detestable manna."

"No water—again!"

"Why are we here? Even Egypt was better than this. We should go back."

* * *

On one day that began like so many others, packing up camp in the cool of the morning and moving on through the increasing heat of the day, at one of our rest stops someone's scream pierced the air. "What could that be?" we asked each other.

Father Caleb went to investigate and soon returned.

"Some of the people have disturbed a den of snakes and been bitten."

No sooner had he told us this than we heard the wailing begin—the keening cry of mourning. Had someone died? From snakebite? If so, these snakes were deadly. I was relieved when we left that spot. Who wanted to camp near snakes?

We trudged on through the day, stopping at last near sundown when the cloud halted. But no sooner had we begun to set up camp than we heard more shrieks. Had the snakes followed us?

In our tent we lifted every cushion, blanket, piece of clothing, and stick of wood with trepidation, careful to check for the poisonous creatures.

Outside, the shrieks of terror and wails of death grew louder and more frequent.

"This is beyond too much!" Cherut declared.

* * *

The cloud stayed still for several days. They were spent dealing with our latest plague. All day and long into the night, screams of terror and wails of mourning filled the air. Many died.

So far, though, no one from our tent had been bitten. We credited that to our vigilance. Cherut helped her daughters-in-law watch their little ones while Devora and I went out to help surrounding families in need. We prepared food, and comforted and consoled bereaved neighbours.

As the situation worsened and more and more were bitten and died, a wave of introspection washed over the camp. Several times a day, people asked us, "Why is this happening?"

At home, we quizzed Father Caleb about how we

should answer. He paused in long silence, then replied with a question of his own. "What was the reason Yahweh sent plagues of illness and death on us before? Was it not for disobedience, grumbling, and criticizing our leaders?

I hadn't thought of the plagues in this light before.

The next day Father Caleb returned home in the late evening, looking happier than he had in a while. "I have convinced them to take action," he said. "We as leaders will go to Moses tomorrow and, as representatives of our people, repent of our grumbling, complaining, and criticism. Maybe then Yahweh will send the snakes away."

Father Caleb returned before noon the next day. "Moses was grateful for our delegation," he said. "He took our request to Yahweh, and Yahweh answered. Moses is sending for Bezalel to cast a metal snake, which he will set high on a pole visible to the whole camp. After the statue is up, whoever is bitten and looks at the snake will be healed."

"Just looking at a snake statue will cure them?" Cherut asked, incredulous. "How will that work?"

"If Yahweh commands it, it will work." The certainty in Father Caleb's voice didn't leave room for any more questions.

* * *

Cherut's scream in the dark of night wakened me with a jolt.

"You'd best see what's wrong," Elah, also awakened, said to me.

I went to Naam and Cherut's room to find Naam leaning over his wife. Devora was there too. We watched in horror as Cherut writhed in pain.

"I've been bitten," she wailed. Her eyes were full of terror.

"Where?" Naam asked.

Cherut lifted her tunic to reveal a red welt on her calf that enlarged, thickened, and darkened before our eyes.

As Naam scrambled to locate the serpent, Devora ordered, ""Make up a poultice, quick and fetch her water to drink."

I ran to mix the poultice, returned with it and helped Devora as we did all we could to counteract the venom. Before we knew it, it was daylight and time to begin the day's activities.

As I prepared the cooking fire outside the tent, I saw, in the distance, workmen, already busy, raising the cast metal serpent onto a pole.

After everyone had eaten, I went to check on Cherut and was shocked by what I saw. She was surrounded by trinkets—Egyptian amulets depicting Hathor and the ankh symbol of life, a variety of gold and faience earrings, necklaces, and armbands.

"What's this?" I ask. "Where did these come from?"

Naam, who sat beside her looked at me sheepishly. "She begged me to get them. I found them hidden amongst her clothes."

Cherut looked at me, fear in her fever-crazed eyes, as she hugged her collection close to her. "You can't take them or I will die."

"No, no," I said gently. "I don't want them. But they won't save you."

"Yes, they will," she said, defiance in her eyes.

Devora came in and all three of us tried to settle her with soothing words and distractions. "The brass serpent is up. Look to it. Moses promises it will save."

But Cherut just turned her back to us and curled up tighter, clutching her treasures.

* * *

All day I was in and out of Cherut's room, bringing her drinks of water, bathing her hot head, and begging, "Cherut, please look at the serpent. All you need to do is look. It will soon grow dark. Look before sunset."

Naam, who hadn't left her side all day, begged her too. But she adamantly refused. "If I look, my charms will lose all their power. Then what help will I have?"

"How much power have they showed you up till now?" I asked.

The long day wore on. Naam left to help with the flock. I kept an eye on Cherut. She seemed worse every time I looked in on her.

And then, just as the sun was about to dip below the horizon, I heard her weak call. I rushed to her side, afraid of what I would find.

"I'm ready," she whispered. "I will look."

I helped her to sit, then stand, and supported her as she walked, unsteady and trembling, to the tent entrance. I pulled it back and pointed to the pole. The brass snake on top of it glowed orange-red as it caught the rays of the setting sun. "There. Look up there."

Cherut looked. The instant she did, I felt a change in her body—a return of vigor and energy.

She looked at me amazed. "It's gone. The pain and fever. I can't believe it!" She was trembling, but now it was with tears of relief and joy. We stood gazing at the snake for a long time until the evening darkness faded it from view.

"Now you will live," I said, giving her shoulders a squeeze with my supporting arm.

She turned to me, her face aglow through her tears. "Yes, I will." Then she walked, unaided, back to her room.

"What caused you to change your mind?" I asked.

"It was a dream I had," she answered. "After you and Naam left, I fell asleep again and dreamt that the cloud that hovers over the tabernacle moved till it rested over the snake. I watched it stop there. As I looked at it, a great sense of peace, well-being, and joy came over me. When I awoke, I knew I would live if I looked.

"Help me get rid of these," she continued as she gathered her collection of charms and amulets into her robe.

"Where did you get so many?" I asked.

"More from my mother," she said. "I found her collection after she died. I loved them but hated them too. It felt like they owned me in some way."

"But not anymore?"

"No. No more. I owe my life to Yahweh of the cloud and the brass serpent. From now on I will be forever free from the gods of Egypt."

She tossed the last gold trinket into the pile and tied her cloak into a knot. Then, with a mischievous twinkle in her eye, she looked at me and said, "Now, I know just what I need to give me the strength to take these outside the camp. A couple of your manna cakes." [51]

Chapter Thirty-one

The snakes were behind us and we were on the move again. The atmosphere in the camp was much improved, perhaps because the loudest complainers had perished during the poisonous plague. It also helped that we were traveling new territory.

We spent a couple of nights in Oboth, then it was on to Ije Abarim and a rest in the Valley of Zered. The Arnon River, our next obstacle, was just a trickle. We crossed it easily, by foot, into the land of the Amorites. There the cloud halted us and Moses gathered the congregation at an ancient well where there was water in abundance.

The joy of water inspired someone in the crowd to break out in song — a catchy tune with words that played in my head till after my day's work was done and I had time to dig out my timbrel and try singing it at the campfire.

"Spring up O well!
All of you sing to it —
The well the leaders sank,
Dug by the nation's nobles,
By the lawgiver, with their staves."

The little ones in the family joined me in the song and soon Cherut, Devora, Caleb, and Naam were singing along. But not Elah. He sat a distance from the fire, his face in shadow, looking on glumly. [52]

* * *

We soon moved again, with each day of travel bringing us to a new campsite. The final hours of one night's travel were a climb into mountains. The Pisgah Mountains, Father Caleb told us. We were exhausted when the fiery cloud finally halted and we could stop and pitch our tents.

We had arrived in the dark, so I was unprepared for the sight that met my eyes when I left the tent the next morning. We were camping high above hills and valleys that stretched as far as the eye could see. In the rose-colored light of early morning, it was beautiful, but also terrifying. What was ahead in the rugged terrain that lay before us?

No trumpet blast commanded us to break camp and move on during breakfast that morning. The men left immediately after eating, Elah and Naam to tend their animals, Father Caleb to meet with the other leaders. When he returned some hours later, he was bursting with excitement.

"Moses is sending more messengers, this time to Sihon, king of the Amorites. He's asking permission for us to travel the king's highway through their territory."

"Does anyone live here?" I asked, recalling the desolate scene I had witnessed in the morning.

"Oh yes. There are settlements scattered all along the highway that leads to the main town of Heshbon."

"Do you think their king will give permission?" asked Devora. "We haven't been too successful with these permissions up till now."

"We need to try. Moses has stipulated that we'll stay on the road and refrain from raiding the surrounding vineyards and fields, or drinking from their wells."

In the days that followed there was tension in the

camp as we waited for the return of the messengers. Perhaps anticipating a "No," Joshua was training our army while we waited.

Elah, his brothers, and Caleb of course, among the oldest soldiers, were part of an extra force. They didn't need to go to drills as regularly as the young men—Kenaz, Raanan, and Lavi. This battle preparation drove home the uncomfortable reality of what I now needed to face again. Our longed-for hope of living in the Promised Land would not come about without warfare.

When the messengers from Sihon returned a few days later, the news was bad. Sihon had refused to give us permission to travel the King's Highway. Even now, the messengers warned, a fighting force of Amorites was coming against us. [53]

* * *

In the days that followed, my fears for our army proved groundless. When the Amorites came against us, our men faced them bravely and won stunning victories. They razed every village around Heshbon, destroyed Heshbon itself, and completely defeated King Sihon. Jubilation replaced fear in the camp.

We moved our tents from the desert to the unscorched areas in the conquered towns to be near water and to look through the rubble for whatever we could find that was useful.

"Grandmother, look what I found!" Cherut's five-year-old granddaughter, little Rebecca, came rushing into the tent one morning with a gold figure in her hands. She had obviously found the figure she was holding when she and her mother Basmat were rummaging through the debris.

"What is it dearie?" Cherut bent down to take a look

at the find, while Basmat looked on. All eyes in the tent went to the figure and it was only when Cherut staggered up, nearly falling, that I noticed that she had grown sickly pale.

I rushed to her side and helped her to a cushion. "Are you okay? What happened? Did you stand up too quickly?"

"No," she whispered, her eyes wide with fear. "It's that thing Rebecca found." In the weeks since Cherut had placed her confidence in Yahweh, the old look of fear had left her eyes. Now it was back.

Little Rebecca, still holding the gold figure, looked surprised at her grandmother's reaction. I went over to Rebecca. "Can I have a look?" I asked.

"No!" she said, clutching it.

"Let Auntie look," Basmat said, prying Rebecca's clinging fingers from the figurine.

I took the golden object and examined it. It was a brass figure on a throne. It had the horned head of a cow, the body of a man with arms held outstretched — a heathen idol to be sure. I squatted down beside Rebecca. "This isn't a toy, sweetheart," I said gently.

"No, it isn't" chimed in Cherut, who had regained her composure. "It's the Moabite idol Moloch. We don't want him anywhere near us. The Moabites build huge statues of him that look like this. They light a fire in the space under his throne, then put their babies and children into the idol's red-hot arms. They sacrifice their children to it so they and their crops will be blessed."

A shudder went through the tent as she described the practice.

"How do you know these things?" Devora asked.

"My mother. She was interested in everything to do

with religion. She knew all about the Egyptian gods and was learning all she could about the gods of Canaan."

Meanwhile, Rebecca pulled at the figure in my hand, and when I didn't let it go, she stamped her little foot. "It's mine! I want it back."

Cherut vehemently shook her head. "No sweetie, you don't want it. This is not a toy. It may be shiny and pretty but it is not a good thing."

Rebecca began to cry. Basmat took her in her arms to comfort her and in the general confusion, I passed the idol to Devora, who wrapped it in her cloak. Later, we found a pile of still smouldering rubble from the city's razing and tossed the idol into it.

I was relieved when, the next morning, a trumpet blast signaled that it was time to move from that place.[54]

* * *

Fearful rumours circulated as we pressed on, following the cloud. We were approaching Bashan, the land of giants. They were threatening to come out against us. Caleb, though, seemed unperturbed. "I hope it's true!" he said, seeming to relish the prospect of meeting them.

He didn't have long to wait. Early on our second day of travel from Heshbon, the trumpet blast sounded a signal to the army to assemble for battle.

It was Elah's turn to serve. I bid farewell to him with a heavy heart, wishing things between us were like they had been before he found out about Pallu. But all my attempts at restoring our relationship had gone nowhere. I felt old and powerless.

Now he allowed me to cling to him as I said my goodbyes. "Take care of yourself," I whispered. "You must come back to us."

"Oh, I will," he said nonchalantly, giving his shoulders a subtle shake as if to loosen my grip. After he left I went to our room and cried. Why was I formerly so blind to what I had in him but never fully appreciated? It was something I would give anything to have again.

As the army left the camp, tension again gripped us. How would our young, unskilled soldiers fare against the warrior giants of Bashan? Only Devora seemed at peace. I could almost hear Caleb's voice as she encouraged us. "With Yahweh's help, our men will overcome these giants. They are well able to overcome them. They will be bread for our army, With Yahweh on our side, they have no protection. It is time for us to take possession of the land."

"I wish I had your confidence," Cherut said.

"It's not foolishly placed," Devora replied, a note of defensiveness in her voice. "Think of all the times Yahweh has helped us in the past. Have you forgotten our victory over King Sihon?"

Her words echoed in my mind as I reminisced over the last thirty-nine years. So many battles we never should have won but did when we went forward at Yahweh's word. As I reviewed how He had been with us, the fear within me dissipated.

* * *

The warriors returned—Elah and Kenaz with them—victorious! They were in the last group to arrive with the spoils of battle—a huge herd of sheep and goats. Elah could now add some of these to his own flock. He looked happy.

Our family gathered around the fire that night to hear the stories.

"Chieftain Og and his army came against us and we battled near Edrei," Caleb said. "He, his many sons, and a host of men advanced on us. But as we approached them, they became confused. In the end, they were an easy prey for us—and we didn't lose a single life!"

"Were they really giants?" Achsah asked.

"Oh yes," Naam replied. "In the rubble of Edrei someone found the chief's bed and measured it at nine cubits long and four cubits wide.

"We didn't just destroy Edrei," Caleb continued. "We went through the region and did a thorough job. Their cities were walled and fortified but we were able to take them with the help of Yahweh! We burned sixty settlements in all. The whole territory of Argob is conquered"

"But we were allowed to keep the spoils—the sheep and goats!" Kenaz said, raising his fist in a victory pump.

"What about the people," Devora asked.

"We destroyed them too—except for some of the young girls. Our men have brought some of them back to camp."

I looked over at my men, Elah and Kenaz. Were they tempted? Their facial expressions told me nothing, but somehow this news troubled me more than I cared to admit. [55]

* * *

The spirit in the camp was jubilant after our victory over Og. The trumpet blast that told us to pack up and move on intensified the excitement.

The cloud stopped after a few days of travel, coming to rest over a vast plain. Here there was plenty of room to set up our tents on level ground. Just beyond our camp was the swift-flowing Jordan River.

Caleb's spirits were especially high. "We're about to enter Canaan at last." Pointing to the waterway, "That is the Jordan and just across is the city of Jericho. Yahweh has been with us in the battles we've just won. I can't wait to now take possession of the land I spied out all those years ago."

No sooner were we settled in our new camp spot—the Plains of Moab—than word came from my family. Bezalel had died. My heavy heart grew even heavier when Elah said he couldn't go with me to mourn because of an emergency in his flock. So Achsah and Devora accompanied me through the tents of Judah. We heard the wailing of the mourners when we were still a great way off.

When I arrived, my brother was already wrapped for burial. As I knelt beside his still form, memories flooded over me. I remembered the clay doll he had made for me when I was five and we were still in Egypt. I remembered the night we huddled together, after walking across the Red Sea, and then, in the morning, watched the Egyptians and their chariots perish in the rising water. I remembered how he warned me in his gentle, big-brother way, when I wanted to marry Pallu.

I had brought with me the beautiful timbrel he had made with his skilled hands. I held it silent under my cloak as I gazed at the motionless bump under the death wrappings—all that was left of those hands, now forever still. Sebia came over, knelt beside me, put her arm around me and we wept together.

* * *

Our new camp spot on the plains of Moab was spacious and pleasant. Now that the day-to-day tasks in our household were spread amongst Devora, Achsah,

Cherut, her daughters-in-law, and me, I had plenty of time to spend away from the tent. In the past I would have sought out Elah and enjoyed the idle hours with him and his flocks. But his coldness toward me made that impossible, so I walked by myself or with the children.

One day little Rebecca and I headed toward the gentle hills that surrounded the camp. We found a footpath and made our way up, till we came to a wide-open space. From that vantage point we looked down on our tents, row upon orderly row of dark goat-hair structures, broken by walkways between tribes. The camping areas of the tribes were marked with banners. It was an awe-inspiring and beautiful sight! It impressed me again with how large a company we were.

"Look Rebecca," I said. "That's where we live"

"Where's our tent? Can we see our tent?"

"Look for the standard of Judah," I told her. "It's the flag with the lion on it. Our tent is just a little to the right of it."

She peered into the distance. "I see the flag. And I think I know which is our tent." She waved and called out, "See me, Mother!"

"I don't think she can see you from here," I told her, with a chuckle.

"What is that cloud in the middle?" Rebecca asked, pointing to the cloud that rested over the tabernacle.

"That's where the Holy One, our God Yahweh lives," I told her. "It covers the tabernacle, a special tent. Inside it is beautiful gold furniture. It was made by my brother, Uncle Bezalel.

"And do you see the middle flag on this side, between us and the tabernacle? That is the flag of

Reuben, the tribe your Grandmother Cherut comes from."

As I went on to point out more flags and named the tribes to which they belonged, I detected movement high on the hillside. I turned to look. Rebecca did too. Together we watched as a procession of richly saddled camels and donkeys wound their way up the hill.

"Who is that?" Rebecca asked.

"I don't know. It looks like the parade of a prince or king, doesn't it?"

I kept my voice nonchalant, but the sight of the retinue unnerved me. It had seemed to me we were camped well away from the eyes of the land's inhabitants. But now that I had seen what a large company we were, and how visible, the sight of this princely procession felt threatening.

"Can we go and see them?" Rebecca asked.

"No," I answered. "I think we'd better head back to camp." [56]

Chapter Thirty-two

"Where is Kenaz?" Caleb asked one evening as we sat around the fire. "This is the third night he has not been with us here."

"He's a grown man, father, and comes and goes as he likes," Elah answered.

I was not surprised by Elah's answer. I had mentioned the matter of Kenaz's evening absences to Elah myself several days earlier but, as he was wont to do these days, he brushed me off, then turned his back to me and went to sleep.

Thankfully, Caleb didn't pursue the issue of Kenaz's absence now. Instead, his eyes swept the rest of the family, taking stock of everyone else sitting around our evening blaze.

* * *

Next morning Basmat and Achsah returned from collecting our supply of manna with news. "Another plague has struck. Young men are falling sick everywhere."

I mulled this over as I prepared our morning meal. In the past, plagues had often come as a result of rebellion or grumbling. Could such a thing be present again?

And how disappointing, to have to deal with plague, and probably deaths and a depletion of our numbers. It was especially serious that it was the young men who were dying—just as we were on the border of the Promised Land and needed a strong army.

We had just gathered to eat, a few minutes later,

when a single trumpet blast interrupted our breakfast. It was the summons for leaders to gather. Father Caleb ate quickly, then threw on his robe and left.

When he returned, he looked grim. All day he was quiet and seemed preoccupied. At the evening meal, he requested that all the family be present around the fire that night, and sent Achsah to tell Iru and Merab to join us. After the tent was tidied and our mats readied for sleep, we joined Father Caleb. He stared moodily into the fire.

"What is this about?" Merab asked Cherut.

"Father Caleb was called with other leaders to meet with Moses today. I think this has something to do with what they discussed."

After we were all seated, the firelight dimly illuminating the circle of questioning faces, Father Caleb began. "Moses called us leaders and judges together today to talk about the plague that has broken out and what is behind it. There are some among us who have been accepting invitations to join the people of the land at their temples and shrines. They are enticing us to not only watch but participate. Some of us have joined in, even to the extent of coming together with their temple prostitutes."

The crackle of the fire was the only sound that interrupted the tense silence. I felt a strange fear over what might be coming next.

"Yahweh looks on this seriously," Caleb continued. "When we join ourselves in physical intimacy with these Baal worshipers, we join ourselves to Baal. And we know the commandment—to worship Yahweh alone. That is why this plague has broken out. Yahweh has withdrawn His protection from these young men.

"Now, Moses has asked us leaders and judges to help purge this sin from our own camps. Everyone who has had relations with a Baal prostitute in this way must be dealt with. Tonight, it is with a heavy heart that I begin my job by examining my own family. Have any of you participated in this?"

As Caleb spoke, fear in me grew. Is this what Kenaz had been up to the last while? Was he involved? And what about Elah, who had defended him? Did Elah know about this? Was he covering up the sins of our son?

Caleb's gaze moved around the circle, probing each male family member in turn. My heart pounded madly as he peered at Elah. To Caleb's questioning gaze, Elah responded with a vigorous shake of his head.

Then Caleb's eyes rested on Kenaz.

His voice was firm as he responded, "No, I have not done this." However, the wave of relief I felt was quickly replaced with apprehension as he continued, "But I knew this was going on."

* * *

The next days were filled with grief and mayhem as the plague continued. The men guilty of joining the Moabites at their religious rites were gathered by Moses and put to death, their bodies left under the hot sun. The sight and smell were another grim reminder that we disobeyed Yahweh at great peril.

A pall hung over the camp. With Caleb involved in judging the idolaters, that heaviness also filled our tent.

Devora announced she was gathering with others at the tabernacle in repentance and prayers to plead with Yahweh to stop the plague. I willingly joined her and hundreds more around the tabernacle.

Here, kneeling under Yahweh's cloud, our camp's idolatry seemed more serious even than when Father Caleb spoke to us. And it seemed unexplainable. Why would someone leave our holy God to serve images? And, I asked myself, to what extent was Kenaz involved in this and how much did Elah know and not tell me? Was my husband tempted to do this too? His distance and coldness toward me continued. But what could I have done differently, after all this time, but tell him the truth? It was all so confusing. My tears were pleading prayers for Kenaz, for Elah, for myself, and for our troubled marriage.

A shout from the crowd cut into my petitioning. I opened my eyes to see people pointing toward the tabernacle. There, an Israelite man was leading a beautiful woman by the hand through the tabernacle courtyard. She was dressed in the colourfully embroidered robes of the Moabites, her arms jangling with gold bracelets. Right before our eyes the man shoved aside the curtain to the Holy Place and they entered it.

Devora saw it too. We exchanged looks of alarm. "Is he one of the priests?" I asked. "What is he doing, bringing a woman into the tabernacle?"

"I don't know. But that woman is not an Israelite."

"Could she be one of the temple prostitutes? Is he trying to bring Moabite worship into our tabernacle?"

Devora's eyes reflected the horror I felt. Along with the crowd we looked on in stunned silence as the significance of what we were witnessing sank in. I looked to Moses to see what he would do but before he responded there was movement in the crowd. A middle-aged man, dressed in priestly robes, rose and made his way toward the holy tent. His face looked angry, he walked with quick determined steps, and in his hand, he carried a weapon.

He strode through the temple courtyard and entered the curtained area into which the couple had disappeared. A moment later we heard cries — a man's voice, a woman's scream.

The crowd came to life in a buzz of reaction.

"What just happened?"

"Did he kill them?"

"What were they doing there anyway?"

By now Moses had also entered the Holy Place. He came out shortly and motioned in the direction of the Levites. "We need some help here."

Levite helpers joined him and shortly they emerged carrying two bodies. The priest who went after the two had also reappeared. His weapon and white robe were stained with blood.

Moses addressed the crowd. "Yahweh has spoken. He said, 'Phinehas, the son of Eleazar, the son of Aaron, the priest, has turned back my wrath from the children of Israel, because he was zealous with my zeal among them so that I did not consume the children of Israel.'"

Moses beckoned to him and, when Phinehas was a few paces away, raised his hand and blessed him in view of us all. "Yahweh says to you, Phinehas, 'Behold I give to him My covenant of peace; and it shall be to him and his descendants after him a covenant of an everlasting priesthood because he was zealous for his God and made atonement for the children of Israel.'"

Moses and Phinehas left the tabernacle courtyard then, and the crowd began to disburse.

"What I have seen today, I will never forget," I said,

as we made our somber way back home.
"Me neither," Devora replied. [57]

Chapter Thirty-three

"Moses has ordered another census," Father Caleb announced on his return from a meeting of Israel's leaders a few days later. He was hardly able to contain his excitement. "I have been asked to help with counting the men from the tribe of Judah twenty years and over."

For the next days, he was away from sunrise to dusk. Despite his absence, his enthusiasm and optimism infected all of us who had witnessed the last census.

"What has got into you, Father?" Achsah asked.

"It was after the last census that we were given the opportunity to enter the Promised Land," Devora told her. "This count surely means that something important is about to happen!"

"When will I be counted?" Acshah asked.

"You won't. It's just the men."

"But why just count the men?" She'era asked.

"They're the ones who will be going to battle against the people who are now in the land that Yahweh has promised to us," Devora replied.

Father Caleb arrived home each night with his head full of numbers. On the final day he announced, "Today we finished numbering Judah. We have an army of 76,500 fighting men. And Moses has totaled the fighting force of all the tribes. It comes to 601,730!

"Moses' prediction from when we refused to enter the land forty years ago has also come true. Not one person who was numbered in the last census is still alive, except for Joshua, and I." [58]

* * *

A trumpeted battle alarm shattered the peace of a lazy afternoon. The census had been completed a few days before and our family's men, on alert after being numbered with Judah's soldiers, were quick to respond.

I watched Elah from the entrance of our room, putting on his makeshift armour, then collecting his sword and shield. "You take care and come back," I said to him.

"I will," he said, giving me a shallow smile. "Moses probably won't even choose me." His coolness toward me was reflected in his eyes.

Later that day, though, not one of our men returned. Kenaz, Caleb, Naam, Elah—Moses had chosen all of them to be part of Judah's 1000-man force to go against the Midianites.

I was comforted to hear that Moses had also sent the priest Phinehas into battle, along with the holy articles of worship from the tabernacle.

* * *

It was a week after the men had gone to war and no word had come back from the front until Achsah returned to our tent with news.

"A scout from the battlefield says all goes very well. Our men have taken every Midianite city, killed all the men, and burned down their settlements. But they kept alive all the women, children, and flocks. They are making their way back to us with these things."

The news struck me as good at first. If our army had been so victorious, then our men must be safe. But the more I thought of it, the more the part about keeping the women troubled me. Hadn't our camp just been through a plague brought on by the presence of idol-worshiping women? What if Kenaz—or Elah—was tempted to take one of the beautiful captives for himself?

In my heart, I feared most for Elah. I worried our estrangement had made him ripe to give in to temptation. But he would never bring an idol-worshiping woman into our home, would he?

I remembered vividly the screams of the Israelite man and woman after Phinehas encountered them in the tabernacle. Could Elah, or any of the men from our family, be putting themselves at risk in this way?

* * *

As the days stretched on and the army failed to return, my fear for Elah's well-being grew—and with it my determination to fight for my marriage and keep idolatry out of our home. But what could I, a simple, aging woman, do?

And then an idea came to me. Could I do what Miriam did... take my timbrel and make a stand, maybe even lead others to do the same? Would women from my family and tribe join me in keeping idolatry from our tents?

I voiced my concerns to Devora and asked her what she thought of my idea. She was skeptical until I reminded her of the plague our camp suffered and the punishment we saw at the tabernacle. Then she warmed to the plan. Together we convinced Cherut to join us. She'era and Basmat took little persuading to come on-side.

The five of us visited Merab. But she was not at all enthusiastic. "I want Iru home no matter what," she said.

When Achsah heard of what we planned to do, she seemed embarrassed. "You'll make a big fool of yourself and all the women with you, Zamri. Our men do as they please, no matter what we women do."

Her words gave me pause. As I walked alone outside in the evening I thought through my plan again. Was I being foolish? Should I call the whole thing off?

I considered that option and quickly realized that something within me would not allow it. Walking past the tabernacle now, I glanced up at the cloud that rested over it, illuminating the night. Its constant glow seemed, at this moment, like a smile—Yahweh's smile encouraging me.

* * *

If my plan was to work, I knew I needed to do some preparing. I took out my timbrel and quietly rehearsed the victorious song Miriam led us in all those years ago.

"Sing to the LORD
For He has triumphed gloriously!
The horse and its rider
He has thrown into the sea."

It brought back that glorious day when we saw our slavers perish and knew we were really free at last. Hope rose as I repeated Miriam's song over and over. [59]

I discussed with Devora and others in our family how we could succeed. We decided we must be ready at a moment's notice to meet the returning soldiers and take our stand before any foreign women entered the camp.

* * *

Only hours after we had this discussion, word came that the soldiers had returned with flocks, booty, and women.

My heart pounded with apprehension as I picked up

my timbrel then led Devora, Cherut, Basmat, and She'era to meet our returning warriors.

To give myself courage I hummed Miriam's song under my breath. Devora heard and sang along. I sang louder. Others joined in. I looked around and saw that more women than from just our tent had joined us. Some also had timbrels. The music lent wings to our feet as we made our way, now in a dancing line, toward Moses.

Gradually our progress was slowed by the mass of people who had joined Moses to meet the returning army. But as we approached him, people opened a path for our company until I found myself face to face with Moses himself and, beside him, Eleazar the high priest. I stopped mid-song and looked into Moses' piercing eyes.

"What is this?" he asked.

"We are here to meet our husbands and sons..." My palms grew sweaty and my voice quavered with nervousness. I continued anyway. "And we also want to guard our homes against idol worship. We have come out against our husbands bringing idol-worshiping women into our tents." As I spoke, my nervousness abated and a strange new boldness took its place.

Moses studied me for long minutes and then his face softened in a smile. His eyes twinkled, but also glistened — with tears.

"You are singing a familiar song. Her song. And you have her spirit. You remind me of Miriam." His voice was choked with emotion.

Had I heard right? A thrill went through me.

"Let's go meet the army," he said.

At his word, our parade of women followed Moses and Eleazar to the place outside the camp where the returned soldiers waited. They were clustered among piles of booty. Some were tending flocks of sheep and goats that grazed on the scrubby greenery. And a short distance from the men, huddled a crowd of women of mixed ages. We halted before the scene.

"Welcome home!" Moses called out. "Officers and captains, I need a word with you."

As the army leaders stepped forward, Moses' expression changed. His face became fierce and his voice angry as he addressed the men.

"Have you kept all the women alive? Look, these women of Midian, through Balaam's influence, caused some in the camp to disobey God at Peor. That resulted in a plague decimating the Lord's congregation. We will not let this happen again. You must destroy every male child and put away all the women who have slept with a man. You may keep only the virgins.

"Then, before you re-enter the camp, you must purify yourselves and your clothes and possessions for seven days."

I looked over the crowd of soldiers for a glimpse of Elah and Kenaz. But I couldn't spot them.

Moses smiled at me before leaving. "That should help," he said.

"Yes, thank you," I murmured.

* * *

The seven days of purification dragged on and on. Though Moses' stipulation that all previously married Midianite women would not be allowed in the camp was reassuring, I was still haunted by the fear that Elah would bring home an untouched young beauty. But, I kept telling myself, I had done all I could.

At last the day came when our men were allowed back into the camp. Cries of welcome from surrounding tents alerted us to their return. I couldn't face, in front of everyone, what I feared I might see, and so I fled to our room. Tense and listening, I heard Caleb's voice first, then Naam's, then Elah's. It sounded nearby, as if he had already entered the tent. I pushed aside the curtain of our room and nearly bumped into him. He was alone!

He engulfed me in his arms in a warm hug. "Zamri, I'm back," he murmured into my hair as he held me tight.

Was I dreaming? Had Elah returned to me not only in body and also in heart?

When he finally released me, I look around at the others. Caleb and Naam had also returned alone, but not Kenaz. He stood waiting to greet me, a young beauty beside him. [60]

Chapter Thirty-four

We talked long past dark on Elah's first night home.

"I left bitter," he said. "But my time away helped me appreciate what we have here. And I was tired of holding onto my jealousy and anger at you for loving someone else."

"I thought I loved Pallu once," I told him. "But I was young and had no idea of what real love was until I met you. Over these last weeks, I feared I had lost you for good. I have come to love you more than ever."

"I heard you even led the women in an attempt to keep the men from bringing home foreign women."

"I had to," I said. "I saw what happened to the man who brought a Moabite woman into the tabernacle and I couldn't bear the thought of that happening to you or anyone from our family."

"I'm proud of you," Elah said. "Perhaps you coming out that way was the reason Moses commanded the men to put away any woman who had been married. Some of the men were pretty upset by that."

"Were you?" I asked.

"No. Not a chance. I couldn't wait to get back to you so I could patch things up and we could start again."

* * *

The army had been home for only several days when the trumpet summons came for the entire congregation to assemble.

A sense of anticipation hung over the crowd of us, gathered before Moses. He stood in a spot where his voice, still strong at 120 years of age, carried over the congregation.

"The Lord our God spoke to us in Horeb saying, 'You have dwelt long enough at this mountain,'" he began. Then he launched into a review of our journey.

He took us through the wilderness, "the great and terrible wilderness," he called it. My mind wandered back to the many long treks in the heat and cold, in daylight or cloud-lit darkness. We were often hungry, thirsty, and had tired, aching feet. I hardly remembered anything different and for most of this crowd, it had been their whole life.

I tuned into Moses again as he recalled sending the spies. He reminded us of the rebellion of the congregation when they listened to the ten spies instead of Joshua and Father Caleb. He even mentioned Father Caleb by name: "Caleb, son of Juphunneh shall see the land," he said, "and to him and his children I am giving the land on which he walked because he wholly followed the Lord."

Elah, who sat beside me now, in companionship like the days before our rift, grabbed my hand, gave it a squeeze, and I felt a shiver of excitement. Our dreams of new life in a new land could come true!

For any in the crowd who hadn't heard the old stories or had forgotten them, Moses reviewed our whole 40-year trip. His words were full of encouragement as he recalled the fearful foes Yahweh had helped us conquer. As if guarding us against giving way to fear again, he emphasized Yahweh's ability to help us win against the fiercest giants we would meet in the Promised Land. "You must not fear them," he said, "for the Lord your God fights for you."

And then he made a startling announcement. "I will not be leading you into the Promised Land, though. I begged Yahweh to let me, but He said, 'No! Enough of that. Speak no more of this matter.' Instead Joshua will lead you into your inheritance. I will only get to see it from a distance."

Moses paused, and as the words sank in, there was a buzz of reaction. Nearby I heard people voicing what was in my own thoughts.

"I can't imagine going ahead without Moses."

"Joshua is a great warrior, but does God speak to him like he does to Moses?"

"What will happen to Moses?"

Moses was not finished, however. He resumed his talk by warning us of the dangers ahead, especially the danger of worshiping idols. "Take heed to yourselves," he cried out, his voice thundering strong across the valley, "lest you forget the covenant of the Lord your God which he made with you, and make for yourselves a carved image in the form of anything which the Lord your God has forbidden you. For the Lord your God is a consuming fire, a jealous God."

His words reminded me of the challenge that we now had in our own tent. How would we teach these things to a beautiful thirteen-year-old Midianite girl who didn't even speak our language, but who Kenaz was intent on marrying? [61]

* * *

Moses called us to gather several more times. It was as if he was loath to finish his farewells for fear he would forget to tell us something important.

A few days after his last talk, the trumpet signaled us to gather once more. When we were all before Moses, he raised his hands over us and called out:

> "The Lord came from Sinai,
> And dawned on them from Seir;
> He shone forth from Mount Paran,
> And He came with ten thousands of saints;
> From His right hand
> Came a fiery law for them.
> Yes, He loves the people;
> All His saints are in Your hand;
> They sit down at Your feet;
> Everyone receives Your words."

Then he named the tribes for blessing. Over Judah he said:

> "Hear, Lord, the voice of Judah,
> And bring him to his people;
> Let his hands be sufficient for him,
> And may you be a help against his enemies."

We sat in hushed reverence under his words for each tribe. And then he said his final words to all of us:

> "Happy are you, O Israel!
> Who is like you, a people saved by the Lord,
> The shield of your help
> And the sword of your majesty!
> Your enemies shall submit to you,
> And you shall tread down their high places."

Moses left us then, taking a path across the plain, toward Mount Nebo. [62]

* * *

Moses never returned. We never saw him again. Some went to look for him, but found no trace. The camp went into mourning the day he left and mourned for him thirty days.

A trumpet blast summoned us to assemble on the thirty-first day. We rushed our morning meal and joined the crowds streaming to the meeting place. There our new leader, Joshua, stood, ready to speak to us. Though we had known him throughout our desert travels, questions hung heavily in the air. Was he up to the job? Did he have the authority, skill, and determination of Moses?

We didn't wait long to find out. No sooner had the crowd settled before him than he began to speak. His voice was strong and confident. But it was his words that transfixed us.

"This is what God has told me. Every place that the sole of your foot will tread, I have given to you as I said to Moses. Only be strong and very courageous, be strong and of good courage; do not be afraid nor be dismayed, for the Lord your God is with you wherever you go."

I must admit I had been feeling weary and, after Moses' departure, wondering where I would find the energy and will to travel on. But Joshua's attitude and what he said quickly changed that. As we left to return to our tents, there was an excited buzz in the air. [63]

* * *

Meanwhile I had taken responsibility for the little Midianite girl Kenaz had brought home. Since we couldn't understand her, we didn't know her name but I gave her one of my own: Nara, "beauty," for she was very beautiful. But she was also scared and sad.

"She sure cries a lot," Elah remarked as we were getting ready for bed.

"She does," I said. "I'm doing my best to let her know

everything will be okay."

The next day officers from Judah's army division passed through the camp with instructions for all of us. "Prepare provisions for yourselves. Within three days you will cross over this Jordan to go in to possess the land which the Lord your God is giving you to possess."

Excitement filled our cooking area as we began preparing food for the days ahead. "We will finally get to enter Canaan," Devora said. Her face hadn't stopped beaming since the messenger came by with the announcement.

"I know," I said, "it's hard to believe this is actually going to happen!"

"Nara is crying again." She'era announced, bringing me back to the present.

I went to her to comfort her, right then feeling more challenged with the task of leading this one than I was when I led the women to petition Moses. But with Yahweh's help I would persevere and have success as I continued to live under His cloud. [64]

The End

Discussion Questions

1. What, in Zamri's view, threatened her close relationship with her older brother Bezalel? How did the young Zamri handle her feelings of jealousy? How have you handled changing family dynamics and relationships?

2. One of the challenges Zamri and other women in this story faced was co-existing with several women in one household. What were some ways they responded to this challenge? In what settings have you faced similar challenges? How did you respond to them?

3. What was the Old Testament Hebrew woman's attitude toward child-bearing and mothering? How was it different from the current attitude of many modern women in the developed world? How was it the same? Is your attitude toward bearing and raising children more like the Old Testament woman or the modern woman?

4. What role did Zamri's timbrel play in the story? What physical objects or events from your life have iconic and/or symbolic significance for you?

5. Despite God's revelation to Israel, idol worship was deeply rooted. Discuss Cherut's obsession with the religions of Egypt and Canaan. How did it start? What ideas, beliefs, and fears kept her enslaved to idolatry? What ideas, beliefs, fears or objects might become forms of idolatry for us?

6. In what ways did God reveal Himself to Zamri? How did she respond? How was the Old Testament pre-Jesus experience of God and with God different from how we

experience God now?

7. Women in leadership positions were rare in Bible times. In what ways did Zamri and other women in *Under the Cloud* show and exercise leadership? How does that compare with women in leadership in the modern, developed world?

8. How does Zamri change throughout the story? What are some of the catalysts of these changes? What aspects of her personality and character stayed the same? What changes have you seen in yourself? What about you hasn't changed?

About the Author

Violet Nesdoly is a Bible College graduate and has a B.Ed. from the University of British Columbia. A freelance writer for over 20 years, she has won awards for short fiction, non-fiction, and poetry. *Under the Cloud* is her second novel.

A mother and grandmother, she lives with her husband Ernie in Langley, British Columbia.

Find out more about Violet, her writing, and her art at her blog/website VioletNesdoly.com.

< https://violetnesdoly.com/>

Also available from Violet Nesdoly:

Destiny's Hands
https://tinyurl.com/y87me9gk

Endnotes

These notes contain the Bible references on which the fictionalized incidents in *Under the Cloud* are based as well as other information. Chapters with no references listed are purely fictional. Directly quoted passages are from the New King James Version of the Holy Bible and the Message Bible as indicated.

Chapter One

[1] Exodus 31:1-11 – Bezalel and Oholiab appointed to oversee Tabernacle construction.

Exodus 39:32-43 – Work done and inspected.

[2] Exodus 40 – The Tabernacle set up.

Leviticus 8:1-13 – Aaron and sons robed and anointed.

Leviticus 9:23-24 – Aaron and Moses bless the congregation and God sends fire onto the offering.

Chapter Two

[3] Exodus 15:20-21 – Miriam's song.

[4] Numbers 7:2-88 – Offerings of Israel's leaders.

[5] Leviticus 8:34-36 – Aaron and sons spend a week at the tabernacle.

Leviticus 9 & 10 – Priestly ministry begins. Nadab and Abihu offer strange fire.

Numbers 6:24-26 – Aaron's priestly blessing.

Chapter Three

[6] Exodus 12:1-13; 31-36 – Israel celebrates the first Passover and leaves Egypt.

Numbers 9:1-5 – Israel celebrates the second Passover.

[7] Numbers 1:1-19 – A census is taken of males 20 years and older.

[8] Numbers 2 – The Israelite camp is organized. The instructions that the tent openings are to face the tabernacle are found in some versions of Numbers 2:2 (example, Amplified Classic version).

Chapter Five

[9] Numbers 10:1-28 – Instructions on how to break camp and leave Sinai.

[10] Numbers 11:1-3; Deuteronomy 9:22 – The fire at Taberah.

Chapter Six

[11] Numbers 11:4-6 – The people grumble about manna.

Numbers 11:16-30 – Moses consecrates 70 elders.

Numbers 11:31-36 – God sends quail.

Chapter Seven

[12] Numbers 12:1-16 – Miriam and Aaron complain about Moses' leadership; Miriam gets leprosy.

[13] Numbers 6:24-26 – Miriam's blessing quoted from the Message Bible.

Chapter Eight

[14] Numbers 12:16-13:20 – Moses sends twelve tribal representatives to spy Canaan.

Chapter Nine

[15] Exodus 17:8-13 – Israelite and Amalekite battle.

[16] Numbers 13:21-14:38 – The spies report, people

refuse to enter Canaan, and are doomed to forty years of desert wandering.

[17] Numbers 14:39-45 – A futile invasion attempt.

Chapter Ten

[18] Numbers 16:1-50 – Korah's and Dathan and Abiram's rebellion against Moses and Aaron.

Chapter Eleven

[19] Numbers 6:47-50 – The plague kills many.
[20] Numbers 17:1-13 – The budding of Aaron's rod.

Chapter Twelve

[21] 1 Chronicles 4:15 – The sons of Caleb named.
[22] Wedding customs and quote adapted from "The Ultimate Wedding" by Bill Risk, <http://www.ldolphin.org/risk/ult.shtml> Last accessed May 30, 2020.

Chapter Fifteen

[23] Exodus 15:20,21 – Miriam's song.
[24] Numbers 14:24; Joshua 14:9 – The promise of land and inheritance for Caleb.

Chapter Nineteen

[25] Exodus 17:8-16 – Israel's victory over Amalek.
[26] Numbers 13:1-14:9 – Twelve Israelite leaders spy out Canaan.
Joshua 14:6-15 – Caleb is promised Hebron.

Chapter Twenty-one

[27] Numbers 13:13 – Sethur named as the spy from Asher.

[28] Remarriage required only 30 days of betrothal, not the one year of a first marriage: "Marriage Laws" by Solomon Schechter & Julius Greenstone, *JewishEncyclopedia.com* < http://www.jewishencyclopedia.com/articles/10435-marriage-laws>, © 2002-2011, last accessed June 3, 2020.

[29] Exodus 10:21-23 – The Egyptian plague of darkness.

Chapter Twenty-two

[30] Exodus 2:1-10 – Story of Moses' parents and infancy.

[31] Exodus 32 – The Golden Calf incident.

[32] Genesis 15:1-6; 21:1,2 – Sarah's story.

Genesis 25:21 – Rebekah's story.

Genesis 30:22-24 – Rachel's story.

Chapter Twenty-three

[33] Numbers 15:32-36 – A man is caught breaking Sabbath restrictions.

[34] Leviticus 10:1-2; Numbers 11:4, 31-34; Numbers 11:3; Numbers 16:1-3, 25-33 – The incidents of rebellion that Caleb refers to.

[35] Numbers 14:36-38 – The unbelieving spies die of plague.

Chapter Twenty-six

[36] 1 Chronicles 4:15 – Kenaz named as Elah's son.

[37] Genesis 49:8-10 – Wording of Uri's blessing is based on Jacob's blessing of Judah.

[38] Numbers 6:24-26 – Grandfather Hur's blessing is the blessing Aaron is given for Israel.

[39] Exodus 17:12 – Hur and Aaron hold up Moses' hands during battle.

[40] Numbers 14:28-30 – The prediction that all those numbered in the original census, with the exception of Joshua and Caleb, would die in the wilderness.

Chapter Twenty-seven

[41] Exodus 14:1-31 – The Red Sea crossing.
[42] Joshua 15:16-17; Judges 1:12-13 – Achsah named as the daughter of Caleb.

Chapter Twenty-eight

[43] Deuteronomy 8:2 – The wilderness wanderings were a test of the Israelites' hearts.
[44] Deuteronomy 1:6; 2:3 – Thoughts from this passage inspired "Long Enough."

Chapter Twenty-nine

[45] Numbers 20:1 – Miriam dies.
[46] Numbers 20:2-13 – The people complain, Moses strikes the rock water instead of speaking to it.
[47] Numbers 20:14-21 – The king of Edom refuses Israel passage through his land.
[48] Numbers 20:22-29 – The death of Aaron.

Chapter Thirty

[49] Numbers 14:39-45 – Israel's futile invasion attempt.
[50] Numbers 21:1-3 – The Canaanites are defeated at Hormah.
[51] Numbers 21:4-9 – The fiery serpents and the bronze serpent incident. The direct quote is from the NKJV Bible.

Chapter Thirty-one

[52] Numbers 21:10-20 – Narrative of travels into foreign territory. The song is quoted from the

NKJV Bible.

[53] Numbers 21:21-23 – The Israelites request passage from King Sihon and are refused.

[54] Numbers 21:24-26 – Israel defeats Ammonite towns and inhabits their land.

[55] Numbers 21:33-35; Deuteronomy 3:1-11 – Israel defeats King Og of Bashan and takes the spoils of war.

[56] Numbers 22:1 – Israel camps on the Plains of Moab.

Numbers 23:8-10 – Israel as seen by Balaam and King Balak after he fetches Balaam to curse Israel for him (full account in Numbers 22-24).

Chapter Thirty-two

[57] Numbers 25:1-13 – The Israelites fall into Baal worship – quote is from the NKJV Bible.

Chapter Thirty-three

[58] Numbers 26 – Moses takes a second census.

[59] Exodus 15:20-21 – Miriam's song.

[60] Numbers 31:1-24 – Vengeance on the Midianites.

Chapter Thirty-four

[61] Deuteronomy 1:6,19, 35-38; 3:23-26; 4:22-24 – Moses addresses the people.

[62] Deuteronomy 33:1-3,7,29 – Excerpts of Moses' final blessing quoted from the NKJV Bible.

[63] Deuteronomy 34:1-8 – Moses disappears on Mount Pisgah.

Deuteronomy 34:9; Joshua 1:1-9 – Joshua assumes leadership of Israel.

[64] Joshua 1:10,11 – Israel prepares to cross the Jordan River into the Promised Land.

* * *